PENGUIN BOOKS

# WINTER'S END

This is John Rickards's first novel. His second, *The Touch of Ghosts*, which also features Alex Rourke, will be available in hardback from August 2004.

D0550365

# Winter's End

JOHN RICKARDS

PENGUIN BOOKS

PENGUIN BOOKS

Published by the Penguin Group
Penguin Books Ltd, 80 Strand, London WC2R ORL, England
Penguin Putnam Inc., 375 Hudson Street, New York, New York 10014, USA
Penguin Books Australia Ltd, 250 Camberwell Road, Camberwell, Victoria 3124, Australia
Penguin Books Canada Ltd, 10 Alcorn Avenue, Toronto, Ontario, Canada M4V 3B2
Penguin Books India (P) Ltd, 11 Community Centre, Panchsheel Park, New Delhi – 110 017, India
Penguin Books (NZ) Ltd, Cnr Rosedale and Airborne Roads, Albany, Auckland, New Zealand
Penguin Books (South Africa) (Pty) Ltd, 24 Sturdee Avenue, Rosebank 2196, South Africa

Penguin Books Ltd, Registered Offices: 80 Strand, London WC2R ORL, England

www.penguin.com

Published by Michael Joseph 2003
Published in Penguin Books 2003

4

Printed in England by Clays Ltd, St Ives plc

# Acknowledgements

Thanks to Beverley Cousins, for prodding me in the right direction with her words of wisdom; to Martin Bryant for keeping me on the straight and narrow while I was doing it, and to everyone else at Penguin for generally being great.

Thanks also to Luigi Bonomi for getting me here in the first place; to Peter Wolverton, for all his help and comments; Whitt, Ade, my parents and others for their respective two cents, and to Jim Doherty, Dave the Pharmacist, Arline Chase and everyone else at the Mystery Writers' Forum for all their help with the research.

Lastly, thanks to Kate, for the colour of sea ice.

# PART ONE

# Happy Returns

'Happy he who still can hope to rise,
Emerging from this sea of fear and doubt!
What no man knows, alone could make us wise;
And what we know, we well could do without.'
– Goethe, Faust

# Prologue

'I don't know why Jimmy insists on playing him,' Sheriff Dale Townsend says, raising his voice over the hammering rain and the swish of the Jeep's wipers. 'It's obvious the guy just isn't on form. His confidence is gone, he's tensed up and he's gripping the bat too hard. Jimmy should rest him a couple of games, give him a chance to get his head right, then bring him back for the end of season run-in.'

His companion, Deputy Andy Miller, keeps both hands on the wheel and his eyes firmly on the pool of light in front of the vehicle. 'Rendall hit three-eighty last year,' he says. 'You can't write off a guy like that, especially when we could still make the title. He'll come good.'

'Maybe.' Dale rubs his hands and stares absent-mindedly out at the darkened landscape. A flash of lightning shocks the trees bordering the highway, a jumble of drenched foliage and stark blue shadows. Darkness returns as a shift in the tone of the wind tells him that they have left the woods behind. Four miles of flat grassland before the trees come back as the road reaches the town. Four miles to home. He checks his watch.

'Your wife waiting to give you hell when you get in?' asks the deputy.

'Naw, she knows I'm going to be home late, even if I can't be sure of the exact time when the weather's so goddam miserable.'

'When's your car going to be finished in the shop?'

'Tomorrow. That's what they tell me, anyway.'

'Well, if it takes longer, you're welcome to keep hitching a ride with me. Until my shift changes next week, anyhow.'

Sheriff Townsend is about to reply when the lightning flashes again and his attention is grabbed by something ahead on the highway. 'What the hell?' he says.

The deputy eases off the gas and, on reflex, hits the blue and red strobes.

The twin headlight beams pick out a man who is bare from the waist up with rain dancing from his exposed skin. Townsend's first, almost unconscious thought is that he must be freezing cold. The man is staring calmly at the ground in front of him, absolutely still, with his hands at his sides. In each of them he holds a hunting knife. At his feet is the naked body of a woman, her flesh white in the glare.

'Andy, call Dispatch,' Townsend says.

He draws his pistol and reaches for the door, then steps out into the downpour. The water hits him like a cold shower as he raises the comforting weight of his gun and carefully sights up on the figure in front of him.

'Aroostook County Sheriff's Department!' he shouts. 'Put down the knives and step slowly over to the vehicle with your hands where I can see 'em.'

To his left, the other door opens and Andy steps out, the dim crackle of the radio still faintly audible behind him. The deputy mirrors Townsend's movements, keeping his gun trained, ready to shoot.

The man, who Townsend guesses is young, no older than his mid-twenties, looks up and his gaze settles on the sheriff. Face pale from the cold. Dark hair drenched. Eyes black pits reflecting the blue and red flashes from the

4

Jeep's lights. A slow, almost mocking smile spreads across his face as he gently places the knives on the ground. Then he strides calmly to the Jeep, keeping his hands in the air.

Andy cuffs him and frisks him for other weapons while Townsend goes to check on the woman. She looks to be in her late thirties, with shoulder-length dark hair and a trim build. Her face is familiar and quite attractive, despite the unreal presence death brings. Her chest is a welter of slashes and stab marks washed clean by the rain. Townsend has little real hope of finding her alive, but checks for a pulse as a matter of procedure. Nothing. Lightning flashes again and, if anything, the rain gets harder.

'Arrest this guy on suspicion of murder,' he calls out to the deputy behind him. 'And notify the Chief Medical Examiner's Office. We'll need to get someone out here.'

# I

The morning is well underway by the time I reach the red brick building in Boston's Fenway district, not far from Kenmore Square, that serves as my office, workplace and home away from home. I can feel the glare of the May sunshine on my back, warm despite the cool air. The sky is glacial blue with scattered flecks of distant cloud. I glance around before crossing the road and see a group of half a dozen students from Boston University, a short way along the river, emerging from Rick's, my local coffee bar. A plastic cup of the establishment's finest is nestled warmly – a little too warmly for comfort, in fact – in my hand. I need it this morning. I'm tired, breakfast was four hours ago in a cramped diner full of truckers and construction workers on the early shift, and I had one too many drinks last night.

All in the line of duty.

I climb the steps and push my way into the burgundy carpeted foyer. Five companies share the building with mine, our names picked out in silvered lettering on a board by the twin elevators. For a moment, I think about taking the stairs on the false premise that the extra exercise would do me good. As always, I push the elevator call button instead.

Inside, I examine my appearance in the mirrored walls. I look exactly like I feel: dog-tired and in need of a shave, a shower and a decent night's sleep. I consider trying to neaten myself up a little, but eventually decide that it's not worth it. If I have to impress any clients today, I'll rely on the remaining store of charm in my weary eyes. On better days, I'm told I bear a vague resemblance to a gaunt version of Cary Grant. Today, I'll settle for a vague resemblance to a member of the human race.

As the elevator doors slide open, I manage to fumble a cigarette one-handed out of the pocket of my battered tan leather jacket and into my mouth. I keep promising to cut down from my current thirty-odd a day, but I never seem to get round to it. I make a left into reception and wave good morning to Jean, our secretary, as I bring up the lighter, spark and inhale. My lungs flood with nicotine, carcinogens and black oozing crap. All the ingredients of a nutritious breakfast.

The sign on the open door behind me reads: 'Robin Garrett Associates'. In smaller writing underneath it adds: 'Licensed private investigators, process servers, business security and criminal consultants'.

I amble through the interior door next to Jean's desk and into our spacious squad room-style office. Five desks, a coffee machine and water cooler, lines of steel shelving and a half dozen filing cabinets. Fake-leather swivel chairs, a couple of potted plants, a few framed photos on the walls. Only two of our trio of junior staff are in at the moment, and both are busy on the phone. As I place my coffee on the worktop and settle into my chair, the man whose desk faces mine across the room calls out, 'Made it at last, I see.'

Robin Garrett is, technically, my boss, which makes me one of his associates. In reality we're more like part-ners, and we've been friends for years longer than the three I've been working with him. He started out as a lone operator, expanding the business as things picked up. Since I joined to make us a duo, we've added Jean, three more investigators and our relatively plush office to the company. A couple of years ago we considered changing its name to something like 'Garrett and Rourke Associates', giving each of us a share of title. In the end, we decided against it, since it would only confuse our existing clients.

'Morning, Rob,' I say as I leaf through the mail on my desk and take a sip of my coffee.

'What kind of time do you call this?'

He's not really annoyed, he just likes playing the overbearing boss every once in a while. It's a routine we're both well used to.

'I call it half past ten,' I say. 'If it's got another name, I haven't heard it.'

'Overslept or hung over? You only live down the road so it can't be the traffic.'

'None of the above. Working.'

He raises a sarcastic eyebrow. 'Well I'll be damned. Who are you and what have you done with Alex?'

'Nothing a month's sleep and a couple of painkillers won't solve. We can tell the Ingrams that Little Jamie is living with his girlfriend, Chrissie Evans, in an apartment on Bedford Avenue. She's still studying at university, he's currently Employee of the Month at Miss Mona's Fried Chicken on Douglas. Having been there, I can only say that he can't have had much competition for the award. He's still not keen on getting back in touch with his folks, but I did manage to extract his permission to give them his number.' I take a long gulp of the gritty, extra-strong espresso. 'I spent yesterday evening with some of Chrissie's friends, and the night in the company car outside her apartment, waiting for her or Jamie to show. Eight-thirty they got in. We talked. Nice enough kid, I guess, even if neither of us were at our best.'

'So we can hand the Ingrams our final bill. Another satisfied customer,' Rob says with a contented smile on his face.

'I wouldn't call them that until they've *seen* the bill,' I retort, flashing him a tired grin. 'Anything new doing down here?'

'A couple of bread-and-butter jobs. The kids are working on them now. I've got some more tidying up work for Tynon, Oliver and Co. on the Sefton case. Oh, and you had a call from some Hicksville County Sheriff's Office, said they needed you to give 'em a ring. Name and number's on your desk somewhere.'

Rob is from Chicago and never ceases to look down his nose at everything from anywhere not covered by city concrete, including my own roots in what he likes to think of as the 'Great White North'. There's no malice in his opinions; like his company boss routine earlier, it's just part of his repertoire.

I scan the desk for a note in my partner's barely legible handwriting. After a couple of seconds, my eye picks out a scrap of envelope bearing a number and the name Dale Townsend. I know Dale. Or rather, I used to know Dale. We both grew up in the same small town and Chris, his younger brother by two years, was my best friend when we were kids. In the seventeen years since I left to go to college, I've spoken with Dale on only one occasion, a year and a half ago. That time, it was business.

A burglar was working stores in the smaller towns around Presque Isle in the east of Aroostook County, Maine. The perpetrator would smash through the front door at night with a sledgehammer, then run inside and grab the cash register before making an equally fast exit. He never worried about setting off alarms or the cameras catching him; he kept his face hidden and relied on his speed to foil attempts to apprehend him. The cops would usually find the register a few streets away, open and empty. An attorney who'd worked in Boston until a few months beforehand suggested to Dale that they might want to give my firm a call, since we'd dealt with a similar burglar for a traders' association in the city. Dale phoned me, and I looked at what his office and the Maine State Police had turned up.

The first robbery, at a place called JP's, seemed the most carefully timed and planned, and consequently had netted the largest haul. I suggested they take a good look at the store's staff and former staff, as well as their friends. The thief turned out to be the boyfriend of the assistant manager's sister, well placed to know when the shop would be at its fattest and what kind of security it had.

No boasting; I didn't solve the crime. A security camera at a truck stop on US 1 caught the licence plate of his pick-up truck during a break-in. But I helped out.

I wonder what Dale wants now. Maybe he has something else to throw at me, or maybe this is just a social call. I pick up the phone and punch in the number. It rings once, twice, before a voice says, 'Sheriff Townsend.'

'Dale? This is Alex Rourke. You tried getting in touch with me earlier. How are things?'

'Alex! Long time, no see. Things aren't too bad up here.

A little hectic right now.' His voice is gruff and throaty. The last time we worked together, we only spoke over the phone, so I have no idea how much he has changed from when I last saw him in person, nearly two decades ago. From the voice, I find myself imagining Dale with a beard and a truck driver's physique.

'How's Chris?' I say. 'Still in the Coast Guard?'

'Yeah. He says he'll be home for a few weeks some time in September. You'll have to come up and get together for a drink.'

'I'll do that. What's on your mind?'

'We've got a funny situation on our hands and I figured you might be able to help out like you did with the Sharp case.'

His use of the term 'funny situation' piques my interest. 'Sure,' I say. 'Fire away.'

'On the night of the fifteenth we took a guy in on a murder charge. We found him standing on the highway nearly four miles south of town, with the body of the victim at his feet and two knives in his hands.'

'South of Winter's End?'

It's where Dale and I grew up, a small town in the wooded hills of north-eastern Maine that make up the tail-end of the Appalachians. Murder has always been rare in the county, and rarer still in the town. I can't remember hearing of a single case in the eighteen years I lived there. This must be a hot crime locally.

'Yeah,' Dale continues. 'According to the medical examiner and the State Police crime scene unit, the knives the guy was holding were the right dimensions to be the murder weapons. The victim had been dead less than an hour, probably less than half an hour, before we found her.'

'Okay, so you've got the suspect at the scene at around the time of death, with the murder weapons in his hands and the vic at his feet. Sounds pretty open and shut.'

'It does, doesn't it? That's where the complications come in,' Dale says. He sounds bothered by whatever these 'complications' are. 'Firstly, we haven't been able to find the guy's prints on the body or the weapons. That might be because of the way the knives' hilts are dimpled, and could have been made worse by the rain.'

'It was raining?'

'Like you wouldn't believe. I nearly got drowned making the arrest. I was on my way home at the time, looking forward to a warm house and a hot dinner. Some luck.'

'So what else was there?'

'In two days we haven't been able to find any blood traces on the guy or his clothing – he was wearing nothing from the waist up, by the way. Nothing on the road either, thanks to the downpour, so we can't be a hundred per cent certain that it actually *was* where the murder took place.'

As I recall, cold water is one of the most effective ways of getting rid of blood. Some time spent in heavy rain might have done the trick. 'Were there any marks on either of them? Any signs that she put up a fight?'

'Not a scratch. Some bruising on her right arm, looks like grip marks from where she'd been held by someone. She was naked and we haven't been able to find her clothes. Again, that means there's a chance she wasn't killed where we found her.'

'Who was she?'

'Angela Lamond, forty, a nurse at the doctor's in town. We checked her house, turned up nothing.'

I nod to myself. 'Who's the guy?'

There's a pause at the other end of the line and a long-drawn breath that might be a sigh. 'That's the biggest problem. We don't know, and he won't tell us. There was no ID on him. We ran his prints through IAFIS, no dice. He doesn't have a record. We've tried what checks we can do through the NCIC and VICAP – pretty sketchy on what little we've got – and also drawn a blank so far. I've sent out the guy's photo and details direct to the rest of the state's agencies, as well as posting them further afield. Nothing as yet.'

'DNA?'

'There wasn't any evidence of sexual assault, so I'm not expecting him to show up on the CODIS Forensic Index. We're checking through the State Crime Lab in Augusta anyway.' There's another pause, shorter this time. 'We've got the guy at the scene, but without knowing anything about him we don't have a motive unless he tells us why he did it. It leaves a gap in the case against him that the DA would prefer to have filled. Hell, we might even have a hard time proving he had the means to do it if it turns out he was just some wandering vagrant. I was wondering if you ever handled anything like this while you were with the Feds. You hold lectures on difficult interrogation for local law enforcement down in Boston, don't you?'

'Not very often but, yeah, I do. Nothing major: just the occasional "guest speaker" thing for rookie recruits. I did courses on it at the Academy and again when I started working for the Bureau's National Center for the Analysis of Violent Crime.' A long time ago, I add in the privacy of my own head.

'Good. If you can, I want you to come up to Houlton

14

and have a talk with our John Doe to see if you can get anything out of him.'

'Don't the State Police have someone who can question him?'

'They're not involved in the interrogation. They did the scene investigation and most of the legwork on the case, but he's our suspect.'

'How talkative is he?' I ask.

'Enough, just not about himself or the murder. Hasn't said a damn thing about either.'

'Who's representing him?'

'So far he's turned down the right to an attorney. Said he had all the lawyers he could ever need, but that he didn't think they were necessary right now.'

I hesitate for a moment, thinking. It's not often that a county sheriff has such a personal involvement in an investigation. Normally, most of the actual work on a murder case would be carried out by the State Police Criminal Investigation Division. Dale must be under a lot of pressure for his department to solve the crime, and to solve it themselves, such is the likely local importance of this case. If he left it to the State or another outside agency he'd lose serious face, and with it perhaps his job.

'Sure,' I say, glancing at Rob. My partner is making 'all quiet here, go ahead' gestures at me from across the office. 'It's going to be a long drive, so I'll leave first thing tomorrow morning and aim to get there about lunchtime. Can you arrange a room for me somewhere in Houlton?'

'No problem.'

Rob is now holding up a piece of paper bearing a hastily scribbled dollar sign.

'One more thing,' I say into the receiver. 'If this takes

more than a day or two, the county is going to have to cover my fees. I've got to make a living.'

'Sure, sure,' Dale replies. 'Our budget got a nice increase this year.'

'I'm not planning on breaking the bank,' I say, smiling. 'Is this going to be sworn or non-sworn work?'

'Sworn, I think. It'll look better on interview transcripts if you've been deputized, and if you have to do any asking around it'll give you a badge to flash.'

The answer doesn't surprise me. As I thought, he wants this to look like his department's work as much as possible. 'Okay. If you can fax me copies of everything you've got on the case I'll go over it before I leave.'

'Thanks, Alex. I'll see you tomorrow.'

'Yeah. Bye.'

As I return the phone to its cradle Rob looks at me with his eyebrows raised and his arms folded. 'Trouble in the wilds, huh?' he says.

'They want me to go and talk to a guy they've got for a murder near my hometown. Sounds interesting.'

'I'm happy so long as they pay the fee. They use money up there, right? They're not going to pay you in moose droppings or something?'

'Yeah, they've just about heard of the dollar.'

He grins. 'Best pack a rifle for the bears.'

'The most dangerous thing I'm likely to meet is an irate potato farmer.'

'Just make sure you take your phone with you. It doesn't seem likely at the moment, but we might get busy all of a sudden.'

I spend the next few hours clearing up some small details on other cases and making out a bill for Mr and

Mrs Ingram. I buy a road map of northern Maine and make sure I've got my various licences: driver's, private investigator's, resident and non-resident weapons permits, for two different states in the latter case. Then I go for lunch. The fax machine finally stops whirring and disgorging paper just shy of three in the afternoon. I bundle Dale's reports together and leave the office for home, then some packing, reading, an early night and an early start.

Unsure how long the trip will last, I settle on a couple of sweaters, three shirts, T-shirts and pairs of jeans, plus socks and underwear for a week. A small bag with an electric razor and toiletries. A camera. Two fresh packs of cigarettes and a couple of spare CDs for the journey. I'm a blues man myself: Roy Buchanan, J.B. Lenoir, Howlin' Wolf. My old but well-tended Colt M1911 with a couple of spare clips of .45 hollowpoint. A knife I took a couple of years ago from a punk kid here in the city. Mostly I use it for digging around in the dirt or, occasionally, letting myself into places I'm not supposed to be. There's a crowbar, some bolt-cutters, a torque wrench and a couple of wire-thin files in my car's toolbox for much the same reason. I don't often have call to use them, but on occasion they do come in handy.

Packing complete, I settle back on my black felt sofa, Sonny Boy Williamson II on the stereo and a bottle of Mexican beer in hand. I start leafing through the files.

## 2

At around 7.45 a.m. on 15 May, two days ago, forty-year-old nurse Angela Lamond left her house on Altmayer Street, Winter's End, on the short walk to the doctor's on Main Street where she worked. She was seen by her neighbour Walter Sarrell who exchanged morning greetings with her. She was also seen by several of the store workers on Main. Nothing in her manner indicated anything amiss. At 8.00 a.m. she opened up the doctor's office as normal, arriving shortly before Dr Nathan Vallence, the town's only full-time physician.

The working day passed normally. None of the people coming for their appointments reported anything strange. Dr Vallence didn't notice anyone suspicious in or around the office. At around 1.00 p.m., Angela Lamond took her lunch break, leaving Jennifer Mitchell, the other nurse on duty, to cover the next hour alone as usual. Angela had lunch in Martha's Garden, a diner not far down the road. She spent just over half an hour inside, chatting with two friends whom she met at the same time most days. Neither friend noticed anything unusual in Angela's manner, or recalled her mentioning anything out of the ordinary. From Martha's Garden, she made a quick stop at a convenience store to buy some milk before returning to work.

The afternoon passed much the same as the morning, and Angela left the office just after its official closing time of 4.45 p.m. She waved goodbye to Jennifer and turned towards home. No one saw her alive again.

At 9.40 p.m., almost five hours after she left the office, Sheriff Dale Townsend and Deputy Andy Miller, both off duty and on their way home, found Angela Lamond's naked corpse on Route 11 some three and a half miles south of town. The best estimate placed her time of death somewhere after 8.40 p.m.

Canvassing failed to turn up anyone who remembered seeing Angela on the route she would have taken home. Similarly, there were no reports of suspicious individuals or vehicles in the area. When police checked Angela's home, they found her mail on the doormat and three unanswered messages on her machine. There were no indications of intrusion or any kind of struggle at her house. An appeal for information uncovered one logging truck heading south whose driver estimated he passed the spot at around 9.15 p.m. He said he saw nothing, unusual or otherwise.

Forensic investigation of the crime scene was badly hampered by extremely heavy rain. Luminol and phenolphthalein testing found highly diluted blood traces in the immediate vicinity of the body, directly beneath the wounded area of the torso, and rapidly decreasing in the direction of water flow. The small amount found, barely enough to be detected, made it impossible to determine whether this was the actual murder site or not. Similarly, neither of the two weapons recovered at the scene retained detectable quantities of the victim's blood.

Examination of the wider site provided little of any apparent worth. Of perhaps most interest was a check of the fields of tall grass bordering the highway before crime scene officers began their search of the area. There were no tracks visible in the grass, which a State Police helicopter overflight later confirmed. The police concluded from this that the victim arrived at the scene by travelling along the highway, not by walking through the fields.

There were no blood traces or foreign fibres on the suspect's clothing, and no hairs belonging to the victim. The tread of the suspect's shoes contained three pieces of highway gravel and a minute amount, barely enough to test, of soil local to the area. There were no traces of plant material or leaf-litter on them. This came as a surprise to the forensic techs, and it's a surprise to me. My shoes would pick up more than that just going for a walk round the block. The report notes that they were scuffed and obviously well-used, so they can't have been new.

The site where the body was found lies within what was once sheep pasture cut out of the local forest. The old fields form a grassy rectangular area four miles long and roughly two wide, running to within two hundred yards of the town limits. Route 11 bisects it almost perfectly. The farmland has been abandoned for some fifty years or more. There are no derelict buildings on site, and no drainage ditches save for small culverts either side of the road, limiting the amount of cover available to the long grass alone.

The county's part-time medical examiner, Dr Gemma Larson, carried out the post-mortem examination of Angela Lamond's body on the morning of 16 May. Cause of death was two stab wounds, cutting some four and a half inches into the victim's chest cavity. One penetrated the right ventricle of the heart, the second punctured the left lung between ribs six and seven, leaving an obvious cut mark on the bone. Entry angles of the wounds suggested they were made from behind, by someone reaching over the victim's shoulder, or from the right-hand side by a right-handed attacker.

There were fourteen other injuries to the victim's chest and upper abdomen. All were made post-mortem and were shallower than the primary injuries, in several cases only penetrating the upper dermal layers.

There were no defence wounds on the victim's arms or hands, although there was faint bruising on her right shoulder. The pattern was consistent with grip marks. There was no evidence of sexual assault.

Scrapings taken from beneath Angela's fingernails revealed nothing. Hair and fibre checks also drew a blank. There were no palm or fingerprints found on her skin, even on initial checking at the crime scene. Preliminary results from toxicological testing of her blood indicated nothing out of the ordinary. Angela's stomach and upper digestive tract were almost empty, indicating that her lunch at the diner was almost certainly the last food she ate.

At this point I'm not interested in the suspect, only in the facts of the case. I can see why Dale is looking for help; this guy is a fucking *ghost*. No prints, trace evidence, blood or anything. There's a famous and long-established principle in forensic science which holds that any contact between one person and another leads to something being exchanged between them, no matter how small the traces. This guy must be made of Teflon. We have him at what may, or may not, be the murder scene, holding what may, or may not, be the murder weapons. And yet if he hadn't stood around waiting for the police to show up, we'd never have known he was there.

My thoughts turn to the murderer. Not the suspect the police have in custody, but the information I can glean about the killer from the facts at hand.

What strikes me first is the extent of overkill injuries to the victim. Whoever did this must have had a lot of anger. This may have been against women in general, or one type of woman, or against the victim in particular. She's naked, degraded, and mutilated in death. Despite her nakedness, though, there's no sign of a sexual element to the crime. And afterwards, the suspect calmly hung around. This suggests to me that there was a personal element to the killing. The murderer's job is done, he is happy. No need to run and hide; no need to continue.

That's not to say that Angela Lamond's killer was a jealous ex-boyfriend. The 'personal' reasons behind the attack might be no more than one paranoid's delusion that she was the Antichrist, here to destroy the world.

The killer snatched Angela unseen shortly after she left for home. That, and the fact that her clothes, and the second crime scene where he presumably kept her, still haven't been found, indicate that the killer planned his deed. He must have known the route she took and found a good hiding place to strike from, along with a safe way to smuggle her away from public view without attracting attention.

If we were still hunting for a suspect, I'd suggest checking the people who lived along and around Angela's route, since grabbing her and whisking her inside would be one easy way to hide her quickly. I'd also look at people whose vehicles might have been in the area on a regular enough basis not to arouse suspicion.

I'd like to know how the killer brought a naked woman three and a half miles out of town on a public highway without being spotted. Surely even the night and the rain weren't cover enough?

I scribble 'Vic's route' and 'Highway walk?' on a piece of paper. Then I turn to the hastily prepared, and rather scant, transcripts of the interviews Dale and his people have had with the suspect since his arrest two days ago.

```
Transcripts of interrogation record,
Aroostook County Sheriff's Department
Case: 'Lamond Murder', A1015-144

Transcript #1 - May 16
Interrogation conducted by Sheriff Dale
Townsend (DT) and Lt. B. Watts (BW).
Subject (SUB) waived his right to an
attorney.

DT: Time is 0035 hours at start of
interview. Present are Sheriff Dale
Townsend and Lieutenant Bruce Watts,
Aroostook County Sheriff's Department,
and interview subject. I remind you that
you have the right to remain silent.
Anything you do say can be used against
you in a court of law. You have the right
to speak with an attorney and have them
present during questioning. If you cannot
afford an attorney one will be appointed
```

for you free of charge. Do you understand
these rights that I have read you?

SUB: Of course.

DT: You do not currently have an attorney
representing you. Are you waiving your
right to legal representation for the
time being?

SUB: I have all the lawyers I could want.
I just don't think I need them here.

DT: So you are —

SUB: (interrupting) Yes, I am waiving my
right to an attorney.

DT: Please state your name for the
record.

SUB: (short pause) I'm afraid not.

BW: Excuse me?

SUB: I won't be adding my name to the
record. Did you know people used to
believe that knowing someone's true name
gave you all sorts of power over them, if
you were so inclined. A nice idea, even
if the superstition is a little outdated.

BW: You know you could face additional
penalties if you fail to provide a name
for the record?

SUB: I'll bear those in mind, although
given that you've brought me here to
question me about murder, I wonder why
you might think additional charges would
frighten me. Has obstruction of justice
recently become an offence punishable by
death?

DT: All right, we'll forget it for now.
Subject will be a John Doe until we know
his proper identity.
BW: We should have it on the record that
the subject is being a pain in the ass.
DT: Leave it, Bruce. Let's start with
what you were doing on the highway, Mr
Doe.
SUB: Waiting.
DT: Waiting for what?
SUB: You'll know when it happens.
BW: Did you kill the woman at the scene,
or did you carry her there from town?
SUB: Winter's End?
BW: Yeah.
SUB: Do you know how the town got its
name, Lieutenant?
BW: I don't know how it's relevant to
this line of questioning.
SUB: A group of settlers were caught by
the onset of winter some way south of the
St John River just as they were about to
set up home in what was then territory
disputed with New Brunswick.
They tried waiting it out, but with supplies running low, they eventually had to
turn south.
DT: Let's get back on to tonight's
events.
SUB: They kept going for weeks. There
weren't any trails, and the going was
slow, especially after they killed their

pack animals for meat. Not enough people
able to hunt properly, I suppose.

DT: Could you describe your movements
tonight until the point where you were
arrested?

SUB: Starving and with their numbers
dropping, they stopped when they saw the
first signs of spring thaw. They called
the settlement they founded Winter's End.
Did you know that makes it older than
everywhere except Houlton and the towns
along the St John?

BW: Fascinating.

SUB: Of course, it sounds like a fine
example of man against the elements and
the pioneer spirit. In reality it was
just a bunch of dumb-ass colonists looking for somewhere where they could
scratch a living out of the dirt. So much
for history.

DT: You're familiar with the town then?

SUB: An astounding deduction. At the very
least, I might have read a tourist
pamphlet about it once.

BW: You got any favourite places to hang
out there? Me, I grab a beer at Larry's
if I'm passing through. Not everyone's
type of place, though.

SUB: (quiet laughter) That was almost
clever, Lieutenant. I'm impressed.

DT: Look, friend, it's late and we're all
tired. Why not stop playing around so we

can all get some sleep? Just tell us what
happened.
SUB: What happened?
DT: Yes.
SUB: If I remember rightly, in the beginning was the word. Or, if you prefer, the
Earth was void. There's more, but it's a
long story.
DT: (sighs) Forget it. We'll try again in
the morning. Interview terminated
at 0105.


Transcript #2 — May 16
Interrogation conducted by Sheriff Dale
Townsend (DT) and Lt. B. Watts (BW).
Subject (SUB) waived his right to an
attorney.


DT: Time is 0945 hours at start of
interview. Present are Sheriff Dale
Townsend and Lieutenant Bruce Watts,
Aroostook County Sheriff's Department,
and interview subject, currently referred
to as John Doe. I remind you that you
have the right to remain silent. Anything
you do say can be used against you in a
court of law. You have the right to speak
with an attorney and have them present
during questioning. If you cannot afford
an attorney one will be appointed for you
free of charge. Do you understand these
rights that I have read you?

SUB: Yes, and I'm still waiving my right
to a lawyer.
DT: I don't suppose you'd like to state
your name for the record, would you?
SUB: No luck in your attempts to uncover
my identity, then?
DT: No. Well?
SUB: I don't think so.
BW: Why don't we start with what happened
yesterday. How did you spend the day?
SUB: I'm surprised to see you here again
in person, Sheriff. I would have thought
a busy man like you would have had better
things to do this morning. What, no town
festivals to open? No schools to lecture
at?
DT: As it happens, John, I do have better
things to do. It's only your pig-
headedness that's keeping me from them.
Why not give us your side of the story?
At least then we'll have two ways of
looking at the situation, and not just
our reconstruction from the evidence,
which I have to say looks pretty bad for
you.
SUB: Should I have my own side to the
story? You seem to be happy with yours.
DT: There must be something.
SUB: Since I doubt you'd believe anything
I say to you, would there be a point in
telling you? I could say I spent the

entire day at a twenty-four-hour New England Steak Lovers' Association whist
drive, or running through the woods trying to escape from a gang of irate
loggers. But what use would that be?
BW: We could check your story. If you
were telling the truth, we'd have to look
again at the evidence.
SUB: Well, thank you for explaining that
to me, Lieutenant. Before today I had no
idea what the word 'alibi' meant.
DT: At least tell us what you were doing
at the murder scene.
SUB: I told you yesterday: waiting.
DT: I remember. Why did you choose that
particular place to do it?
SUB: It seemed appropriate.
BW: Did you know Angela Lamond?
SUB: Do you have a family, Sheriff Towns-
end? Wife and kids?
DT: Is that some sort of threat?
SUB: Simple curiosity. I'm locked firmly
in jail, hardly a position from which to
be making threats. So, do you?
BW: Let's stick to the events of the
fifteenth.
SUB: I'd rather talk about something
else.

There's more but I skip through it. The suspect doesn't
give anything away, dodging questions whenever he's

asked about the crime, and occasionally digressing on to other subjects: history, sport, religion. I don't need to read the rest in depth; I have what's necessary. I know the case and I have a feel for the suspect. Everything else will come later.

# 3

It's six o'clock the following morning when I step, yawning, out of my front door and trot down the steps towards my car. The day is cool and still has the fresh, undisturbed air that comes with the dawn hours and lasts until ruined by the waking world. I slide into the leather driver's seat, dropping my bag in the passenger footwell. The immobilizer, a retrofit since my car is way too old to have one as standard, switches off as I turn the key in the ignition. When the engine growls into life, I rest my hands on the steering wheel and reflect for the millionth time that I'm driving an anachronism given form. I don't often take it out for a spin; it's a bit too awkward for use around Boston. Perhaps it's best that way.

The car that eases out of my residents-only slot before turning north towards the bridge over the Charles River is a 1969 Stingray Corvette. Pale metallic blue bodywork which hides a seven-litre V8 throwing out somewhere over 400 horsepower. It's not the most powerful 'Vette of its time, but it's close.

If I had a shrink, he'd probably say I was compensating for something.

Maybe so. Most of the parts like the air-conditioning, heated windows and power-assisted brakes are factory fitted, or at worst modern replicas. A few, like the immobilizer and the CD player, are wholly new. My car takes a lot of work to look after and it's expensive to run; on a good day, I can squeeze about fourteen miles to the gallon out of it. In many ways, the 'Vette compensates for not having a family.

Like my choice of attire and my personal appearance, it also represents a complete break with my time at the FBI. Agents are expected to be smart and presentable at all times. The requisitioned unmarked brown sedan is a little clichéd, but it's not far from the truth. When I quit, I dropped the look of a Bureau man, and when I happened to spot the 'Vette at a collectors' auction, I couldn't resist.

I only use it when I have to go out of town. The city's overcrowded roads and the pitched mêlées that break out whenever someone spots a spare parking space make it too hard to drive for everyday purposes. I don't mind; at least on the interstate I can open her up a little.

And so I do just that, cruising up I-95 at sixty-five with the strains of Hound Dog Taylor's 'Sitting at Home Alone' wailing above the roar of the engine.

The concrete sweep of the highway cuts relentlessly north, through Massachusetts and New Hampshire, then dives a short way inland from the picture-postcard Maine coast, which even now will be starting to fill up with tourists. Vibrant trees and hedgerows, some Victorian-era New England architecture. Grim truckers heading north to Portland or south to Boston and beyond, steering clear of the coastal fringe and US 1, which is packed with vacation traffic and usually slower.

Winter's End never gets many visitors. There's usually some hikers, snowmobilers, people who come for the fishing or hunting and a few adventurous types looking for something a little off the beaten path, but nothing like the infestation that the coast and the mountain resorts endure. Hell, the whole eastern chunk of Aroostook County is the same. Nothing but woods, cold weather and potato farms.

I wonder whether I'll have time to visit my hometown on this trip. I've not been back since I started at college down south. It might be interesting to see how much the place has changed, or how much it hasn't. It could also be a depressing experience.

I wonder whether anyone will remember me. I also wonder how many would remember my parents – my dad a lawyer and one of the town's volunteer firefighters, my mom a kindergarten assistant – and how many of those would know about the crash. Retired down to Florida with some of my mom's relatives and a couple of my dad's friends. Two years into the quiet life in the sun, I was visiting, driving them into town, when my car was T-boned and wrecked by a stolen sedan. The cops never caught the driver. I was thirty-one when I buried my parents in Hamworthy Cemetery a little way north of Miami. Six months later came the breakdown that finished me as a federal agent.

I found the NCAVC – the FBI's violent crime subdivision whose staff help local police forces on request – a hectic, messy assignment after the easier surroundings of the FBI field office in Atlanta. The latter was where I began life as an agent and where I first met Rob Garrett. With the NCAVC, people's lives were on the line in almost every job we took, and we never seemed to have enough staff to cover everything as we would have liked. Quantico's internal politics didn't help matters. While I'm still proud of the work we did, it was a pressure cooker of an assignment. Maybe I don't handle pressure very well. Maybe my parents' death was just one thing too many.

One October morning I suffered complete physical and mental collapse. For weeks I'd been growing more and more irrational, convinced that I was being deliberately overworked, and equally that it was all more than I could cope with. I wasn't sleeping or eating properly, drinking too much caffeine and smoking almost continuously. I'd had several full-blown psychotic episodes, thankfully while no one else was around to see, and when I did manage to sleep I'd have terrible nightmares, seeing the victims of the people we were trying to stop; murder, pain and torture like some horrible late-night cable channel. Not only that, but the Bureau was having one of its periodical reorganizations, making everyone unsure what they'd end up assigned to. Eventually, it all became too much.

Some time later, I found myself in a hospital in Kansas City. Paid leave on health grounds. The early days were a haze of tranquillizers, anti-depressants and anti-psychotics. I drifted in and out, from zombie to human and back again. After a while, the drugs were phased out and I could go home for a few months' less intense therapy. Then, just as I was starting to wonder about my future as a thirty-two-year-old FBI burnout, Rob got in touch and offered me a job with his agency in Boston. Easiest decision I ever made.

There has been a lot of water pass under my particular bridge, then, since the last time I pulled off I-95 at Exit 62, not far short of the Canadian border, and turned south into the town of Houlton.

I let the engine tick over, humming to itself as I cruise towards the town centre. Well-kept brick houses with a slightly bleached look to them, something that comes with the climate. Rows of box-shaped stores selling groceries, outdoor clothes, footwear. The Stars and Stripes flutters from the front of one, its colours washed out and faded. The people are dressed for spring and early summer – bright hues and lighter cloth. Couples chat to one another and kids play on the sidewalk, enjoying the freedom that Saturday brings. Some can't help glancing at the car. I cross the Meduxnekeag River and the steadily thickening knots of people and shopfronts tell me, if I didn't already know, that I'm almost at my destination. Further confirmation comes when I pass Market Square and see the line of stores on Main Street, some of them over a hundred years old. On the right-hand side of the road I spy a glass-fronted diner selling the kind of food that would have several health-freak lawyers I know back in Boston quivering and reaching for their vitamin supplements. I had a coffee at a rest stop on I-95 three hours ago and by now I'm starving. I make a mental note to grab lunch at the diner once I've met up with Dale.

I hit Military Street and the red brick of the Houlton Superior Court building, which also holds the main offices for the Sheriff's Department, is right in front of me, a stone's throw from the smaller District Court and the Aroostook County Jail. I swing the 'Vette into the Superior Court parking lot and pull up next to a Jeep Grand Cherokee with strobes on the roof and the six-pointed star of the Sheriff's Department on the side. There's a State Police blue-and-white not far away. I climb out of my car, which looks as out of place here as a ski shop on a Pacific island, and haul on my leather jacket. I feel like the bad guy in an action film, leaving his flashy sports car outside the bank before explosions fill the air and chaos ensues.

I push through the courthouse doors. A wooden sign on the wall inside directs me to the stairs if I want to find the Sheriff's Department offices on the first and second floors. There, a pair of open doors lead into a small but tidy room occupied by a handful of polished wood desks set with computers, file trays and assorted personal clutter. A man wearing a uniform shirt marked with a 'Dispatch' badge looks up from the short wooden counter he sits behind as I walk in. Him aside, there's a single deputy drinking coffee and staring at the glowing monitor in front of him, and otherwise the place is empty. There are two closed doors at the far end of the room, each of them marked with lettering too small to make out from where I stand.

'Can I help you, sir?' the dispatcher says, his expression neither friendly nor unfriendly, just blankly neutral.

'Yeah, my name's Alex Rourke. I'm here to see Sheriff Townsend.'

The man nods as if he'd already guessed my response and gestures at the left-hand door. 'The chief's in his office, go right on through.'

'Thanks,' I tell him.

'Alex!' says Dale as I step into his office. He's not quite as I've pictured whenever we've spoken on the phone. His gruff voice suggested a beard – he has a moustache – and a gut, which is just beginning to protrude as he heads for forty on a carbohydrate-heavy diet. His dark hair is starting to thin on top, though I'd give him another ten years before he faces the choice of whether to completely shave off what's left or not. Lines show around his eyes and his cheeks have begun to sag. The resemblance to his father is startling.

We have that moment that all people experience when they meet someone they haven't seen for years: studying, judging, remembering.

'Good to see you, Dale. It's been too long.'

'You too. You're looking well. Good trip?'

'All right,' I say. 'I'm starving, though. Is it okay if we talk over lunch? I passed a diner on the corner.'

'Pete's? Sure. I could do with a bite myself.'

As we enter the sun-splashed parking lot he points at my 'Vette and laughs. 'That's not yours, is it?'

'Saw it at an auction three years ago and couldn't resist.'

'I don't imagine you use it much in the line of duty.'

'It is a bit conspicuous for surveillance work,' I agree. 'Mind you, I don't have to do too much of that in Boston. If I do, I take a cab. At least then it's not me that has to worry about finding a parking space.'

We cut across the junction and into Pete's Diner. It has the same fried potato smell as every other establishment like it all over the world. Staff in red and white striped shirts weave between the tables like ballroom dancers. The café is busy but not packed, and we have no trouble finding a table and getting served quickly. I order a rare steak while Dale plumps for grilled fish with mashed potato. His wife has him on a diet, he explains. When the food arrives, I see why. It's huge. It's not a steak; it's practically half a cow. That's not salad; it's a forest. Those aren't fries but some distant mountain dusted with salt instead of snow.

I have a feeling I'm not going to be starving for very much longer.

'Has there been any change in our guy's story since you sent me the transcripts?' I ask Dale between mouthfuls.

He shakes his head. 'No. He gives us the same stuff every time; still no name. You ever encountered anything like this before?'

'I've heard of suspects refusing to tell the cops who they are, but they've always given in after a few hours. Since most of them that do it are trying to hide the fact that they've been busted before, their prints are on file anyway.' I swallow a mouthful of black coffee. 'Has the guy been arraigned?'

'Yep,' Dale says, 'had his hearing the day before yesterday. The judge slapped him with contempt of court since he wouldn't identify himself.'

'He refused to do it in court?'

'Same performance. They won't set a trial date for a while; they're giving us a chance to find out who he is.'

I nod and finish mopping up my lunch. 'Where have you got me staying? I might as well drop my stuff off and pick up a key before I talk to the guy.'

Dale looks a little sheepish. 'Well, I figured you might want to see the old town again, so I got you a room at the Crowhurst Lodge in Winter's End instead of somewhere here in Houlton. It's less than an hour's drive. I still live up there.'

'That's okay.'

'Sure?' Dale places his cup in front of him. 'Hey, Alex, I meant to ask you back during the Sharp case: how come you never came back to visit after you went to college?'

'Angry teenager,' I tell him. 'Had a fight with my folks

right before I left. By the time I patched things up, I was too busy to come back.'

'Yeah, Chris said something about that. Hope you didn't mind me asking.'

I shake my head and polish off the last of my coffee. 'I'll pay for this lot, then we can go meet your mystery man.'

I watch from behind the one-way glass as two deputies wearing Corrections Division uniform escort the guy into the interview room and sit him at the table. Although I've seen black and white reproductions of his mug shots, photos never compare with seeing a suspect in the flesh. Untidy straight black hair a couple of inches long. Guarded oval eyes coloured a blue so deep it's practically black. A narrow nose and thin mouth. He's a couple of inches shorter than I am, and I can see that beneath his orange County Jail overalls he's well built, though not hugely muscled. Mid to late twenties, I guess. He moves without any hint of rancour for his captors, even nodding at them when they show him to the chair. Then he just sits and stares, Zen-like, at the wall. He doesn't twitch. He doesn't blink.

'Good luck,' says Dale, patting me on the shoulder. 'He shouldn't give you any trouble; we haven't had any. I don't know whether you'll get much out of him, though.'

'Well, we'll see.'

The man glances up as I open the door to the interview room carrying a cup of coffee and a manila file. I walk to the seat opposite him and place both items on the table. Then, as I'm about to sit, I act as if I've just remembered something. 'Oh,' I say, 'did you want a cup? I should've asked.'

'No. Thank you.' He is quiet and softly spoken. His tone is polite and his accent hard to place, as if he moved around the country a lot while he was growing up.

'Well if you feel like one later on, just ask.' I spark up a Marlboro and leave the pack and my lighter on the table. Then I turn on the tape recorder and give the time, identify myself as Deputy Alex Rourke, and run through the guy's Miranda rights. I don't bother asking for a name.

Then I begin. 'Well, John ... That's kind of a silly sounding name – "John Doe". Is there something more personal I could call you? I'm not asking for your real name; if you don't want to give it to me, I can't force you.'

The guy regards me calmly, head cocked slightly to one side as if I'm a new lab rat whose quirks he finds interesting. Dark blue eyes reach out to me like they can see my thoughts, but without any hint of emotion. Whatever my thoughts are, they're obviously nothing to get worried or excited about.

'If you'd prefer, Deputy, you can call me Nicholas.' He smiles faintly. 'Not my true name, of course.'

'Sure. And you don't need to call me Deputy. Mr Rourke, Alex, whatever you want.' I take a drag on the cigarette to give him a chance to respond, but he stays silent and still. His eyes continue to track mine. 'How are you finding the jail? It's been renovated since I last saw it. Probably for the best; the paintwork used to be pretty drab.'

'I can think of worse places.'

'Me too. You get to see some real shitholes in my line of work.'

The eyes continue to stare at me. They suck in the conversation, leaving me talking to myself in an empty room. One-sided interviews are the bane of an interrogator, a sure sign of things going wrong. I change tack.

'It's got to be tough,' I say. 'Being stuck in a place like this on your own. No family to speak to, no friends. I take it you aren't a local?'

'You can take whatever you want, Mr Rourke.'

'Is there anyone you'd like us to contact for you, just to let them know you're okay? Even if it's just to cancel the morning papers.'

John Doe – Nicholas – smiles faintly again. 'I'm not a great reader of the news. I prefer to stick to less salacious subject matter. It's more stimulating.'

'Well, a man should always try to broaden his horizons. You study history?'

'Not specifically, no.'

I check my polystyrene cup, only to be disappointed; I've already drunk the contents without realizing it. I hate it when that happens. 'You know how Winter's End came to be founded, though.'

'I see one of the sheriff's people has been hard at work typing up our earlier conversations.'

I nod as if that's obvious. 'Of course. I wasn't going to come here without knowing what to expect.'

'And what did you expect?' Although his tone is steady, Nicholas leaves a slight pause before the final word. The effect is one of disdain.

'An apparently intelligent man who, for some reason, hung around a murder scene until the cops found him. There's three thousand miles of public highway in the county, Nicholas, and the Sheriff's Department has three patrol cars. Strange stroke of luck that Dale came along when he did.'

'Are you saying my timing was deliberate?'

The eyes are still fixed on me, but I just stare back through the cigarette haze. 'I'm not saying anything in particular. Maybe you were just unlucky. Maybe you wanted to get caught so people could marvel at what you'd done.'

'So what else did you learn from reading the transcripts, Mr Rourke?'

'Nothing definite,' I reply, brushing off the question and taking the opportunity to switch to a fresh cigarette. 'If you wouldn't mind, though, I'd like to hear why you were standing in the middle of the road on the night Angela Lamond died.'

'I've already given an answer to that.'

'Waiting. What were you waiting for?'

'Do you believe I'm a murderer?'

'That's what I drove all this way to find out.'

'Ah yes, how is Boston, Mr Rourke?'

Nicholas leans forward slightly, the only movement his frame has made since he first sat down. At the same time, his eyes widen slightly. His mouth opens further when he speaks, revealing the tips of ivory-white teeth. For some reason, the change in his posture and manner, slight though it is, unsettles me. The icy water feeling that not all is as it seems washes over me, quickly gone.

'Or should it be Agent Rourke?' Nicholas continues. 'Tell me, why did you leave the FBI?'

The question takes me aback, but I try not to let it show. 'You know I was in the FBI?'

'Why did you leave?'

'What else do you know about me?'

'Why did you *leave*, Agent Rourke?'

I take a long, soothing drag on my cigarette. Most successful interviews are based on trust. Suspects open up to you because they want to justify their actions to you, because you're someone they trust. Trust is the hook on the end of the fishing line, with confession the nice fat trout.

'Health reasons,' I say. 'Then someone I knew from the Bureau offered me a job in the private sector.'

'Health reasons?'

By now, Nicholas has returned to his original stance. His eyes are slightly wider though, less guarded. The sneering half-smile has become a permanent fixture. The tip of one white incisor is visible through the gap between his lips.

'Stress. Too many cases, not enough time. I had a breakdown.' I stub out the cigarette. 'I spent some time in an institution.'

'I would have thought the Bureau prepared you for the effects of the job while you were in training,' Nicholas says.

'They do, but nothing like that ever works all the time. Anyone can snap.'

'True.'

I sense an opening. 'Has that kind of thing ever happened to you, Nicholas?'

'Not as such, no.' His voice softens even more, barely louder than a whisper. I wonder whether the microphone will be able to pick it up. 'I came close once, a long time ago,' Nicholas says, eyes no longer looking at me, but back through time.

'What happened?' I ask. My voice is as low as his, as if we're holding our conversation in a church.

'I could feel myself starting to go. Then I made a decision, set myself a goal. Everything became clear again.'

'What did you decide?'

Nicholas seems to snap out of his reverie and his eyes harden again. 'That's private, Mr Rourke. I doubt you'd understand it, either.'

'You could try me.'

'I don't think so.'

This seems like a reasonable time to take a quick break. 'Do you want a coffee, Nicholas?' I ask him. 'I'm going to get one for myself.'

'No thanks.'

'Fair enough. Help yourself to a cigarette if you'd like one.'

I stand and walk out of the interview room. First I head to the coffee machine and help myself to a cup. Then I let myself into the darkened viewing room, where Dale is still watching the suspect from behind the mirrored glass. 'How does this compare with your earlier chats?' I ask him.

'Good,' he says. 'I'm impressed.'

'Get someone to send his pictures to mental institutions all over the north-east. There might be something in the breakdown angle that could identify him.'

'Sure.'

I walk back into the interview room and place my coffee on the table. My cigarette pack and lighter are lying where I left them. I sit back down. 'Did you know Angela Lamond, Nicholas?' I say once I've settled into my seat.

'What was there to know?' By now, his face has resumed

its Zen-like façade. I have no more idea what is going on behind the mask than I know what it's like to walk on the moon.

'She was a forty-year-old nurse who'd lived in Winter's End for her entire life. Her parents moved to Portland when her father changed jobs. They'd get in touch with each other every few weeks. The last time they saw her was to identify her body.' I take a long slurp at my coffee. 'She was a smart, attractive woman with no steady boyfriend, but plenty of friends and no enemies. She wasn't rich, didn't hang around in bad company and, as far as we know, had no reason for anyone to hate her. Yet someone abducted her, stripped her and stabbed her to death on a lonely highway in the middle of the night.' I finish my coffee and light a fresh cigarette.

The half-smile makes another fleeting appearance. 'By "someone", I assume you think it was me.'

'I just want to understand why it happened. I'm sure her family do too.'

'Why do you want to understand?' The question is posed so flatly, I can't tell whether he's being sarcastic or whether there is a real reason for asking.

'Their peace of mind.' I drag on the Marlboro and stub it out. 'Besides, the more people understand, the more we can stop things like this happening in the future.'

Nicholas's face stays impassive as he stares at me in silence for a moment. Eventually he says, '*Eripere vitam nemo non homini potest, at nemo mortem; mille ad hanc aditus patent.*' When I remain blank, he translates. 'Anyone can stop a man's life, but no one his death; a thousand doors open on to it.'

'Who are you quoting?'

'Seneca. I don't suppose you had much of a chance to study the classics at college, Mr Rourke. Criminology and law, wasn't it?'

I stay silent.

'And at high school I suspect you were too busy chasing cheerleaders,' Nicholas continues. 'Not really the sort to spend all your time in the library.'

'True enough.'

Nicholas smiles at me, like an indulgent parent at his child. 'I'm feeling tired, Mr Rourke. I wonder if we could continue this later.'

For a moment I think of denying this request, forcing him to stay until he answers my questions. However, something tells me that his resentment wouldn't make my job easier, and that I'd be better off letting him get relaxed and waiting for him to slip. It'll also give me a chance to find out how he knows so much about me.

'Sure,' I say. 'We'll stop here.'

I note the time, which is later than I'd thought, and turn off the tape recorder. Then I call for the two deputies to take Nicholas back to his cell. As he heads for the door, he stops and looks back at me.

'You asked what I was waiting for,' he says. 'I was waiting for you, Mr Rourke. You.'

# 4

The sun is dipping towards the distant humps of the Appalachians by the time I reach a spot on Route 11 marked with a couple of small bouquets of flowers. I bring the 'Vette to a halt at the side of the road and climb out. Small blooms of yellow and purple wrapped in cones of clear plastic. The petals are curled and wilting. I hear the door of Dale's Jeep shut as I bend to check the notes left with these floral memorials, curiously pathetic in the middle of the empty countryside.

> *Angela – Always in our memories, forever in our hearts.*
> *We love and miss you more than words can say.*

Neither card bears the names of its senders. I'm not sure whether they're sincere or not, just half-hearted offerings left by people who think they should care even if they don't.

'Folks from town, probably,' Dale says behind me.

I nod and stand up. 'Whereabouts was she when you found her?'

Dale leads me to a spot in the middle of the northbound lane no more than twenty feet from the hood of my car. There are still some faint marks from the crime scene investigation on the blacktop, the rest presumably washed away. 'Here,' he says. 'Head to the north, lying on her right side. You sure this is necessary?'

'There was a reason she died, and we need to know what it was,' I say. 'I need to check the scene, then walk the route Angela would have taken from work. I'd also like to look at her house. You said you'd got nothing in detail on her personal history?'

'Some, but I reckon we could get some more if we dug further. You think it's important?'

I bend to touch the asphalt. 'Always try to know the victim, Dale.'

'Speaking of which, our suspect seems to know a lot about you. What do you think he meant by "waiting" for you?'

'I don't know.'

Dale's coat rustles as he wedges his hands in the pockets to keep off the chill. 'He sounds educated,' he says. 'You think we should try asking colleges and universities whether they recognize him?'

I shrug. 'You can try, but I don't think it'll work. For one thing, you're talking about remembering one student in thousands. For another, I don't think he is well *educated*. To me he sounds more well *read*; no formal teaching, just what he's picked up for himself.'

'How do you get that?'

'The way he talks.' I stand and take a summary of the crime scene notes out of my jacket. 'He quotes stuff and brings out information, but there's no pattern to it. It's like having someone read poetry without giving it any sense of rhythm. You remember science at school?'

'Yeah, sure. Wasn't great at it back then.'

'Well, you know how you get taught to write up science experiments? Aims, apparatus, method, results? It gets ingrained in your brain, and once you've been taught, you'll do it that way for the rest of your life. Like riding a bike. Nicholas talks like he's hopping from results, to apparatus, to conclusion.'

Dale nods. 'I follow you.'

I glance briefly at a couple of police photos taken at a wide enough angle to show her entire body. Then I let my gaze wander over the roadway and the narrow concrete-lined culvert and fields to either side. 'You say there were no tracks in the grass?'

'No.'

The thigh-high stalks that fill the former farmland bordering the road are now bent and twisted into tufts by the crime scene unit's inch-by-inch search of the area around the site. The edge of the forest surrounding the oblong patch of grassland is visible as a dark line in the distance, three and a half miles north, half a mile south and a mile to the east and west. The fields are flat and empty. A breeze blows down from the west, setting the pale green strands dancing in rippling waves. A burgundy station wagon cruises past our little roadside scene, the family inside gawking openly at the curious conference taking place between the county sheriff and the stranger in the leather jacket.

'Why did he choose here?' I say, ostensibly to Dale, although we both know it's a rhetorical question. 'This is either a really stupid place to dump a body, or it's really clever and we've missed something. Fingernail scrapings on the vic turned up nothing?'

'No. What have you got in mind?'

I gesture up the road, towards town. 'If he didn't come across the fields, he must've come along the road. He couldn't walk openly with traffic, even sparse traffic, going past. If he walked her along the culvert, he could've laid them both flat whenever a vehicle came by. But if he did, she'd have grit and mud under her nails. Did the ME examine her toes?'

'I don't know.'

'Okay, I'll ask her tomorrow. Let's check out Angela's route home. Drive slow – I'd like to scope out the woods around town when we reach them.'

The thin belt of spruce and birch trees that separates the fields from the town itself offers no obvious sign that they were used as cover by the murderer. The area beneath the brilliant green canopy is open and airy, with scattered bursts of wiry undergrowth. Dog-walkers' countryside.

Then I'm through and driving past houses of red brick and whitewashed wood. Wide lawns carpeted with the kind of thick emerald grass that always sprouts after the spring thaw. Four-by-fours in driveways. Pick-up trucks and sturdy sedans. To a tourist, this would simply be one more picture-postcard Maine town. I, on the other hand, can see peeling paint under the eaves, loose boards, curtains in need of a wash. Winter's End is just an ordinary town with ordinary people and ordinary problems.

Ordinary in part because it's so familiar. I've been away for seventeen years and if you allow for certain changes in fashion – mostly cars and clothing – it seems as though nothing has changed. I could have left yesterday. Like anyone visiting their old stomping grounds after a long time away, I find myself scanning the faces of the people I pass, looking for features I recognize from my youth. Street names and buildings evoke surprisingly strong feelings of familiarity, and with them the memories. Skinner Street, where Rhona Garde lived when we were at high school. Making love while her parents were away – the first time for both of us – was probably the scariest five minutes of my life. Renfrey's Liquor, now a hardware store, where my friends and I used to buy six-packs before heading for Boynton Campground, a beauty spot in the woods just north of town, to get wasted. The grocery store, now a chain 7-Eleven, where I got my first part-time job to help pave my way to college. I push the memories aside and park opposite the doctor's office on Main Street.

I light a cigarette while Dale clambers out of his truck and straightens his jacket. A balding guy in a sweater and pressed corduroys waves at Dale and walks over. 'Evening, Sheriff,' he says with a bright voice.

'Hello, Leonard. Figured I might run into you.' Dale turns to me. 'Leonard works for the *Bangor Daily News*. He's been covering the Lamond case for them.'

'So who's this, Dale? Outside help?'

'Alex Rourke,' I say, extending my hand. He shakes it briefly, his eyes flicking over my face.

'Alex has been deputized to help us work on the case,' Dale tells the reporter. 'We grew up together here in town, so I wouldn't call him "outside help". Not exactly, anyway.'

Leonard regards me. 'What law enforcement experience have you got? If you don't mind telling me, that is. It'll save me a lot of digging and I'll know I've got my facts right.'

'I'm ex-FBI,' I tell him, 'now working privately down in Boston.'

'Any new discoveries, Dale?'

'When there are you'll be the first to hear about them, I

promise. Look, we've got to get going. If you want anything more out of Alex, he's staying at the Crowhurst Lodge. Have yourselves a beer later.'

'Sure,' Leonard says. 'Seeya, Dale. You too, Mr Rourke.'

Dale waits until we're crossing the road before he speaks again. 'Normally I've got no problem with Leonard,' he says. 'We don't usually have much intrusive journalism up here, and he's never shown the inclination. We get along just fine. But when he wrote his first story on Angela Lamond he included a whole string of "town in terror" stuff – you know, about folks being afraid to step outside or leave their kids playing unsupervised. Bull, mostly, or it would have been if he hadn't stirred things up with his writing. The first murder around here for years, we've got the guy, but the whole damn town's on edge. Byron wasn't best pleased.'

'Byron?'

'The mayor. You'll probably meet him at some point; I told him you'd be coming.'

By now, we're standing in front of the doctor's office. It's past closing time and the building is locked tight. Now that Dale has mentioned how tense the town is, I can feel it too. Winter's End is like the village in a western when the gunslinger rides in. Shutters slam, ordinary folk hurry off the street. I can still see people out and about, but they're just getting from here to there. No window-shopping. No time to stop and chat except to talk about murder. I haven't seen a single kid playing in the street since I got here.

I turn to the south and begin walking down Main Street under the indigo sky. Past storefronts with handwritten cards in their windows advertising garage sales and lost pets. The shops are typical small town fare: a couple of grocery stores, a place selling outdoor wear, a tiny book-store. Nothing large, and most of them pretty much as they've been for years. The only ones that ever change hands and move into a different business are the stores that have never done well to begin with. Right now, those that are open look quiet; a couple of bored clerks glance through the windows at me as I pass. The rest are shut. A block from the doctor's office, I make a right on to Carver.

'She went this way?' I say to Dale.

'As far as we know.'

Carver is a curving road flanked by neat red-brick houses with tidy little front yards, all almost identical to each other. Not one looks a day under fifty years old. Windows are shut for the most part, and the curtains framing them give the buildings a dark and walled-off aspect. Every time we pass one, though, I get the feeling that someone inside is watching. Twitches at the curtain. A glimmer of a shadow moving out of the corner of my eye. Some houses have cars in their driveways, some by the kerb. A red Toyota, a blue Cherokee, a brown pick-up. Further up the road, a short woman in her fifties or sixties is walking a dog.

Carver hits Altmayer after a couple of minutes' walk. The houses are bigger, although only marginally so, and many have white-painted wooden boards covering their stonework. Altmayer used to be where the town's better-off folk lived, though that had almost ceased to be the case by the time I was old enough to know it. Now it just holds most of Winter's End's oldest houses. Angela lived a few doors down from the junction. Her salary can't have been bad to afford one of these places. Half a dozen bouquets lie by the porch and the front door has a strip of police tape across it. Dale unlocks the door and ducks underneath the tape. I follow.

There are notes, mostly reminders and friends' phone numbers, stuck to the mirror in the hallway. A couple of spare coats hang on hooks behind the door. The living-room furniture is well-kept but starting to show threads. A TV, the remote control on the coffee table, and a TV guide on the sofa. Hi-fi with stacked CDs – Mozart, Vivaldi, some soul from the late sixties and a couple of modern compilations. The kitchen at the back is tidy, although there's an unwashed mug and cereal bowl in the sink. The calendar on the wall has a few dates marked in biro.

*Auntie Jean's birthday.*
*J, E, C, 9.00 pm at the Sawmill.*
*Dentist – 2.30!*

'"J", "E" and "C"?'

'Jenny Wright, Evelyn Reilley, Caitlin Hill. Friends of hers. They went out together every so often.'

I glance through the kitchen window at the back yard. Shrubs along the borders, a few flowers and a well-kept swathe of grass. Tidy and very green, lush with spring growth. Dale follows my gaze and tells me that the state crime scene people checked it.

Upstairs, the picture is much the same. The bed is unmade, and there are a couple of stray items of clothing discarded on a chair. One of the dresser drawers isn't fully shut. On top is a wilted rose in a glass vase.

'Present from an admirer?' I ask.

'She didn't have a boyfriend,' Dale replies. 'Forensics

checked it for latents and fibre *in situ* but all they got was a partial print from her left thumb on one of the leaves. Guess she might have bought it herself.'

'Uh-huh. I guess.'

A shoebox in the closet contains certificates, employment records and 'thank you' notes from past colleagues and patients from the office. The trappings of a life that's over. I start to replace them. Then a thought strikes me and I flick through the bundled papers.

'What are you looking for?' says Dale behind me.

'There's old job stuff in here. I'm wondering whether Angela ever worked anywhere where they got mental patients, just in case our boy Nicholas does turn out to be a nut.'

'I doubt she has – we don't have anything like that round here. As far as I know, she used to be the in-house nurse at the children's home before she worked at the doctor's office.'

I pause in my flicking. 'St Valentine's? Up where the old Wade House used to be, just outside of town?'

'Yeah,' Dale says. 'It closed after a fire about six years ago.'

'After my time,' I tell him, glancing over my shoulder. 'My dad used to visit the home occasionally when I was young, taking presents for some of the kids. I went with him a couple of times. I never heard about a fire.'

'The staff quarters burned to the ground one night, taking the director and a couple of others with it. The insurance company wouldn't pay up, so the home closed down. Come to think of it, your dad must have been one of the ones called out to tackle the blaze.'

I shrug and replace the papers. 'That's what volunteer

firefighters do, Dale. Are there any records of the kids who lived there?'

He shakes his head. 'Up in smoke. The county or the town council might have copies, though. You think there's a chance Nicholas spent time in St Valentine's?'

'Maybe. It's certainly worth a look.'

We head back downstairs and I wait on the porch while Dale locks up. The shadows of evening are beginning to deepen, painting the town a dull blue-grey. From here, Winter's End seems still. A couple of birds are wheeling high over the trees to the west, indistinct black shapes against the skyline. That aside, nothing moves. There are sounds, though. I can hear faint traffic noise from the highway and a radio or TV turned up too loud somewhere down the road.

'So what do you think?' Dale asks.

I glance at him. His face is expectant, as if he's hoping I've learned something that will help get Nicholas to talk. I know that what I have to tell him could come as a disappointment.

'Nothing definite,' I say. 'As far as I can see, there's still no clear reason for anyone to want Angela dead, so still no clue to Nicholas's motive.' I let my gaze wander down the road. 'There's something else too.'

'What?'

'I'll tell you over a beer, if you've got time for one before you go home.'

We walk to the Sawmill, one of the town's two bars. For some reason, despite the name, it's the other, Larry's, which is most often visited by the men working for the lumber companies further north. The Sawmill is a non-descript building with few windows and an open doorway.

The inside is floored in new-looking emerald carpet tiles. The counter, tables and other fittings are all of dark wood, although the inherent gloom that this creates is partially offset by the bright blue and white lighting behind the bar and over each table.

The barmaid appears to be a year or two younger than me. I take a good look at her while she's getting the drinks, trying to work out if I know her. Then I dismiss the idea as pointless, and content myself with paying for the beers. Business seems pretty slow right now. The day hasn't worn on long enough for there to be more than two staff on duty, and the handful of regulars look like the usual variety of barflies. Not drunks, necessarily, save for the big guy dozing in a tattered brown jacket in one corner, just people whose comfortable little routine involves downing a few after work, if they have a job. Comfortable routine is about all a town like this has to offer by way of a life. I don't see anything particularly wrong with how the Sawmill's regulars choose to fill theirs.

I knock back one bottle of Bud and start on a second before I tell Dale what I've got in mind. 'What if Nicholas had an accomplice, someone local working with him?'

Dale frowns at this suggestion. 'Is this just a hypothesis, or something you want me to take a serious look at?'

'It's a hypothesis. What have we got?' I start counting off the fingers in my spare, non-beer hand. 'A woman disappears on a journey that would've taken about five or six minutes at most. The locals don't remember seeing anyone suspicious. The woman vanishes for nearly five hours, during which time she is stripped naked. Then she turns up three and a half miles down the road, still naked, and we're fairly certain she hasn't come across country.

'The suspect we've got doesn't have a car that we know of, so presumably he snatched her on foot in the middle of a residential area. Then he takes her somewhere – we don't know where – and gets rid of her clothing. No one sees any of this. Then he walks her out of town along a public highway without being spotted by a truck driver we know passed that way twenty-five minutes before you did. I don't buy a truck driver failing to spot a naked woman on an empty road.'

'So where does the accomplice come in?'

'Let's say that Angela is walking home when someone living on Carver or Altmayer calls at her from his front door. He asks if she can give him a hand with something. She goes inside, he grabs her. Did the State Crime Lab run a toxin screen on her blood?' Dale just shrugs, so I continue. 'Anyway, this guy and Nicholas strip her and keep her inside for a few hours. Then they take her down to the garage, stick her in the accomplice's car and together they all drive out to the highway. The accomplice drops her and Nicholas off, then turns round and heads back into town.'

Dale thinks for a moment, giving me a chance to finish my beer and reach for a cigarette. Then he shakes his head. 'Suppose someone saw her going into the house?' he says. 'It'd be too risky. And we'd have picked up fibre traces from the car's seats on her body.'

'Plastic covering. Hell, keep her clothed, then strip her off when she gets to the place you found her. Take the clothes away in the car. The house is trickier, but suppose the accomplice picked her up in his vehicle rather than calling her into his home. It would be less obvious, particularly if you knew which neighbours were going to be in and which were at work. You could pick a spot on the road where as few people as possible would see.'

'True, though no one acted funny when we did door-to-door along her route the morning after.' He pauses for a moment. 'How about if Nicholas stole one of the locals' cars and used it to snatch Angela?'

'You'd have a report of a stolen car.'

'Not if he left her unconscious somewhere while he returned it.'

Now it's my turn to shake my head. 'That's as risky – no, more risky – than someone calling her into their house. Anyone could have seen him stealing or returning the vehicle, and he'd have to leave the body unattended while he did it. What if Angela's corpse got found? If the owner was home – pretty much a certainty since their car would have to be there – there'd also be the risk that they might want to go for a drive somewhere and find it gone.'

'Okay, maybe it doesn't quite fit. Let's leave it until you talk to Nicholas tomorrow. Maybe he'll let something slip.'

Dale stands and finishes the remaining dregs in his bottle. 'I'd better get going. Oh, before I forget, Laura wants you to come for dinner tomorrow. She'd make it tonight but her sister's down from Presque Isle.'

'Sure, no problem.'

'You remember where the Crowhurst Lodge is?'

I smile. 'The town hasn't changed that much. I'll see you tomorrow.'

I take a couple more drags on my cigarette, then finish the Bud and drop the empty back on the table. I decide to check into the hotel and leave my car there while I get something to eat. Outside, the gloom is deepening. What traffic there is, mostly people returning from work in the larger towns to the north and south, is hurried and purposeful, as if people are anxious to be off the streets before nightfall. The same is true for pedestrians, walking quickly, heads bowed.

Then one calls out to me. 'Alex? Alex Rourke?'

I turn to face a nervy-looking guy with short dark hair, glasses and the beginnings of a double chin. I have a feeling I should recognize him. 'Yeah?' I say.

'Cochrane, Matt Cochrane. We were at high school together.'

'Oh, hell, yeah! How's it going?' The memories are slower to return than my voice implies. Cochrane. Cochrane. A damp, slightly nerdy kid who I remember being better at maths than me. A little tubby, but not excessively so. Hand-me-down clothes. Not enough of a target to be bullied, not fun enough to have a lot of friends. I remember him getting drunk at one of our post-graduation parties and hurling on the lawn. I wouldn't be surprised to learn he'd gone on to become an accountant.

'It's good, good. I'm an accountant. Up in Ashland.'

That figures. 'Yeah? Good work?'

'I do all right.' A touch of pride in his voice. Without meaning to, we've entered the game of one-upmanship all old acquaintances fall into. 'I heard you became a cop.'

'FBI. Went into the Academy after college. I left to go private three years ago,' I say, trying not to make it sound like a challenge, another item to be trumped.

'Are you here on the nurse's murder case? Terrible business.'

'Dale Townsend called me in. It must be big news round here. I don't remember there ever being a murder in town.'

Matt nods. Then his face changes as he thinks of something else. 'What are you doing tonight?' he says.

'I've got to check into the hotel and get something to eat, but aside from that I've got no plans. A few notes to write up, maybe.'

'How about coming out for a drink with my wife and I? You remember Rhona, don't you? Her surname was Garde when we were at school.'

I concede the game to him. The aforementioned Rhona Garde, ex of Skinner Street. Sure, Matt's an accountant who never managed to escape the smallsville we grew up in. But he's the one who married my high school girlfriend.

'Great,' I say. 'What time, and where?'

'Meet you in the Sawmill at half-eight?'

'Okay, I'll see you then.'

Matt waves goodbye and I head for my car once more, helping myself to a cigarette to stave off the feeling of defeat. I wonder whether Matt and Rhona have any kids. Then I'm back in the 'Vette's welcoming interior and the smell of motor oil, old smoke and leather banishes such thoughts. I drive to the hotel.

The Crowhurst Lodge has been a hotel and guest house for almost its entire life. It is a 1920s building fashioned in neo-gothic style, with high windows and scattered chunks of decorative masonry around its ledges and cornices. Its white limestone facing seems to glow in the twilight. Twin mosaics, each depicting a smiling face, indistinct in the shadows, look down on me as I park, like grimacing circus clowns picked out in green and terracotta tiles.

We used to tell stories about the place years ago. How in the 1950s, a honeymooning couple were butchered in their sleep by a lunatic who'd escaped from an asylum near Bangor and was making his way north. How the ghosts of the dead could still be seen on the upper landing and in the room where they were slain. How their screams would still sometimes split the night, setting dogs barking and cats yowling. How the killer himself stalked the parking lot and trees nearby, where he was shot dead by two deputies. Kids' talk. Dares to see who would be brave enough to walk through the hotel grounds after dark.

The outer door, double-glazed frosted glass, is open and leads into a short, stubby porch lined with pamphlets, some of them practically antique, and adverts for local businesses. At the end of the porch is a second door, solid wood blackened through age, with a cast-iron knocker moulded to look like a snarling . . . whatever. The ring is missing, though, and it's probably no more than a leftover of the building's youth. I push the door open and step into a warmly lit foyer, which has the same neo-gothic leanings as the exterior, carpeted in slightly faded green. Doorways are arched, the ceiling is high. Light comes from sconces holding candle-shaped bulbs. The air smells slightly stale.

'Yes?' says an elderly man in a faded cardigan as he emerges from the doorway behind the desk. Lifeless grey hair clings to his lined head like a frightened child.

'My name's Alex Rourke. Sheriff Townsend booked a room for me.' I notice that my voice echoes faintly but the old man's, perhaps because of its different timbre, does not.

'Hm.' The man opens a ledger that looks no younger than himself and leafs through it. Pages filled with lists in faded, spidery handwriting. He finds the most recent page and runs his finger down it. 'Mr Rourke, yes. Room fourteen, at the top of the stairs. Sign in, please. Do you have any other baggage?'

As I autograph the book, I try to imagine the old man struggling up the stairs with armfuls of luggage. 'No,' I say. 'The room's at the top of the stairs?'

'First door on the right,' he says as he hands me a fob with two keys on it. One of them looks like it fits the front door. 'Breakfast is from seven to nine, dinner from six to eighty-thirty if you request it.'

I thank him and head up to my room. The stairs are old and solid, made from some sort of dark wood, winding around a central space and breaking on to a new landing every half-turn. The building is deathly quiet. Every floor seems identical: off-white paint and an air of neglect. I unlock my door and find myself in a small but clean and tidy room with a single bed, TV, dresser and closet. There's a phone on the dresser. A small door leads into the en suite toilet and shower.

I use the phone to send out for pizza – the number of the only place in town was in the porch – then take a quick shower and get changed. A buzzer sounds just after I flick on the TV and I assume this means the pizza guy has arrived. I check out the window and see his bike parked out front. As I'm about to turn away, I spot what looks like a figure lurking in the shadows beneath the trees which surround the hotel's small parking lot. I can't make out any details, just a dim silhouette and a glint of what could be a face with the same glow as the building's walls. The shape remains still as I stare at it. Then I blink and it's gone.

I go downstairs and collect my dinner. The scent of

melted cheese and a mixture of tomato and basil wafts from the warm box in my hand. The parking lot is empty save for the delivery boy's bike and my Corvette. The hotel is silent, too. It looks as if I'm the only one here. Even the old man behind the desk has vanished.

Once I've finished the pizza – which is pretty good, given that Winter's End isn't exactly Little Italy – I sling on my jacket and make my way back down to the Sawmill. Night is heavy on the town, a blanket of sable with only the barest hint of the indigo tones of the day just gone. Winter's End isn't silent, but has an edgy quiet amplified by the swish of the trees around the parking lot and the faint murmurings of TVs glowing behind lit windows on the streets leading off Main. Life is taking place behind closed doors tonight and I'm outside, alone in the dark. The feeling I have is that I might as well be on a different planet.

Then I push through the door of the Sawmill and into the quiet Saturday night hubbub inside, and everything changes. The faint *clunk* of pool balls comes from the back, and the jukebox is playing softly. People are talking, socializing. Normality. Matt is sitting at a table near the wall and with him is a woman facing away from me. Shoulder-length black hair and a violet sweater are the only details I can make out. He waves at me and I walk over.

'Alex!' he says as I reach the table. 'You and Rhona know each other, of course. See,' he says, turning to her, 'not changed a bit, I told you.'

'How are you Alex?' she asks. 'It's been a long time.'

'Too long.'

'Drinks are on me,' says Matt. 'What'll it be?'

'Beer, thanks.'

'Rum and Coke,' says Rhona. 'Actually, make that Diet Coke.'

Matt goes to the bar, giving me a chance to study my former girlfriend. She hasn't aged badly, the beginnings of laughter lines around her eyes are the only sign of her years, and while I guess she's trying to lose four or five pounds – *Diet* Coke – she doesn't look in bad shape. Her dark eyebrows are still fine and arched high over her deep brown eyes. Those same eyes have a slightly dead, flat look to them; resignation, perhaps. The eyes of someone whose dreams of a grand life elsewhere have slowly been eroded by the small town whose gravity well she could never escape. I knew her as a cheeky cheerleader-type, slightly too sure of herself, always ready with an acid put-down if she thought you deserved it. Perky figure, smooth skin. Warm, soft. Surprisingly tender behind the public façade, as nervous as I was on the evening when we both took our first serious step to being full-blown adults.

In many ways, I prefer the memory to the reality.

'So, how have you been?' I say. 'Matt seems to be doing well for himself.'

She nods. 'He is. I'm teaching English at the elementary school. Where did you get to after high school?'

'College, then the FBI. Now I work with an old Bureau buddy of mine down in Boston.'

'How are your parents? I haven't seen them since some of us threw them a going-away party.'

'Dead. Car accident three and a half years ago.'

'Oh, Alex, I'm sorry,' she says.

'Don't worry about it, it happened a long time ago.' I pull out a cigarette and light it, then hesitate as I take my first drag. 'Sorry, I should've asked if you minded me smoking. I've picked up some bad habits over the years.'

'It doesn't bother me.'

At this point, Matt returns with the drinks. He's on what looks like whisky sour. 'So,' he says, 'have you two caught up yet?'

'Rhona says she's become a teacher.' I grin, trying not to look like I'm faking. 'Who would have seen that coming?'

We laugh. 'I just wonder how she'll handle it when Seth's old enough to go to school,' says Matt.

'Seth?'

'Our boy.' Rhona looks at Matt, almost as if she's sheepishly admitting some shared secret. 'He's nearly five. How about you, Alex? Are you married? Any kids, a family?'

'I had a cat once.'

We chuckle. I can see that they're both being a little hesitant, unsure whether this is a sensitive subject for me. I swill some beer and decide to expand further. 'His name was Rusty. Got hit by a truck about eighteen months ago.'

What else can I tell them? That I never formed any successful long-term relationships while I was with the Bureau? That even if I had, I wouldn't have wanted kids? Sure, a lot of agents have perfectly happy home lives and perfectly normal families. But there are a few, particularly those whose work has them tracking the real monsters, who turn into the Paranoid Control Freak Parents From Hell as soon as they get their first child. Their exposure to society's darkest corners, which in all probability their offspring will never get closer to than the six o'clock news, scares them into putting up a barrier between their kids and the world outside. That was stress I could well do without; I had enough problems already.

When I was with the Bureau, I didn't want a family because I didn't want to leave them with only half of my life, the part outside the job. Since I left, I haven't made a serious effort to start one because I'm not sure that any sensible woman would want a failed FBI agent who burnt out at thirty-two as the father of her children. Maybe it's a self-esteem thing, but I've stuck with casual relationships at most.

'Whereabouts are you living now?' I ask, changing the subject.

'Spruce Street, not far from the library. The house needed a little work, but now it's all finished we've got more space than we know what to do with. Rhona thinks we could do with a couple more kids just to fill up the place.'

'Oh, Matt, stop it,' she says, slapping him playfully on the arm.

'Sounds nice,' I tell him and mean it, pretty much. I take a long gulp from the bottle and finish my cigarette. 'I live in a shoebox with a bed. But I still get residents' parking, so it's not all bad.'

'What do you drive these days?'

I pause for a moment, reflecting that perhaps there's still a last round of one-upmanship to be played and won. 'A '69 Stingray Corvette. When I drive, which isn't that often.'

Rhona laughs. 'You always were one for flashy cars, Alex. Maine's answer to Don Johnson.'

'Well, if I'm going to be remembered for something,

that's an image I can live with.' I grin and finish my beer. 'I'll get these. Same again?'

I fetch another round of drinks from the bar. The jukebox starts playing 'Ramblin' Man' by Hank Williams.

'Matt told me you're here working for the Sheriff's Department,' Rhona says once I've returned. 'To do with Angela being killed, I take it.'

'That's right. Dale Townsend asked me to help him out.'

'Is it going to be a complicated job? The only police work I've ever seen has been on TV.'

I shrug. 'Not complicated, but it might drag on for a while. It's mostly just a question of getting the guy to talk.'

'The man they arrested?' asks Matt.

'That's the one.'

Rhona sips her rum and Coke. 'It must have been awful for poor Angela. Has the man given you any idea why he did it?'

'I can't say. You know how it is with police work.' I light up another cigarette. 'How many of our old classmates are still in town?'

'There's a few,' says Matt. 'Jimbo's a mechanic, Brooke married Tristan Maitland – they've got two kids now – and Grant owns the pizza place. There's more, but I can't remember who right now.'

Rhona is about to cut in with some additions of her own when a hand slaps me firmly on the shoulder and a voice behind me says, 'So you're Alex Rourke. Dale told me you were coming.'

I turn to look up at a floury man in his mid- to late-forties. Brown hair shot with grey, combed neatly back from a widow's peak. A suit but no tie. The firm handshake of someone who likes to make out that he's as tough as the next man and won't stand for any bullshit. His flaccid eyes are constantly moving, judging, assessing. 'Byron Saville, mayor,' he says. 'I see you've done some catching up with old friends.'

'That's right. Do you know Matt and Rhona Cochrane?'

Saville nods. 'Sure. How's the case coming?'

'Well, this is the first day I've been on it. I'm fairly confident of having everything settled in a few days, though.'

'That's good, Alex, very good. The murder's got the whole town rattled. The sooner we can all put it behind us, the better. Dale spoke very highly of you.'

There's no answer to that and I don't give one. 'In any case,' Saville continues, 'if you need anything while you're here, just give me a call and I'll see what I can do.' He hands me a business card. 'In the meantime, I'll leave you to your drinks. Goodnight.'

'Goodnight, Mr Mayor.'

Saville struts away as if he's having a hard time keeping his inflated ego tethered to the ground. A big man in a small town; I know the signs. 'Word gets around fast,' I say to my two former classmates.

'Angela's death is a big thing,' says Matt. 'No one can believe something like that could happen to someone like her. She was always so quiet. Not like the other seniors. Did you hear about the time Scott Robson dared her and a couple of her friends to go with him to Mason Woods after nightfall? She got so freaked out by his spook stories that he had to drive the lot of them home. A sixteen-year-old still scared of the dark.'

'No, I don't remember. I remember Scott, though.' An

asshole, if I recall correctly, though my opinion of him may have been coloured by the natural disdain and fear younger kids hold towards their elders.

I also remember Mason Woods, an ill-defined area of forest east of town. Every kid growing up in Winter's End hears the various ghost stories set beneath its tangled boughs. A massacre of one of the local Indian tribes by French troops in the eighteenth century; a lynched trapper and his wife who committed suicide when she found his body; the spirit of a priest from the town who fell into a ravine.

Back in fifth grade, Dale's younger brother Chris and I spent a night camping out in Mason Woods. I told my folks I was going to be sleeping over at his place, and he told his folks the opposite. We spent so much time in and out of each other's houses that we figured they'd never bother checking.

We hiked into the woods, scattering into the trees by the road whenever we heard a car approaching, just in case the driver knew us and might tell our parents. A week or so before, Dale had told Chris a bunch of ghost stories about the Blue Axeman and suggested he'd be too chickenshit to spend a night out in the woods. It was the kind of challenge that a couple of kids like me and Chris couldn't help but take up.

The Blue Axeman was supposed to be the ghost of a tribesman who was pressed into service as a scout by a French officer back in colonial times. He didn't want to leave his family, though, and soon deserted to return to them. The officer who recruited him took a handful of soldiers and headed back to their homestead, making it there first. He hung the Axeman's wife and daughter from a tree to punish him for his crimes, then his men ambushed the Axeman as he tried to cut them down and bury them. According to Dale's stories, the Axeman's ghost had prowled the woods ever since, hunting the French officer so he could avenge his family. His spectre was supposed to appear on nights when the moonlight made the night sky appear a deep blue rather than black, hence the name, and to kill all who stood in his path.

There was a lot more to the tales, most of it pretty gory, but I've forgotten it down the years. The crucial point made by Dale was that the Hanging Tree, where the Axeman would begin his nightly rampages, was the huge and ancient fir which stood in the clearing outside Thachel Burrow, a cave running down underneath Golson Ridge. It was this small clearing, full of the bitter scent of pine resin, where we were going to spend the night.

We got there an hour or so before nightfall, laid out our sleeping bags and, with the trepidation of the young and parent-paranoid, lit a small fire. We huddled by its meagre flames, eating chocolate, drinking Coke and talking about kid stuff. Then darkness fell.

The sky was a deep velvety purple, touched by the slowly growing light of the moon rising in the east. The wind dropped to the kind of breeze which you can't feel, but which is still strong enough to rustle leaves and set branches scraping against each other. We tried to get to sleep, but between the chill of the night, the sounds of the forest and the stories of the Axeman, it was impossible. All the place needed was wolves howling to make it complete.

Then, around midnight, there was a noise from the cave behind us. A kind of snorting growl, distorted by the rock and sounding ever so loud in the quiet. Something moved in the darkness.

I don't think we stopped running until we made it home.

We were both grounded by wrathful parents for a week or two and had to go, shamefaced, back to the woods by daylight to retrieve our sleeping bags. Dale had a good laugh, as older brothers will, our folks soon forgot their anger and the incident passed into memory. I don't know what made the noise; probably just some animal out looking for food. But Chris and I never forgot the Axeman. If I had stayed in town rather than moving away, I'd probably be telling my own children stories about his ghostly quest for vengeance, smiling inwardly as they huddled closer and glanced fearfully at the shadows.

Everyone knows the stories, because everyone from town hears them when they're young. Some get embellished over the years, but not all. They never get forgotten, though. Kids save them up for when they're at high school, because Mason Woods is a favourite place to make out. You park at the old picnic spot on the edge of the forest, sit in your car and try to creep out your girlfriend with spooky tales to put you both in the mood before getting up close and personal. You stay in the car, though. They might just be stories, but still no one goes into the woods, except on the occasional dare like Chris and me. You never know, right?

My attention returns to the Sawmill and I realize that the conversation has – unsurprisingly – petered out. Matt and Rhona are both sitting uncomfortably, glancing at the bar, looking at another customer, sipping their drink, reading the beer mat, anything to make it look as though they're silent through choice and not necessity. Rhona eventually manages to find a way to break the deadlock.

'How long do you think you'll be up here for?' she says.

'At least another day, probably more. Dale's invited me to dinner tomorrow night.'

'Did you know that Chris joined the Coast Guard?'

I nod. 'Yeah, Dale filled me in the last time I worked with him, a year or two back.'

'I didn't know you were in town back then.'

'I wasn't. We did it all over the phone.'

Things go quiet again. Then Matt makes a show of checking his watch. 'It's getting late,' he says. 'We'd better be going. It was nice seeing you again, Alex. We'll have to keep in touch.'

'Sure,' I say. We both know it's bullshit. I hand him my card anyway. 'It was nice seeing the two of you again.'

Rhona leans close and kisses me on the cheek. She's wearing store-brand perfume. Cheap without being unpleasant. 'Take care, Alex,' she says. Then she and her husband leave.

As I finish my drink, I reflect on how little some people change over the years. It took an hour to get seventeen years of catching up out of the way. For some reason, I find that fact depressing.

I wedge a Marlboro between my lips as I step out of the bar and into the night. The lighter flame leaves bright blue spots dancing in front of my vision. It's a chilly evening, with no moon as yet and the stars partially hidden by tufts of cloud. Traffic is almost non-existent and the town is even quieter than it was before, as if the people safely tucked away indoors are now talking in whispers with their TVs muted. Occasional chinks of warm golden light leak through the gaps between curtains or at the edges of windows, but beyond that the only illumination comes from streetlights, the tip of my cigarette and a yellow neon sign advertising Coors in a closed liquor store on the far side of the road. A breeze I can't feel blows ghostly notes on the telephone lines spanning the street. I can hear, or imagine that I can hear, the same wind hissing through the trees on the edge of town. I glance at my watch. 9.40 p.m. The same time that Dale came upon Angela Lamond's body.

I walk home with nothing but the night's imaginary demons for company. A movement in the shadows: just a cat on the prowl. A voice talking in a hushed whisper: a TV turned up just loud enough to be audible. Footsteps that echo my own, but quieter and more hollow: someone walking the same path as me, too far behind to be visible. It's the kind of night when the superstitious subconscious fights with the rest of the brain to see who rules the roost, and actually has a chance of winning. When I can almost hear a lone, dead voice calling for revenge like a wolf howling in the distance. When I can almost hear others, victims of past crimes I never knew about or couldn't solve. When I can almost feel their anger.

I tell myself not to be so stupid and spark up another cigarette. While I'm doing it, though, I pull my collar up around my neck and quicken my pace. I don't want to be out in the cold for any longer than I need.

The Crowhurst Lodge is in darkness when I arrive. There isn't even a welcome light over the front door. The hotel's limestone facing has a sickly look to it; no longer glowing as it seemed to before, but now the colour of bone or milk gone sour, leaching away the starlight. This change in aspect makes the mosaic faces leer hungrily and

I wonder why the architect included them in the design for a hotel. I manage to slide my key into the lock on the second attempt, then find myself in almost complete blackness in the porch. Relying on memory, I avoid tripping over anything and when my questing fingers meet the rough boards of the inner wooden door, they do so without stubbing against the dark-stained wood. My hand brushes against the snarling face of the old knocker and I use its warm iron features as a convenient handle with which to push the door open.

A single candle-effect bulb in a socket above the main desk illuminates reception, albeit faintly. Its feeble glow and my night vision, by now well developed, are enough to guide me to and up the stairs. Memory finds my door, touch locates the keyhole and then I'm in and home. The instant brightness as I switch on the lights is a welcome relief.

I drop my jacket on the bed, then turn on the TV and splash some water on my face. I sit up for over an hour, skipping through random channels, before I douse the lights and fall into bed.

I can't sleep.

It's a combination of factors, but they add up to several hours of insomnia. I'm in new surroundings; primal instincts latch on to the building's unfamiliar smell and heighten my alertness. There also seems to be a draught coming from somewhere, although I can't pin down its source. The trees outside keep up a continuous whispering, loud enough to hear and not regular enough to lull me to sleep. I'm not comfortable lying on my left. I'm not comfortable lying on my right. Back. Front. Arms in. Arms out. Pillow. No pillow. I run through conversations in my head — the afternoon interview with Nicholas, the questions I'm going to ask him tomorrow. Picking apart my chat with Matt and Rhona.

I've suffered from insomnia on and off since college. It's not usually a problem if I'm somewhere familiar — at home or in my car (stakeouts being what they are). If there was a time *not* to have an attack, this is it.

The last time I remember seeing the clock by the bed, it reads four fifteen. Finally, sleep claims me.

# 5

Seven o'clock. The grating beep of the alarm drags me out of a surreal dreamscape I can barely remember. Something about snow-covered trees, but the details are fading fast. Perhaps it was a throwback to my youth; I used to have a recurring nightmare about the winter when I was growing up. Maybe it was the first sign of the trouble I've always had with sleeping, maybe not. No matter how many times I had it, it was always enough to wake me in the middle of the night. I'd sit in bed, arms wrapped around my knees, and try to clear my head so I could go back to sleep. It rarely worked.

My mom used to tell me that if you tried to remember the dreams you had, it would ruin your memory. I couldn't help it, and the nightmare is still locked solidly in my head. My memory doesn't seem so bad, so I think Mom was just trying to stop me worrying about what I'd see when I slept. Maybe it made it easier on her. She also told me that when you cracked your knuckles, the sound was made by the cartilage inside snapping and that you'd end up with arthritis when you grew up. I believed *that* one for years, until she admitted that she only said it because she hated the noise.

The nightmare would always begin as something else. I'd be dreaming about being an astronaut in the future, or a soldier in some far-flung country, when the details would start to change. If I was that soldier, for instance, I'd start to notice snow on the leaves of the jungle I was marching through. Pretty soon, the foliage would be rimmed with ice and inch-thick snow and I'd be trudging through the bitter cold. People with me would fade out and disappear as the temperature dropped. An icy wind would pick up, peppering my face with grains of snow that stung like sand thrown against my skin. Then I'd hear the voice behind me.

'You said we'd be somewhere safe by now,' it would say. A man's voice, rasping and dry. 'Now where are we? Where are we going?'

I'd turn to see a man with a straggly beard, dressed in leather and tattered furs. Never modern clothes. His face was always pale and his skin looked raw, unhealthy. His eyes scared me most, though. They were flat and cold, the eyes of a dead man, yet at the same time they had a sense of pleading in them, a desperation I could do nothing to alleviate.

Behind him would be a line of battered wagons, old wooden ones, and thin, gaunt people clad like the bearded man. Some would have blackened and burned patches of skin. Others I would see were missing fingers, or walking with the aid of crutches to spare feet wrapped in ragged bandages soaked with blood and dirt. Their eyes were all alike, and they'd all stare at me.

'Where are we going?' the man would ask again, a question I never knew the answer to. 'What are we supposed to eat? We're down to our last scraps of food.'

The expression on his face would harden and his eyes grow even colder and more unfriendly as I continued to struggle for words. 'We should never have come this way,' he'd say, stepping closer. 'Are you going to get us back? Do you even know where we are?'

I could never hold firm in the face of his sheer hostility

and would always start backing away. 'I don't know,' was all I could usually say.

'Don't know? What the hell do you mean, you don't know? This was your idea!' he'd shout, coming after me. 'This is all your fault! We're dying because of you!'

I couldn't take the cold, dead stares of the people in rags, and the fury of the bearded man scared the hell out of me. I'd turn and run blindly into the forest, crashing through the snow and ice, scraping my face and hands on the branches as they whipped past me. I'd hear the bearded man chasing me, his footfalls smashing through the undergrowth. He always seemed to be faster, but not fast enough to quite catch me; dream logic, I guess. Usually, I wouldn't be far into this panicky escape before I'd catch my foot on something and fall headlong into the snow. Cold, like liquid dread, or the sudden realization that something seriously bad has happened, would smother me and I would wake up with a pounding heart, out of breath and shit-scared.

If I did have the same dream last night, at least it didn't wake me. As it is, I feel as if I've only been asleep for a couple of hours. Zombie-like, I head for the bathroom and autopilot my way through the three 'S's – shower, shit, shave. Dress, slowly and mechanically. Have my first cigarette of the day. Double-check to make sure I haven't forgotten anything. Then I make my way downstairs with the intention of grabbing breakfast and plenty of coffee.

The building is lighter and now, without the gloom and darkness of the night before, quite airy. The stairs wind around an open central space, which reaches from the green carpet downstairs to the vaulted ceiling. There's still no sign of anyone other than myself in residence, although the smell of cooked food emanates from the doorway next

79

to the reception desk. There's no sign at all of the old man I saw yesterday. The dining room is large enough to seat a couple of dozen people at six round tables. A buffet off to one side holds a surprisingly good range of breakfast offerings on hot plates, although the actual amounts on offer bolster my belief that I'm alone in the hotel. I help myself to some cereal and orange juice, then a big plate of fried stuff and an entire pot of coffee. All this time, the building stays strangely silent. The rattle of my cutlery echoes and I find myself trying to eat more quietly.

Finished, I leave the dining room and cross the foyer, taking a quick look behind the desk to see if I can spot any sign of the manager's recent presence. Nothing. Outside, the day is bright but the sky is peppered with small clumps of cloud. There are darker patches of grey over the rugged foothills to the west. The peaks and valleys occupy most of the horizon, marching from it like a green-clad sea frozen in time before its waves could break upon the beach. The shreds of low cloud above them make them look as though they're frowning at me, showing their displeasure for some misdemeanour I'm not even aware I've committed.

As my car leaves the gravel driveway and turns on to the road, the engine its usual comforting snarl, I catch sight of a dark-haired girl. For one brief moment she seems familiar. Then I get closer and it passes. She's young – seventeen or eighteen – with short hair and neat, colourful clothing. The girl watches my 'Vette as I drive by, and continues to stare at it until she becomes too small in the mirror to make out. Just a small-town kid, maybe, gawking at a big-town car.

Perhaps because of this, or perhaps because of my

tiredness, I'm driving fairly slowly as I cut through the old fields, past the murder scene, and re-enter the woods on the far side. A few hundred yards in, an overgrown track winds away to the left, disappearing as it passes behind ranks of dead-looking brown trunks and thick, matted undergrowth that doesn't seem to have started its seasonal greening yet. The silhouette of a building is just about visible at the far end of the trail, peeking out through the trees maybe half a mile away. A high gable and a roof that seems to sag in the middle. The track is unsignposted, but I know the building. The old Wade House, then the St Valentine's Home for Children. I wonder whether Dale and the State Police crime scene unit checked it at all. I make a mental note to ask him.

The primeval forest, dark with new spring growth, continues almost unbroken along miles of rolling hills before turning abruptly into grass and farmland as I head east on Route 212. The change is sharp, a sudden switch back to the modern human world, away from the endless woodland. From here, it's over half an hour of empty country, great swathes of flat farm earth blanketed in green shoots, and small towns to reach Houlton. I leave my car in the lot by the sun-washed walls of the Superior Court, then walk back up to Houlton Regional Hospital to see Dr Gemma Larson, the medical examiner who carried out the post-mortem on Angela Lamond. It's a nice day and I could probably do with the exercise.

The morgue is situated in the bowels of the hospital, well away from the areas frequented by patients. At least, those frequented by living patients. A corridor painted white and pale blue turns through a double set of aluminium doors and into an office containing a couple of desks, computer terminals, lockers and a coffee machine. A second set of doors leads into a spacious, well-lit chamber lined on one side by the usual chiller cabinet with its drawers marked by name and serial number, and on the other by three examination tables and neatly arranged banks of surgical tools and scientific instruments. Through one of the windows looking into the mortuary proper, I can see a blonde woman in a lab coat and gown supervising the loading of a fresh addition to her collection. I tap a couple of times on the glass and she turns around, then beckons me inside.

In my experience, pathologists tend to fall into three categories. The first act no different at work than they do when having a drink over dinner. They chat, tell jokes and discuss the latest football scores while cutting into brain matter. The second are those who seem to have gravitated to the job because they lack some of the necessary social skills to get on well with their living counterparts. The third are usually the oldest, weary of the job and looking forward to retirement.

I have no problem with morticians or their work. It can be quite grisly at times, but in some ways I'd rather do their job than work in an abattoir. At least here, what goes under the scalpel is already dead when it comes through the door.

I hang back a couple of paces while a pair of morgue assistants place the body of an elderly man on one of the drawers. Then, once the two have wheeled their empty gurney away, Dr Larson scribbles down his details on the identity card and turns to me. She has high cheekbones, eyes like smooth jade and blonde hair tied back in a ponytail. She's a few inches shorter than me, slim and pretty. It's not as though she's just stepped out of a swimsuit modelling shoot, but she's *definitely* attractive, with a delicate elfin look to her. I guess that she's three or four years younger than I am.

'You must be Mr Rourke,' she says, her eyes giving me the same quick once-over mine have just given her. She extends her hand, which I shake. 'I'm Gemma Larson.'

'Call me Alex, Dr Larson.'

'Gemma,' she says, giving me a quick, bright little smile. 'How can I help you?'

'Angela Lamond, a murder victim from a few days ago. When you worked on her, were scrapings taken from underneath her toenails as well as her fingers? I know it's not something that often comes up.'

She stares into space for a moment, then says, 'I'm not sure. Come into my office and I'll check my notes.'

I follow her back into the outer room and over to one of the computers. 'We covered her hands and head with plastic bags at the scene to protect them,' she says after a moment of scanning the screen. 'We didn't do it with the feet, but I did check her toenails during the exam. Two specks of tar-covered gravel, almost certainly from the road, but nothing else. It's possible other traces may have been washed away.'

I nod. 'Were there any kind of dimple marks on the soles of her feet like she'd been walking barefoot on the road or on another rough surface?'

'There's nothing in my notes, but the feet weren't my main area of interest.' Gemma dips one eyebrow, half-frowning. 'With surface water there could well have been dimpling anyway, like you get after you've been in the shower or bath. I could check again. I would have spotted any visible areas of broken skin, but there might still be tiny pinpricks if the edges of the stones dug in.'

'What about blood toxins?' I say, then give an embarrassed laugh. 'Sorry, I'm being very officious. I didn't sleep well last night. Normally I'm much more easy to get on with.'

Gemma flashes me her smile again, then her gaze shifts down at the desktop. 'That's all right,' she says. 'I have mornings like that. The lab in Augusta did screen her blood, but from preliminary results it doesn't look like there's anything out of the ordinary in it.'

'Ah, nuts. An otherwise good theory out the window.'

'If you give me your phone number, I'll give you a call when I've checked the feet again,' she says, finished with the monitor screen. 'It shouldn't take long, but I've got a couple of other things to do this morning as well.'

'Do you normally work on Sundays?'

She shrugs and tucks a stray hair back behind one ear with her fingertips. 'My shifts vary, but it does happen when the hospital's busy.'

'Irritating, isn't it?'

'I don't know; sometimes it has its moments.' Her eyes meet mine, then quickly look away again. 'Anyway, you were going to give me your phone number,' she says.

'Sure. In fact, if we swap numbers I'll be able to get in touch if there's anything else that jumps to mind.'

Hastily scribbled notes are exchanged. 'If you try to get through and find my phone's switched off, it's because I'm in interrogation,' I say once I have her number safely in my pocket. 'You can leave a message or get me to call you back.'

'Okay. I'll call you later.'

I grin involuntarily. 'That'd be great, thanks. I'll say bye for now, then.'

She waves at me and smiles again. 'Goodbye.'

As I head for the County Jail, a voice in the back of my mind points out that there weren't any photos on her desk, and no wedding ring on the hand that touched her hair. I remind myself that they might be in her locker, or might not be allowed at work. For now, there are more important matters at hand.

Nicholas is waiting in the interview room when I walk through the door.

'Mr Rourke,' he says without turning around. 'How nice to see you again.'

'Good morning, Nicholas.' I drop into the chair facing him and turn on the tape recorder, then run through the usual identification procedure and read him his rights.

'Sleep well?'

I glance at him. Nicholas is sitting, as always, perfectly still and calm. His voice is level and without inflection, like a shrink trying to ask questions without leading his patient. I light a Marlboro.

'Not really, no,' I say.

'You look rather tired. How was your return to Winter's End?'

'What's to say I've been back?'

He permits a half-smile to break the stillness of his features. 'You came all this way and didn't visit your hometown? I don't think so. I wouldn't be surprised if you were staying there.'

'As it happens, I have been back. I took a look at the spot where you were arrested. I've been wondering what route you took there. North or south?'

'How do you know I didn't come from the east or west?'

'The police didn't find any tracks through the fields. How could you have avoided leaving a trail?'

'You're asking because you don't know how I or the woman's body turned up on the highway without being seen. Work it out. The information is there.'

'You'd prefer me to do that? Why not just tell me?'

'I'm *relying* on you to do that, Mr Rourke. Believe me when I say that there's nothing to be gained by revealing all.'

I take a long drag on my cigarette and regard the man in front of me for a moment. Tone alone provides his emphasis. As usual, his posture and body language don't change at all. His ability to sit like a barely animate statue makes him infuriatingly hard to read. I have no idea what he means by 'relying' on me. I decide to let it pass for the moment.

'I've done some checking and I still can't work out why Angela was chosen as a victim. Assuming she was chosen,' I add.

'Have you ever been fishing, Mr Rourke?'

I shrug. 'I've been once or twice.'

'Taught by your father? Where did you go?'

'Claye Lake. Why?'

Nicholas seems to ignore my question. His eyes meet mine and he says, softly, 'Claye Lake. A small cabin thirty yards or so from the lake. Trees running all the way down to the water's edge. A young boy with his adoring daddy. Pleasant picture.' A trace of emotion passes over his features, a twinge at the corner of his mouth. It's not there long enough for me to work out if it's sadness or pride. 'Did your father explain why there are different types of fishing, with different types of bait and different techniques?'

I pause for a moment. His description of the cabin where my father used to fish, which I visited a couple of times as a boy, is startling in its accuracy. But then I figure, trees down to the water and small cabins are a dime a dozen in these parts. I don't much like the thought of someone like Nicholas talking about my dad, either, though I don't want to show it. 'Not really, no,' I say.

'Then I'll use a different example. Do you believe in God, Mr Rourke?'

I shake my head. 'Not really, Nicholas.'

'No?'

'I've never really seen the point. A pleasant afterlife might be something to look forward to, but I'd rather make the best of the one I've got right now.'

'I have a hard time imagining a policeman who wouldn't take comfort in the idea of heavenly judgement whenever the bad guy walks free from court.'

'Nice idea, but I've always preferred to get the judgement correct here on earth.'

Nicholas smiles, showing the tips of his teeth again. 'Yet you can rarely rely on getting the result that's right even when you do have a good case. I admire you, Mr Rourke, for your faith in man's efforts at justice.'

'You prefer divine retribution?' I say.

'Divine?' He chuckles dryly. 'I never said anything about *divine* retribution. Entirely the wrong way of looking at it. Sometimes people's actions put them in the service of the Devil. If God won't forgive them, he'll eventually come to collect.'

'What do you mean?'

'Say, for example, that I committed a murder and got away with it. Then one day, I get hit by a car and killed. My borrowed time is up.'

'Did Angela Lamond get away with some crime that no one knew anything about? Was she living on borrowed time?'

Nicholas smiles and gently shakes his head. The movement is rare enough that I take far more notice of it than I would in a normal conversation with a regular human being. 'Until you know the answer to that yourself, I'm afraid I can't help you,' he says.

'Well, I've looked at her history but I can't see anything there. Maybe there never was. Maybe she'd never done anything to put her on to borrowed time.' It's my turn to smile. 'If she had, I doubt it would have been to anyone important.'

There's a moment of silence. When Nicholas replies his face stays emotionless but his tone is different, more controlled. I can't tell whether he's angry or laughing. 'Maybe so; importance is relative. But you're in no position to know.' He relaxes again. 'Trust me on that.'

I continue to press home my questions. 'I'd like to trust you, Nicholas, but at the moment I don't understand what happened. To me, it looks like any other random killing by a nut who needed to vent his anger on someone. I can't see any bigger picture. Perhaps you could show it to me.'

'I've already told you I won't do that. But believe me, Mr Rourke, when I say that by the time you return to Boston, you'll know the reason why the nurse died.'

'Are you saying you killed her?'

'I'm saying I know why she died. You will too.'

The promise is spoken as flatly as if he had just said he

was going to buy the next round of drinks or pay me back the ten bucks he owes me. Despite his choice of words, there's no sense of him being in love with his own cleverness. Normally, I'd start pushing my suspect at this point, driving forward to get a confession, or at least a coherent statement, out of him. Two things stop me from doing that with Nicholas. The first is that, while he's no longer being so evasive, I don't have the feeling that he's about to break. The change in his manner seems too deliberate and calculated, a slow release of information rather than a guilty flood. The second reason is harder to quantify, a gut instinct that tells me to go along with it for the time being.

I help myself to another cigarette and change tack. 'You said you believe in God, Nicholas. Are you a follower of a particular faith or church?'

'Why do you ask?'

'We can try to accommodate any individual religious leanings at the jail. Are you a Christian?'

'That question is an amusing one, coming from someone from your part of the country, Mr Rourke,' he says. 'Very amusing.'

I raise my eyebrows, baffled. 'What do you mean?'

'Surely you know your own civic history. Didn't you learn about Charles Ryland when you were at school?'

'I never paid much attention in class.'

'He was a rich businessman who spent a year building a new church for your hometown when the inhabitants had barely finished hacking land out of the forest. At the height of the first sermon in the chapel, the building was struck by lightning and Ryland, the priest and eighteen others died in the fire that followed.' Nicholas smiles at me, almost contentedly. 'I'm not a Christian. Nor a Muslim,

Jew, Buddhist or anything of that nature, but I am a great admirer of God's sense of humour. Even if His jokes are sometimes a little cruel, His timing is usually impeccable.'

'So you believe in God and the Devil. And you think Angela Lamond is, what, burning in the fires of Hell?'

'The "fires" of Hell aren't really appropriate here, Mr Rourke. Do you know where the Bible was written? The eastern Mediterranean. A hot climate. Deserts. Sand-storms, drought, sunstroke, plague. Hot weather evils. I suspect that's where the association comes from. In this part of the world, I'd say that "icy wastes" would sum it up better.'

'And that's where Angela Lamond is?'

'Yes.'

'What did she do to deserve it?'

'You're repeating yourself, Mr Rourke.' Nicholas sighs.

'That's because I seem to be wasting my time,' I say. Maybe it's the way he sighs, or maybe it's the feeling I have that he's patronizing me. Maybe I'm just getting fed up with the bullshit he's spouting. 'I'm hoping that you're eventually going to be smart enough to realize that giving me your side of the story is the only chance you have of avoiding jail.'

'I doubt it.'

'We'll never know if you don't stop being an asshole and actually give me something useful.'

'Language, Mr Rourke. I'm sure your parents didn't bring you up to swear at people.'

'You obviously didn't know my parents, Nicholas. They'd swear like anyone else if they got annoyed.'

He smiles like I've said something funny. 'And you're annoyed?'

'Smartass pricks trying to be clever always do that to me. So why not help me out?'

'I already have, Mr Rourke. You just don't know it yet. Come back and see me tomorrow, or perhaps later today. As you become more aware of your destination, I'll illuminate more of the path for you.'

I think for a moment, then nod and stub out my cigarette. 'Okay, Nicholas. I'll see you later. Let's hope you can start talking to me then.'

I have the deputies outside take the suspect back to his cell, then I go to find Dale. He's in his office, talking to another man in uniform, when I knock on the door.

'Alex Rourke,' he says, 'this is Owen Marsh, Chief Deputy. He's been handling most of my civic duties while I focus on the Lamond case.'

'Owen,' I say, extending my hand. Dale's second in command looks about the same age, with a slimmer build and a nose rouged by burst capillaries just beneath the skin.

'Mr Rourke,' he replies before turning back to Dale. 'Morris said he'd like you there if possible. He said it's good for the town's image, and since it's only a short way up the road I told him I'd ask you.'

'When is it?' asks Dale.

'Tuesday at midday.'

'All right, tell him I'll be there unless anything urgent crops up.'

Owen nods and walks out.

'Monticello Town Fair,' Dale explains as I claim the chair opposite. 'Mayor Morris likes having as many of the county's dignitaries there as possible. A policeman's work is never done. How's our man coming along?'

'I'm starting to feel like I'm getting somewhere, but it's not going to happen quickly. On my way here this morning I caught sight of St Valentine's,' I say, changing to the subject I came to talk about. 'Was it checked when the murder site was examined?'

Dale thinks for a moment, then shakes his head. 'We didn't have any information to suggest it might have been relevant, so we didn't go up there. Why?'

'It struck me that the turn-off for the old building is only half a mile from the crime scene, and the driveway itself isn't any more than half a mile long. We've been assuming the guy brought Angela to the scene from town. What if he came the other way, from the south? He wouldn't even have been on the highway at the time the truck driver passed through.'

'You want to go up there?'

'Yeah. Just in case.'

Dale nods and I catch something in his eyes, a glimpse of a fleeting thought or emotion, quickly gone. 'Do you want me to go with you?'

'Shouldn't be necessary. I've got my badge to flash if anyone asks what I'm doing. I'll give you a call if I find anything. Otherwise, I'll see you for dinner tonight. Whereabouts do you live?'

'Francis Street, number fourteen. Come by about half six or seven,' he says. 'You're not going to be returning here after you have a look at St Valentine's?'

I shake my head. 'Not unless I find anything staggering. I might do a bit of talking around town, then try and grab a few hours' sleep before dinner. I didn't get much last night.'

'No? You do look a bit worn out, now you mention it. Nothing wrong with the hotel, is there?'

'I just get insomnia every so often. I'll see you later.'

I've just stepped out of the building when my phone rings. 'Alex,' says a woman's voice, 'it's Gemma Larson at the hospital. I've just checked Angela Lamond's feet again.'

'Hi, Gemma. What did you find?'

'A few pinpricks of broken skin. I'd say she'd been walking on the road barefoot. It's impossible to determine age on such minute cuts, though.'

'That's okay,' I say. 'It seems likely that she did walk to the scene and wasn't driven, and that's good enough for me. I don't suppose there were any grit traces in the breaks?'

'No such luck, sorry.'

'Can't win them all, I guess.'

'I guess not.'

'Well, thanks again, Gemma. It's really nice of you to get back to me so fast. I'll give you a ring if anything else comes up.'

'Sure,' she says. 'You're welcome. Bye for now.'

'Goodbye.'

I breathe out slowly, then slide into my car and start back towards Winter's End.

The gravel and aggregate of the St Valentine's Home for Children driveway crunches beneath my tyres as I gently coax my Corvette up the slope towards the building's hunkering mass. Grass and weeds are slowly establishing themselves between the stones as the forest embarks on reclaiming the land carved out of it years before. The trees around are in full spring bloom and the drive is roofed by a green vault of birch and ash leaves. A hundred yards from the derelict hulk, I come across a set of wrought-iron gates set in the mouldering remains of a wall which seems to surround the establishment. The gates are yawning open, rusted in place, and I park the car just inside. The building sits in a wide clearing that would once have been its grounds. Green shoots blanket what was, I guess, the gravel parking lot, and the lawn is a knee-high field of grass stalks. A couple of cherry trees in blossom rise out of the overgrown sward, occasionally dropping petals in the breeze. It looks as though it would once have been a pleasant place to live.

I step out of the car and into air that has the damp, organic smell of fresh grass and leaf mulch. The clearing is quiet, but seems somehow watchful. A forgotten place alert to a new intruder, wondering how many of its secrets risk exposure, how many of its ghosts are to be disturbed.

A single feature immediately draws my attention. What look like a double set of tracks, lines of bent and crumpled grass across the former parking lot. I think about calling Dale and getting him to send for a crime scene unit, but since the trail doesn't mean a thing by itself, I decide to leave it until I've checked the building. This isn't a fresh scene, so the CSU can afford to wait for a while.

I check my gun, just in case, and drop my bolt-cutters in my belt before picking up my camera and flashlight and heading for the building, careful to avoid walking over the track marks.

St Valentine's looms above me, a four-storey edifice of red brick and aluminium siding with the lines of the original house still visible beneath. The old brass plaque by the main entrance is still in place, now coated in a slime of green algae. Several windows are broken and the rest are dark. A padlock and chain that once barred the front doors have been wrenched out of place, taking the handles with them, but I notice that there are no scrape marks in the leaf litter on the top step. Leaving the doors as I found them, I switch my flashlight on and clamber in through a nearby window.

Things have changed since my last visit. From what little I remember, St Valentine's used to be a clean place, if somewhat clinical and spartan. I wouldn't have fancied living there; the staff seemed very austere and the building itself had an unfriendly air, the cause of which I couldn't put a finger on.

Now the structure smells of old sawdust and years of disuse. Damp is busily attacking the walls, flaking the paint and leaving blue-black bubbles in the paper. Windblown leaves are scattered on the mouldering carpet tiles near the window, mingling with pieces of detritus left over from when the children's home closed – a couple of plastic bags, a discarded stuffed bear. Somewhere deep within the gloomy structure I hear something patter over the floor. I move through the room and further inside, searching for some evidence of recent visitation. The entire building sighs whenever the breeze passes through its shattered windows; the noise makes it seem as if the old house is breathing long and slow, asleep. Everywhere my flashlight beam roams, it picks out signs of years of neglect. Beetles are nesting in the ruins of the old front desk, the carpets are decaying, eaten away a thread at a time, and moisture has started to warp the wooden fittings. The air is chilly inside, noticeably cooler than in the grounds.

The main house seems to have been mostly occupied by facilities for the kids staying here. I walk through a number of dormitories with many of their bunks still intact, though now riddled with damp and mould. A dining room and kitchen, showers, and what looks to have been a small classroom. Something I recall from my few childhood visits to St Valentine's as being a playroom, now empty save for the broken shards of a toy robot in the detritus on the floor. Store cupboards. A staff room. A couple of wooden doors with corroded brass locks still intact. There's a small administration office on the fourth floor, littered with empty filing cabinets and galvanized drawers.

Downstairs, soot in whirls and leaf patterns streaks the walls of the corridor leading to what were the staff quarters. The carpet underfoot is blackened in places and in even worse condition than the floor elsewhere. The door at the other end is shut, and when I open it, I find myself in the ruins of the old staff wing. The walls of the building continue for a little way in each direction, albeit dark and buckled. Charred beams criss-cross above me, and I can glimpse patches of the sky beyond. A few yards into what remains of this extension to the building, I can only guess at its shape by the height of each jumbled pile of masonry, charcoal and debris. The staff wing runs for a good sixty or seventy feet in all, and almost everything within has been razed. Nothing has disturbed the ashen silt on the floor in a long time and my footprints cut a lonely path through the blackened rubble.

The basement is the last place I check. It's small and occupied mostly by laundry and washing equipment, long since disused. Rust-coloured residue smears the bottom of sinks and hulking lines of washing machines like so much dried coffee. Power and water are both dead and aside from an old bundle of towels covered in cobwebs, the place is empty. There's a gas boiler larger and older than its domestic cousins tucked in one corner, dead and dusty. Past it is a steel door hanging temptingly ajar. Opening it, I scan my flashlight over a short brick-lined corridor with two doors on either side. All are sturdy and, like the corridor itself, plainly an addition to the original house. They have equally sturdy steel locks on them, like prison cells. The air is old, stale and cold.

I return to the outside to see if I can find where the tracks went. At the back of the building I catch sight of the twin dark lines in the grass again, leading away from the wall and towards the treeline to the north. At the point where the marks vanish under the tangle of wiry brown branches, beyond my limited ability to follow them, I catch sight of something glittering in the leaves. A heart-shaped locket, looped over a twig at head height. Tempting though it is to remove it, I instead take one last look at the trees, then head back towards my car and call the department on my cell.

Three hours later, when the forensics truck containing the crime scene technicians loaned by the State Police is vanishing down the drive, the locket nestles in an evidence bag in my pocket. I'm planning to show it to Angela's friends and colleagues to see if any of them recognize it. Inside the locket, one photo is missing and the second shows a slim young woman with dark hair, my guess is in her twenties, smiling uncertainly at the camera. I don't recognize her, though I have a vague feeling I've seen her before.

I take one last look at St Valentine's, then start up the 'Vette and drive into town, my earlier weariness beginning to return. Winter's End already seems to be firmly closeted away; Sundays here are much quieter than I'm used to. The streets are almost deserted, and what people are about have the focused air of those heading home for the day and not intending to leave again until the following morning. While stopped at the intersection just short of the doctor's office, I'm surprised by a tap at my window. Mayor Saville leans down to talk, wearing the same obsequious smile as yesterday.

'I heard there were cops up at the old kids' home,' he says once I've lowered the window. 'Did you find anything?'

'Yeah, maybe,' I reply. 'I can't say much about it, though, you understand.'

'Sure, sure. It's just that if you had any questions about the building or the area, I might be able to help you.'

'Off the top of my head I can't think of anything right now, Mr Mayor. I'll give you a ring if something does crop up.'

'I'd appreciate that, Mr Rourke. Anything at all, mind, not just questions. I'd like to see this case wrapped up as much as anyone.'

The light changes to green ahead of me and I slip the car into gear. I'm about to cross the intersection and head for home when a thought strikes me and I hang a sudden right on to Verger Street. Fifty yards or so down is the small box-like public building that houses Winter's End Museum, an equally small set of exhibits charting the town's history for the benefit of local schoolkids and the occasional tourist. I remember visiting once on a class trip, but that was a long time ago. I've got no idea if it's open. I park the car and make my way up the weather-beaten paving towards the building, which is made from heavy, dark wooden boards, a cross between a log cabin and an old barn.

The old woman behind a flyer-covered desk looks up as the door tinkles shut behind me. 'A dollar for adults,' she says, blunt but not unfriendly, then stops to look me over. 'Don't get many tourists out here this early in the year.'

'I didn't expect you to be open, not today. I only tried on impulse.'

'Spring's here. We're just about in season. You from out of town?'

I fish around for the money. 'I'm a local boy just returned home, came here once when I was a kid.'

'Local, huh? What business are you in these days?' She feeds the note into the register.

'Sheriff's Department.'

The woman raises an eyebrow and looks at me afresh. 'Alex Rourke, right? News travels fast, even getting as far as me,' she adds when she sees my expression. 'Don't remember you when you were a kid, but I remember your parents. Good people. Good people. So, you here for some catching up? I don't reckon cops have too much use for history.'

'Actually I am here on police work. Kind of,' I add. 'Someone mentioned something about the town's past and I thought I might as well check it out. Say, you wouldn't remember if you'd had a visit from a white guy in his mid-twenties, slim, about so tall, with short dark hair, dark-blue eyes, would you? Quite neat and polite, probably on his own.'

The woman thinks for a moment, then shakes her head. 'We don't get many lone visitors, and most of those are older guys up here for the area's "atmosphere". Truth be told, we don't get many visitors of any kind. If the town council didn't fund this place, and if I had something better to do during my retirement, the museum would've shut by now.'

'Oh well, it was a long shot anyway.'

'If you think of anything else, sonny, just holler. Meantime, enjoy yourself.'

I thank her and move off to examine the small collection of glass cases and framed photographs that fill the museum's three rooms, separated according to historical period.

The first has as its centrepiece a model depicting a wagon train moving through the forest.

*Our community began as a hundred people heading for Acadia and the rich forests near the St John River to find somewhere they could log and trap in peace. They were led by Samuel Parnell and Nathan Laroche of L&P Milling and Mining Co.*, says the card stuck to the glass case holding the vignette.

According to the notes which follow to accompany a battered diary from the period, a string of minor mishaps delayed them and they were still well to the south of the river by the time winter set in.

*Our ancestors made camp and tried to wait out the months of cold. But before long, the ice and snow, dwindling supplies, exposure and frostbite facing the settlers were bad enough to drive them back southwards,* the card next to a moth-eaten pair of leather gloves reads. *By the time they saw the first signs of thaw the following year, 1806, and stopped at the place that would become Winter's End, Parnell and Laroche had only sixty folk with them.*

Another glass case in the corner of the room holds a

couple of pieces of period costume as well as an old map, a faded copy of land deeds, and a model of the town as it was to begin with. The sixty seem to have been busy, wasting no time in clearing the forest and building a mill on the west side of town, homes, and a small chapel dedicated to St Francis. A second case holds another set of costume and a musket, noting that the discovery of a skeleton clad in rotting native-style leathers and a musket started rumours of a massacre of local tribes by French or British troops.

I'm pleased to see that the ghost stories I learned as a kid had some basis in fact, even if it is only a loose one. The source of my childhood nightmares also seems pretty clear. I guess I must have heard about the original settlers even younger than I thought, or maybe I mixed up the time that I visited the museum before and it was actually when I'd just started school. Something must have struck a chord with me, if that was the case. Maybe they had bones or something on display back then, or maybe the woman who runs the place had been keener to make an impression on our young minds and had embellished the story with her own rather morbid additions.

I read on. *Charles Ryland*, apparently one of the early settlers' more affluent members, *further fuelled these rumours when he cleared some of his land and found a patch of forest burned out and regrown years before, scattered with bones*. The case holds several of these bones.

Ryland must be the guy Nicholas was referring to. There's a small and rather dusty portrait of him hanging in a corner. A chubby guy with bushy sideburns and narrow eyes. In 1815, with the town unaffected by the war of 1812, he apparently decided that Ryland Hill, the place where the bones were dug up, would make a fine site for a proper church for the town. Not everyone agreed with him. Nevertheless, the Chapel of St Valentine was finished in spring the following year. The first service in the newly consecrated church took place on an April evening during a thunderstorm. At the height of the sermon, the chapel was struck by lightning and burnt to a cinder. Twenty people died, including Charles Ryland and the priest. Plans for a church outside Winter's End were abandoned, and St Francis's remains the town's only place of worship to this day.

God's impeccable timing, Nicholas called it. Although the museum case includes a yellowed copy of a newspaper article written at the time, as well as parish pamphlets and other scraps, I can't think of anywhere outside Winter's End where he could have learned of the town's history in such detail. The St Valentine's connection also interests me, assuming the site is the same. I move further around the room.

Bad luck, or God's sense of humour, didn't stop with Ryland's death. Winters were ferocious for the next two years, and in December 1818 the L&P mill burned to the ground with Samuel Parnell and half a dozen workers inside. Some said it was Laroche moving to gain sole control over the company, by then doing all right for itself. Others said it was a curse on the town. Laroche himself died in 1821, a bitter and miserly man.

*Winter's End held its breath in 1827 when Boston businessman Gabriel Wade bought Ryland's land. He demolished Ryland's run-down house and built a newer and far grander home up the hill, on the site of the old chapel. There were rumours that he had a priest exorcize the place first. There were no more strange happenings and*

*the town prospered, mostly as a supply stop for the bigger lumber
camps now springing up further north.*

I pass quickly through the next room, which deals with
the town up to the end of World War Two, looking
for more information on the house that would become
St Valentine's. In the last room, amidst the pictures of
town festivals and small-time news, I find it. The Wade
family evidently moved out in the 1960s, but the place
wasn't sold to become a children's home until a few years
after I was born. There's a photo of some of the original
staff. Henry Garner, director. Sarah Decker, night manager. Dorian Blythe, day manager. Deborah Pierce, nurse.
I vaguely remember Garner from the couple of times I
visited the home with my father. They seemed to know
each other; hardly surprising, I guess, since Dad used to
go there every so often with toys for the kids.

There's a bunch of stuff on the fire that led to the home's
closure: news clippings, photos, interviews. The blaze
started in the middle of the night and quickly took hold of
the staff quarters. The evacuation of the building was
chaotic, but eventually everyone got out save for Garner
and a couple of other workers. By the time the volunteer
fire crews arrived from town, they could do little more
than stop the blaze from spreading to the rest of the
building while it burned itself out. My father was one of
those called out on duty; I spot him in a couple of the
photos taken at the time. Regular pillar of the community.

The remains of those who died were never properly
recovered. The emergency crews didn't find any whole
bodies, and what they had they couldn't positively identify.
The newspapers don't say why, but my guess would be
that if they found a burned skull that was crushed by a

fallen piece of masonry, even dental records wouldn't be much help. And I do know that the building was an absolute wreck. Arson was the verdict of the official investigation, although no one was ever charged with the crime. The insurance company cited a loophole in the home's cover and refused to pay up, and St Valentine's closed for good.

'Find anything?' The old woman's voice startles me out of my thoughts.

'Yeah, thanks,' I say, turning to face her. 'More than I expected.'

She taps the glass case in front of me. 'I've heard it said that the place was cursed,' she says matter-of-factly. 'Nothing good ever came of anything built on that land.'

It sounds to me as if she's launching into her spiel for the tourists. I feign rapt attention anyway. 'Really?'

'It's because of all the people that were burnt there, before the town was built.'

'Two fires in nearly two hundred years doesn't mean a curse, not to my mind.'

She shrugs. 'They're just stories. I don't know if there's any truth to them. Don't much care, either. So long as people still want to hear them. Kids, mostly.' She laughs, dry and rattling. 'Probably told them to you and your classmates when you came here. You sure you don't remember?'

'That was a long time ago.'

'Maybe. It's not often I get to try them on the same audience twice.'

'You gave me nightmares last time. I'm hoping you don't manage it again.' I make my way towards the door, trying not to seem impolite. 'Well, thanks for your help. Most informative.'

'Just be sure to recommend this place to your friends,' she calls after me, then laughs again. The sound follows me until the door swings shut behind me.

The drive back to the Crowhurst Lodge takes five minutes in the slowly advancing evening. The sun is already touching the horizon, turning the sky a deep orange and lighting the scattered clouds a brilliant yellow. The forest that blankets the hills around town is already in shadow. As I approach the turn-off, I again see the girl who watched me leave this morning. She's standing a little way down the road and stares continuously at me as I drive past and make the turn.

The hotel itself is already starting to glow faintly in the failing light, although it's a long way from achieving the leprous hue of the night proper. The smiling images above the door have yet to start leering as the shadows distort their features, and for that I'm thankful. Inside, the air is flat and lifeless, like that of some long-forgotten tomb. I wonder how often the elderly manager bothers to show his face. Tomorrow I might even try phoning to catch him out. I make my way up the winding staircase, a fixture too grand for this kind of building, a result of its pretentious design. Back in my room, I drop into bed with the intention of snatching an hour's shut-eye before making my way round to Dale's house. Instead, I spend a sleepless sixty minutes staring at the locket and letting my mind wander. The face of the woman whose photo lies inside floats before my vision, tantalizingly out of reach. I wonder who she is, or was. My weary mind, perhaps returning to last night's dream, mingles her image with thoughts of the biting cold, of the feeling of plunging into the snow, hands outstretched in a futile attempt to stop myself, of ice cutting into my skin.

The woman's face is still lurking at the back of my mind when Laura Townsend opens the door of the four-bedroomed house she shares with her husband.

'You must be Alex,' she says, standing aside to let me in. 'I don't know if you remember me from high school. I was in the year above you.'

I smile politely, trying to remember as I step into the hallway. Something vague stirs in the attic of memory and I say, 'Laura Redfern?'

'That's right. Dale!' she yells in the direction of the lounge. 'Alex is here!'

'How long have the two of you been married?'

'Twelve years,' Laura replies, 'and I'm still trying to civilize him. Dale!'

I grin, as always a little uncomfortable around others' apparent domestic bliss. 'That's not a job I'd want to take on.'

'Hey, Alex,' says Dale, finally emerging from the depths of the house. 'You want a beer?'

Bottles in hand, we make our way into the dining room and assist Laura, as best we can, in getting everything ready. In between shuffling plates and looking for cutlery, I run through what I found at the hospital, along with the results of the crime scene technicians' work.

'No usable impressions?' Dale asks once I've finished.

'They got enough to say that there were two sets of footprints, moving from the north, around the building, probably along the gutter at the base of the wall, and then away to the west. One set, which we might assume to be Nicholas, may have stepped up to the front door to break the padlock, but we can't be sure. But they couldn't find a single identifiable tread-mark that we could match with a shoe.'

'What about the locket?'

'No prints, no hair, no fibre. I don't recognize the girl inside.'

'It might be no more than a coincidence.'

I shake my head. 'Right where a murder victim was led on the way to where she was killed? You've got to be kidding.'

At this point, Laura emerges bearing plates of steaming fish stew with potatoes and the conversation breaks up somewhat to accommodate chewing and swallowing. I steer clear of 'shop talk', since I don't know whether it would bore Dale's wife to death. Instead, I let her run through the usual questions – do I have a family, how's Boston, have I run into any of my old school friends since I've been back – and I give all the usual answers. Once the stew, which is excellent and extremely filling, is out of the way and the fudge cake dessert has been similarly dispatched, I take out the locket and show it to Dale and Laura. Keeping it in its bag, I flick the catch with my thumbnail to reveal the picture within.

'No,' says Laura after a moment's thought, 'I don't recognize her. I don't think I've ever seen her around here.'

Dale shakes his head too. 'Doesn't ring any bells with me either, Alex. Are you going to ask Nicholas about it?'

'Yeah. Maybe he has a family, or maybe he took this from some past victim we don't know about. I'll check with the people who knew Angela whether she owned a locket like this first, though.' I stifle a yawn.

'You look tired,' says Laura.

'I didn't sleep well. Hopefully I'll have better luck tonight. Say, do either of you know a girl, about seventeen, eighteen, with short dark hair, about so tall? Slim, pale, dark make-up.'

Dale nods. 'Sounds like Sophie Donehan, maybe. Why?'

'I've seen her up near the hotel a couple of times. Always staring at me.'

'She's a messed-up kid,' says Laura. 'Sophie's mom killed herself, what, six years ago. She overdosed on sleeping pills. They never found out why she did it, but Sophie's dad hasn't been the same since.'

'Six years ago, huh?' I say. Around the time of the St Valentine's fire.

'I've heard a couple of stories that she's pestered tourists from out of state, trying to get them to take her away with them,' Dale chips in. 'Maybe she thinks you might be another potential ticket out of town.'

'Great. A screwed-up adolescent is just the souvenir I've been looking for. Rob would have a good laugh when I got back to the office, if nothing else.'

We chuckle and the conversation moves on again. Around half past ten, tiredness begins to tell and I say my farewells. I leave Dale's warm, tidy house and walk back through the deserted streets, past curtains drawn tight and doors firmly closed, towards the pallid glow of the hotel and the sighing of the wind in the trees.

# 6

I'm walking through town and it's the middle of the night. I don't know what hour it is exactly – I left my watch in the hotel – nor how long I've been out wandering, unable to sleep. The moon is up, though; a half-full orb of white, casting a silver sheen on the mist which drifts through the streets. The moist tendrils swirl about me, probing at closed doors and darkened windows, wreathing the widely spaced streetlights with haloes. Winter's End is utterly silent. Even the breeze and the distant sound of the trees are no more.

I have no idea what I'm doing out here. Everything's hazy. I don't even remember leaving the hotel.

Then I catch movement out of the corner of my eye, away to the right. A whitewashed stone church is visible behind a couple of stunted trees, the mist smudging its pale outline. As I glance at the building, the low gate at the end of the path leading to its doors clicks shut. The noise sounds clear and sharp in the deathly quiet. The wooden gate and the lower end of the path are veiled in misty darkness. As I walk slowly across the road, curiosity dragging me onwards, I wonder who could be about so late at night; the good folk of Winter's End seem to hide away from well before midnight until daybreak. Images of Nicholas's hypothetical accomplice drawing me into a trap, or trying to hide some as yet undiscovered evidence spiral through my mind. They are followed by more fantastic scenarios – fresh murders, new killers, demons and all the monsters of the human subconscious that no amount of modern rationalization can banish once the sun goes down.

Nothing lurks by the gate, which I allow to swing shut behind me. The small church rises before me like an ivory pinnacle in the fog. I can see now that the grounds are littered with gravestones and burial markers. Carved cherubs, crucifixes and, here and there, a larger statue depicting the Angel of Death or some long-dead saint. The mist weaves in and out of these monuments, distorting distances and imparting a never-ending sense of movement to figures half-glimpsed in the gloom.

As I crunch cautiously up the path I catch sight of a woman's figure ahead, at first no more than another silhouetted shadow in the moon's thin light. She turns her head briefly towards me before she steps behind a cluster of stones further inside the graveyard. A flash of dark hair and the briefest glimpse of bone-pale skin are all she allows me before she disappears, but for some reason I feel certain she is the woman depicted in the locket. I pick up the pace, jogging as quickly as the darkness and uncertain footing will allow along rows of stone markers rising like teeth out of the ground.

Turn left around the corner of a mausoleum-type structure and she's right there in front of me. Cold arms clad in a rotting shroud reach up towards me as the woman smiles, mouth turned up at the corners but eyes dead and clouded. *Things* scrabble at my feet and I can feel their scratching nails through my shoes. One questing appendage finds the leg of my jeans and the flesh underneath, and cold pain flares from my shin.

I turn and run wildly, heart threatening to burst out of

my chest. I tear myself free from whatever undead hands are grappling for me through the earth and flee from the graveyard, pursued by a hideous high-pitched keening, like screaming infants or cats in heat. Out through the gate and into the town, buildings and streets blurring through fright and fatigue.

Eventually, exhaustion triumphs over panic and I collapse on to the sidewalk, fighting for breath. My head swims and my vision whirls drunkenly before going completely black.

# PART TWO
# A Measure of Darkness

'Because of thee, the land of dreams
Becomes a gathering place of fears:
Until tormented slumber seems
One vehemence of useless tears.'
– Lionel Johnson, 'The Dark Angel'

# 7

I wake up in bed, my head a confusion of thoughts and memories. The sheets are twisted and balled around my feet and my heart is thudding audibly in my ears. Adrenalin makes my vision sharp but my eyes nervous, jumping at the movement of the curtains, the shape of a shadow by the TV, or the creaking sound as the hotel shifts in its slumber. My throat is dry but I'm sweating and the pillow beneath my head is damp. I check the clock next to the bed. It's 2.30, no more than an hour and a half since I drifted off to sleep. I go to the bathroom to get a glass of water from the sink, down it, and take a refill back into the room. Then I sit on the edge of the bed and wait for my system to relax. I feel more awake right now than I did at any time yesterday.

Breathe in. Breathe out. Think calm thoughts.

I sit like that for half an hour, sipping the water. Then, once I'm feeling nice and tired again, I try to get back to sleep. It doesn't work. Three o'clock becomes four o'clock, and all I can do is twist and turn, trying anything I can think of short of bashing my head on the wall to return to the blissful but elusive state of unconsciousness. By four, I can feel a point of bright light developing behind my eyes, an oncoming migraine. By half past four, I consider making the trek downstairs to my car in the hope that its surroundings will be familiar enough for me to grab a couple of hours' slumber. In the end, I reject the idea. The walk through the gloomy interior of the hotel does not appeal to me, and once my migraine starts kicking in good and proper I know that it'll take more than familiar seats to knock me out. I find a couple of ageing paracetamol on the bathroom shelf and swallow them in the optimistic hope that they'll do something. They don't, as ever. I wish I'd remembered to bring my emergency supply of tablets with me. I should have thought of it, but it's been so long since I've had one that it must have slipped my mind.

Five o'clock turns into six turns into seven. Two more hours spent lying like a beached dolphin or a coma patient, staring blankly at my surroundings as the migraine makes sections of my vision blur and wheel.

The sun's up and I'm feeling so desperately tired and drained that all I can wish for is that it'll go away again so I can make another try at this whole sleep business. I take a brief shower, keeping my eyes closed and my head as still as possible, then dress and head downstairs, taking the locket with me.

I eat another lonesome breakfast in the Crowhurst Lodge's empty dining room, with its yellowing walls and starch-scented linen. The food on offer is the same as yesterday, but my weary senses are in no state to enjoy whatever flavour it may have. After my warm but tasteless meal, I walk into town with the intention of asking Angela's friends – if I can remember who they are – about the locket. When I speak to Dr Vallence, I'll take the opportunity to mention my insomnia and see if he can give me something for it.

I wedge my hands in my pockets to keep them out of the breeze and squint against the glare reflecting from the washed-out buildings along Main. The town is gearing itself up for another day. People are on their way to work, lights are springing on inside stores, shutters are rattling upwards.

My first stop is Martha's Garden, the diner where Angela used to have lunch. It's a pleasant enough place, and I'm thankful it's neither been turned into 'a genuine slice of Maine' for the tourists, a pointless job in somewhere like Winter's End, nor been bought out by a restaurant chain. As it is, with plain decor that's faded around the edges, it's got the kind of character that only comes when the same people go to the same place to have something simple to eat, month after month. Unpretentious. I have a couple of cups of coffee, more for the caffeine than anything else, and ask the staff on duty if they knew Angela and whether they've ever seen the locket before. I also ask whether they recognize the woman depicted inside. They don't. The old guy grilling bacon at the back briefly gets my hopes up as he looks as though he does, but then he shakes his head like the others and says, 'Sorry. Don't recall her face.'

I arrive at the doctor's office almost as soon as it opens. The small waiting room is devoid of patients and the nurse on duty looks up from a magazine as I walk in. I show her my badge and tell her I'm with the Sheriff's Department.

'Oh, you'd be the one investigating Angela's death,' she says. Her eyes take in my haggard expression. 'I'm Jennifer. I work . . . worked with Angela.'

I show her the locket. 'Did you ever see Angela wearing this? Was it hers?'

'No, I've never seen it before.'

'How about the woman inside, do you recognize her?'

'No, sorry.'

'That's all right. Is Dr Vallence available?'

She buzzes the intercom and informs the doctor of my presence. He tells her to send me through. The doctor's office is compact, filled with books and pieces of medical paraphernalia without looking untidy, like a private study or a Victorian-era drawing room. Nathan Vallence is white-haired, with a lined face and a long nose. He regards me from above this haughty proboscis as I shut the door behind me and sit in the chair at the far side of his desk.

'Good morning, Deputy Rourke,' he says. His voice is dry and cultured, but wavers slightly. His lips smack dryly together as he speaks. 'How can I help you?'

'I'm looking into Angela Lamond's death. I was wondering if you recognized this locket as belonging to her.'

'I was under the impression that the man responsible had been arrested,' he says as he briefly regards the battered gold in front of him. 'No, I never saw Angela wearing anything like this.'

'Do you recognize the woman inside?'

He peers at it again, swallows once, then slides it back to me, jerkily shaking his head. 'No, I'm afraid not.'

'Was there anyone Angela might have encountered while working here who might have had a reason, however mistaken, to hate her? Do you ever treat mental illnesses or anything like that?'

'Rarely, and never anything serious. I usually refer them to Houlton or Presque Isle where they're better equipped to treat such cases. As to Angela making enemies amongst the patients . . .' Vallence shakes his head. 'Not that I can recall.'

I shrug and clamber to my feet. 'Thanks for your time, Doctor. If anything else comes to mind, get in touch.'

As I turn to go, Vallence draws breath and calls hurriedly

after me, 'While we're speaking of patients, if I may say so, you don't look well, Deputy Rourke. Is there anything I can help you with on a professional basis?'

'As it happens, there is,' I say, glad for the invitation. I sit back down. 'Insomnia – I have attacks occasionally, which my doctor down in Boston gives me stuff for. I've also got a thundering migraine and I left the pills I take for them at home.'

'If you can give me the name and number of your doctor, I'll give him a ring and see what I can do. I take it these are regular prescriptions you have.'

I nod and rattle off Dr Hansen's phone number. Vallence calls him up and the two talk briefly. Then he writes a couple of prescription notes and tells me to go to the pharmacy.

'Thanks,' I say, and hand him one of my business cards. 'If you think of anything, give me a ring. My cellphone number's there.'

Fifteen minutes later, I emerge from the town's dispensary, which like much of Winter's End is a curious mix of modern fittings overlaying the original Victorian work. I am now the proud owner of two sets of pills. The first are ergotamine tablets for my headache, to be taken once every half-hour until the migraine is gone. The second bottle contains lorazepam, according to the faded print on the label; it looks as if the machine was about to run out of ink. Two capsules every night before I go to bed should deal with my insomnia. The bottle contains twenty.

I start on the first of six migraine capsules as I head back to the hotel to pick up my car. Then I set off south to Houlton. On the way through town, I catch sight of the Church of St Francis down a side street. While my dream had the building itself correct, the cemetery around it is smaller and far simpler. I guess I should have remembered that, but clarity of thought is a rare commodity in dreams.

The journey is eventful, if only because I have a hard time keeping my eyes focused on the road. Every so often, my head nods and my eyeballs feel as if they're rolling up in their sockets. In reality, it's my tired lids fighting to close. The risk of nodding off at the wheel is serious enough that I don't pull on to I-95 when I reach the eastern leg of my L-shaped journey. I stick instead to the smaller US 2 all the way into Houlton. It means I avoid most of the truck traffic, even if the risk of smashing into something by the side of the road is greater on the narrower highway.

'Jesus Christ, Alex,' says Dale when I clamber out of my car in the Superior Court parking lot. 'You look like shit.'

'Thanks, Dale,' I reply. 'I appreciate the sympathy.'

'I'm serious. You're not coming down with something, are you?'

I shake my head, blinking the sleep from my eyes. 'Just another bad night's sleep. Had a migraine this morning, too. Dr Vallence gave me some stuff for both.'

'Are you sure you want to speak to Nicholas right now? We can ask him about the locket tomorrow if you want.'

'No, it's just the long drive. A couple of cigarettes and some coffee and I'll be okay.' I change the subject to something other than the state of my health. 'I spoke to Angela's colleagues about the locket. They don't remember her owning anything like it. They don't recognize the woman in the photo either.'

'So maybe it really was just coincidence, it being left there,' Dale says, frowning.

I spark up one of the aforementioned cigarettes and suck contentedly on the filter. 'I don't think so. You know what this whole thing looks like to me? One big case of staging. You know, like a single crime scene on a bigger scale.'

'Yeah, some guy shoots his wife then puts the gun in her hand to make it look like she killed herself. I know what staging is. I just don't see it here.'

'Everything that we've been able to learn about the crime itself looks like a set-up. We only have the guy in custody because he stuck around to get arrested when he could have vanished in seconds. Hell, he needn't even have left the woods if he'd wanted. We look into what he did and find tracks leading towards the house. Someone breaks the lock to make it look like he went inside, but doesn't actually bother to do so. Someone hangs a piece of jewellery that seems significant, but which we can't identify, at the place where he emerged from the woods.' I puff a couple of times more, then flick the butt into the gutter. 'It's like we're following breadcrumbs, but don't know where we're being led.'

Dale just shrugs as I head for the jail and the sterile, unfriendly surroundings of the interview room where Nicholas awaits. The accused murderer is sitting as always in his orange jailhouse overalls. If it wasn't for the fact that I see the deputies taking him away every time, I could almost believe he never moved from his seat.

Once the usual legal pleasantries are out of the way, I begin. 'Good morning, Nicholas. How are you?'

His eyes gaze flatly back at mine, his expression as blank

as if he had been carved in jade. 'I'm well, Mr Rourke. You look a bit under the weather, though. Nothing catching, I hope.'

'Insomnia. Sometimes I can't sleep if there's something bugging me. The doctor's given me pills for it, but I'd rather deal with the cause than the symptom.'

'And what is the cause of your little problem, Mr Rourke?' Nicholas asks. His pitch has become higher, his tone almost amused.

I light yet another cigarette. 'You. I can't figure out why you won't give us a name if you're not someone who's already got a record. I also can't figure out what you were doing with a dead body on a highway in the middle of the night.'

'You must have a theory.'

'To me it looks as though you abducted Angela Lamond, walked her through the woods to the old St Valentine's children's home, and then down to the road. Then you killed her.' I blow smoke at the lights above us. 'It fits the facts, even if I can't see why someone like you would do that. Maybe I'm wrong. Maybe you were just out for a walk or something and you came across the body and the knives. But unless you tell me something, my theory is what's going to put you away for murder.'

Nicholas's eyes don't so much as twitch. 'Kids' games, Mr Rourke. Did you ever play the one where someone would choose a word, and everyone would then do their best to get you to say it?' One corner of his lips twitches upwards. 'Your questions bring it to mind.'

'I went for a stroll up near St Valentine's yesterday, Nicholas.'

'Really?' he says. His eyes are even darker and more empty than usual.

'I found something interesting while I was there.'

'And what was that?'

I take the plastic bag out of my pocket and place it on the table. 'This locket. I found it at the edge of the woods. Do you recognize it or the woman in the photo?'

Nicholas smiles. 'From your tone, I take it that you don't.'

'I'd like to find out, though.'

'Well then, yes, I know who the woman is.'

'Who?'

'I say "is", but I suppose "was" would be more appropriate. She was a victim, Mr Rourke. A victim.'

I light a Marlboro. 'One of yours?'

Nicholas does something totally unexpected for a man of his apparent composure. He laughs, long and loud, eyes pinched shut. His wide-open mouth is the colour of raw meat, with a bright red tongue lolling between teeth of perfect whiteness. Eventually, he calms down, wipes his eyes and looks at me. 'Oh, I'm sorry, Mr Rourke,' he says. 'You'd have to be sitting on this side of the table to see how funny that question was. No, not one of mine.'

'Then what happened to her?'

The blank mask returns, although the eyes are no longer as guarded as they were. Nicholas changes the subject. 'Tell me a little about your childhood, Mr Rourke. I'm interested in the small-town boy who ended up chasing murderers for the FBI.'

'The locket, Nicholas,' I say, trying to keep him on track. I don't want to talk about my family life.

'Son of a lawyer and a part-time teacher, weren't you?

Daddy part of the volunteer fire department in Winter's End?'

My instinctive reaction is to ask him how he knows this, but I don't. Try to keep focused, stay on track. I maintain an emotionless façade and correct him. 'My mom wasn't a teacher, she helped out at the kindergarten. But so what?'

'Childhood events shape the rest of our lives, Mr Rourke. Basic psychology. Did your father ever have any near-misses as a fireman? Times when you feared for his life? Stress as a kid might have made you more prone to stress as an adult.'

I stub out my cigarette, but don't reach for another. Too many more and my lungs will feel like I've run a cheese-grater over them. 'No, nothing like that,' I tell Nicholas.

'And where are mom and dad now?'

Bile rises and I feel the muscles at the sides of my neck tense as I stare at him, teeth clenched. Perhaps it's his tone of voice, perhaps it's just because I'm tired, but for a brief moment I consider slamming his smart-ass face into the table until his nose splits and his mouth fills with blood. Three years ago, right before the breakdown, I might have done it. Today I satisfy myself with the glare, force the anger back. 'That doesn't fucking concern you, Nick,' I say, keeping my voice steady.

'I'm sorry if I hit a nerve,' he says, and I'm certain that he's not. 'But you're wrong: it does concern me, in so much as I'm now real curious to know the answer to my question. What happened to your parents?'

In my mind, I hear the sound of the sedan screaming towards me from the right a split-second before a mind-numbing collision. Glass rains around me as my car grinds along the road on its side. I don't know at the time, but the passenger door has been shredded and driven inwards. Something sprays on to my face; it might be blood.

'They're dead,' I say. 'They died three years ago.'

Either he detects something in my reply that satisfies him, or his digression is at an end, because he sighs and relaxes a little. 'The woman in the locket was a victim of a crime which went unpunished for a long time,' he says. His tone is different, no longer laced with the all-knowing calm I had taken for arrogance, now direct and focused as if we have dispensed with the trivia and are only now getting to the serious business at hand. 'As we discussed before, sometimes the Devil comes to collect. He did so in this case. You won't find what happened to her in police records or on your computer databases, Mr Rourke.'

'So what does she have to do with Angela Lamond's death?'

'It's a belief in some religions that our actions are all connected to each other in a myriad tiny ways. The Devil collected on Ms Lamond, Mr Rourke. He never acts without a reason.'

'What does the marker mean? Did you put the locket there?'

'I wouldn't like to say.'

'So you did?'

Nicholas stays silent. His body language, leaning back in his seat with his mouth firmly shut, seems to suggest that he regards the interview as over for today. At other times, I'd try to press him further, but I'm too tired right now. Instead, I have the deputies take him away.

I step out of the room and go to find Dale, who as before has been watching from the viewing booth, hidden behind the one-way glass.

'What do you make of that?' he asks.

I shrug. 'Nicholas seems to think he had a reason to kill Angela, and I get the impression he'd be willing to spill everything if we can figure out what that reason is. Let's make a copy of the photo in the locket and send it out around the state to see if anyone recognizes the woman. It's probably a good idea to get hold of the records from the doctor's in town to see if there were any deaths while Angela worked there. It might be that this woman died after she went for treatment and Nicholas blames the staff. See if you can dig up any records of parents who had their kids taken away by the authorities and put in St Valentine's as well. Maybe she was an unfit mother or something.'

'For all we know, Alex, she might have been killed in a hit and run.'

'That's not a bad thought. Let's ask the State Police about fatal accidents over the past few years, while I'll check the records we've got here. Her face might be there somewhere.' I stop Dale as he's about to turn and leave. 'Have any of the guards at the jail been talking to Nick, do you think?'

He frowns. 'What do you mean?'

'I just wondered how come he knows me. Some of the things he's said run very close to the truth.'

'I doubt any of our people in Corrections could tell him much at all about you, even if they did chat to one of the inmates. Which they wouldn't.'

Lunchtime and the early afternoon tick away while I plough through old accident reports, looking for the woman in the locket. Crash photos, drivers' licences, victim details, injuries laid out in full. She isn't there.

Half past three comes around and I start the drive back to Winter's End. I'm feeling somewhat light-headed, as if I'm stoned or suffering from a concussion. I don't know whether this is a result of general fatigue or an after-effect of the migraine pills I took this morning. I concentrate as best as I can on the road, knuckles turning to white as I fight to keep a firm grip on the wheel whenever I see one of the massive logging trucks looming ahead of me. Hit one of those head-on and there wouldn't be enough left of my corpse to bury. I'm just thankful it's not raining and I don't have to worry about slippery conditions.

Since I could do with a pick-me-up, I stop off at Martha's Garden and order a coffee. The diner isn't empty but there are no more than half a dozen people inside. I spend a quarter of an hour doing nothing, just drinking and hoping the warmth will somehow creep from my stomach into my nerves and tired muscles. Then the bell above the door tinkles and an old guy, maybe in his late sixties or early seventies with thick white hair and a beard, takes the seat next to me. In a red checked jacket and well-worn jeans, he looks like an ageing lumberjack or a country musician. Something about him is familiar.

'Hey,' he says, gesturing at the waitress for a coffee, 'you're Alex Rourke, aren't you?'

'That's me.'

'Ben Anderson.' He extends his hand, which I shake. 'Last time I saw you, you were still at high school.'

'You were one of my dad's friends?'

'Sure was. Knew him since before he met your mom. We used to get together for a drink every once in a while.

Used to go fishing with him and Josh and a couple of others back when I was a lot younger; haven't done that in more than twenty years, though.'

I light a cigarette and offer him one. 'I remember you, I think. You came round to our house a couple of times at Thanksgiving.'

'That's right. I helped your dad build a new porch when you were a boy, too.'

'Yeah, I remember, now you mention it. Did you hear what happened to my parents?'

Ben nods and slurps at his coffee. 'Terrible shame. They were good people, both of them. There was this time, back in the winter about thirty years ago. We had a clear couple of days, snow on the ground but blue skies. Then this gale came down one night, bringing a blizzard like you wouldn't believe. We heard there was a family staying with their folks here who'd gone out for a winter hike in the woods, up north by the river. Your mom and dad rounded a bunch of us up so we could get our gear together and go looking for them. Took us the best part of five hours, but we found them huddled in an old cabin a few miles from the Penobscot County line, freezing cold but still alive.'

He nods to himself again and repeats, 'Good people, your mom and dad. Come to think of it, they left some things with me when they moved away. Just a couple of boxes of junk, probably. They've been sitting in my attic ever since. You can have them if you want.'

'Sure.'

He downs what's left in his cup and fumbles for some change to cover the cost. 'I'll give you a ride down to my house and you can pick them up.'

'Only if it's okay with you.'

We walk outside. 'I'm retired, son. Don't have anywhere to be in a hurry. What about you, what are you up to these days?'

'You haven't heard?' I finish my Marlboro. 'The way gossip spreads around here, you must be about the only one. Right now, I'm working with the Sheriff's Department on the Lamond murder. Normally, I'm a private detective down in Boston.'

'I don't hear much gossip these days,' Ben says. 'I spend most of my time patching up my RV' – he gestures to where a battered but obviously well-tended vehicle is parked by the side of the road – 'or fixing up my house, or fishing. By the time you hit my age, you've got plenty of time for gossiping but you find you don't care since none of it concerns you.'

I grin. 'I thought you old-timers did nothing else except wag beards on your driveways.'

'Not me, son. I keep to myself.'

Ben's house stands at the end of a two-hundred-yard muddy track that joins the northern end of Altmayer Street. The two-storey building nestles there like a cottage from some fairy-tale forest, only with cream-painted wooden siding and a garage off to the side. When we pull up and climb out of the RV, I see the hand-painted sign that hangs from the door-handle: 'Gone Fishin''.

I shake my head as Ben unlocks the door. In anywhere bigger and not as quiet as Winter's End that kind of message might just as well read: 'House empty. Burgle at will'.

Inside, the house displays the habitual quasi-neatness of most long-time bachelors and has a faint dry, earthy odour. With nothing particularly impressive about its decor, Ben's house has a character of its own only because it's plainly been lived in for a good many years.

'It's not much,' he says as if acknowledging my thoughts. 'But it's enough.'

'I like it. It's nicer than my place in Boston.'

We make our way upstairs while I get the usual feeling of vague disorientation I always have when entering someone else's home on my own. Every sense is alert, soaking in all sorts of information about my new surroundings, while my subconscious, which like anyone's can instantly tell the difference between a newly built show apartment and a place that's been inhabited for some time, feeds me a constant stream of tiny facts and observations about the building's owner. The slight scuff mark on the carpet, the collection of muddy boots standing on newspaper on the landing, the framed map of the county listing almost every watercourse within its borders.

At the top of the attic ladder Ben pulls the cord to switch the light on and says, 'They're in here somewhere.'

Shadows scatter and run into the corners of the room like a carpet of bugs disturbed by the sudden glare. They lurk behind the scattered bags and boxes, waiting for a chance to reclaim the floor for themselves, as we hunt through Ben's collected detritus for my dad's things.

Eventually, he drags out two rather desiccated cardboard boxes near the back of the roof space. My chest tightens involuntarily as I rest my hands on top of them. I'm curious as to what, if anything, lies inside, but I also catch myself wondering whether I should open them at all. What's within is personal. Then I tell myself not to be so stupid and slide the boxes over to the hatch where the light is better. The ageing card has a dusty, fibrous feel, almost like suede or soft leather to the touch as I open them and run my eyes quickly over their contents.

The first, the heavier of the two, contains a couple of faded high school yearbooks, a collection of crinkled papers from my dad's legal work, a ten-years' service certificate from the town's volunteer fire department. A bunch of old keys, a bottle of mysterious liquid with a brightly coloured label in Spanish – an old souvenir from a vacation in Mexico, I guess – and a couple of books on fly-tying.

A flurry of dust kicks up from the second as I open it. Inside, I find a couple of old photo albums scattered with blank white spaces where my parents took favourite pictures away with them, as well as a bundle of loose prints held together with string. I flick quickly through the musty-smelling photos out of curiosity. Family members, some people I don't recognize – presumably distant relatives or old friends – and a couple of shots from what look like fishing trips.

I've got fond memories of my own times at Claye Lake and other places with my dad. After twenty-nine years I can still picture the first time he took me with him. Maybe time has coloured my recollection, a psychological editing process reinforced by the times later in my life when the two of us didn't get on. I still look back fondly at it though.

I watch the water shimmering as it laps beneath my feet. Light glints with every wavelet that reaches the battered wooden jetty. The wind periodically gusts at my back, flicking my hair over my eyes despite the effort I put into pushing it back again. The cooler behind me feels rough where I'm leaning against it.

'You're not getting bored, are you?'

I lift my head and turn to look at my dad. His expression

is part genuine concern, part hope that I'm not getting fed up only a day into our fishing trip. 'I'm fine,' I say, raising the rod in my hands to emphasize my interest. 'I was just watching the water.'

He grins. 'Hypnotic, isn't it? I always like the way the lake looks in the sun. It's relaxing.'

'Uh-huh.'

'It's nice to get away from everything for a while and not worry about anything much.'

'Why doesn't Mom come?' I ask with a six-year-old's grasp of married life.

Dad smiles. 'It's as much a break for her as it is for me. Besides, don't you like it just being you and me?'

'Yeah. You think we can catch dinner?'

'It doesn't matter if we don't. I brought a couple of steaks with us.' He leans conspiratorially towards me. 'Don't tell Mom. I'm supposed to be watching what I eat.'

I smile at the shared secret. 'Sure, Dad.'

'Reach behind you and get me a beer, would you? Get yourself a Coke if you want one.'

I place the rod on the wooden planking and stand to open the cooler. The catch is difficult for my small hands and when it finally pops up the sudden release is enough for me to lose my balance. I stagger for a moment, trying to hold myself upright by rocking on the balls of my feet, then topple backwards into the water.

Cold. A burst of pressure and a roaring in my ears.

Then my feet bite into the stony bottom of the lake and I stand, a little unsteadily, uncomfortable with the water sloshing against my chest and the sudden weight of sodden clothes. I look up at the jetty and see my dad leaning over, sudden worry pinching his face.

'Alex! Are you all right?' he says, trying to keep from yelling.

'Yeah,' I nod, hair plastered to my forehead.

For a moment more he stands, looking at me, then he stifles a chuckle. Seeing me glaring with childish outrage at his expression, he says, 'I'm sorry, Alex. It's just – you should have seen your face.' A snigger escapes. 'I'm sorry,' he says again, eyes creasing.

I do what most kids would in my position. I hurl an armful of water up at my dad. Not a lot splashes him, but he throws up his arms in mock panic anyway and I slosh another load up towards him.

Dad is laughing out loud by the time he jumps off the jetty, fully clothed, and joins me in the lake as the water-fight begins in earnest.

That evening we eat steak by the fire, wrapped up in sweaters. I fall asleep on the sofa, curled up by my father.

At least, that's how I remember it. How I like to remember it.

Years later, I'm sitting in my room at college with the phone against my ear. At the other end of the line, my dad's asking me whether I'll be home for the summer. He's being very polite about it; we had a string of arguments about my future career direction before I left. I haven't been back since.

'Sorry, Dad,' I tell him. 'Kurt's invited Howard and me out to Rochester to stay at his aunt's place. We're going to work at her diner for a while to get money together and hang out there all summer.'

'You're not going to be home at all?'

The answer is 'no'. Things are okay between us, but I'd

prefer to stick with my friends right now rather than go back north. 'Maybe, I guess. It depends how things go.'

'Well, give me a ring if you can make it back to see your mom and me. Do it anyway, just to let us know how you're getting on.'

'Sure, Dad.'

There's a pause which I use to take a swig from the beer in my other hand. Then my dad says, 'I'm still proud of you, whatever you do. You're my only son.'

I didn't go home that summer. I never went home again. My parents visited me at Thanksgiving, then again the year after. By the next time I actually went to see them, for the first time in fourteen years, they'd moved down to Miami.

I sigh and close the boxes again before the two of us manhandle them out of the attic and down to the waiting RV. Back in the centre of town, Ben helps me get them into the trunk of my 'Vette, then stands back and brushes the dust from his fingers.

'Thanks,' I tell him. 'I never got round to sorting through most of my folks' things after the crash. I'll go through these properly.'

'No problem, son. Just a favour for old friends. Say, if you find yourself with some spare time, I'm heading for a few days' fishing on the McLean River. There's a dirt road meets Route 11 a short way north of Ashland. I'll be parked a few miles down. If you fancy taking a break for a while, feel free to drop by.'

'That'd be nice,' I say, nodding. 'I'll do it if I get a moment. Haven't been fishing in years, though, not since last time my dad took me up to the cabin he used to rent at Claye Lake when I was a kid.'

A strange look passes across his eyes. Sadness, perhaps.

'That's all right. I go mostly for the quiet and the country-side. I don't much care what I catch.' Ben scribbles something on the back of a scrap of paper. 'My number's on there. Give me a ring if you can't find my truck. It was good seeing you again, Alex. Take care.'

'You too.'

Ben clambers back into his RV, which sputters into life and pulls away from the side of the road, heading north. I watch as it fades into the distance, then turn back to my own car. I'm about to climb in when I hear a voice calling my name.

I look around to see Mayor Saville walking briskly towards me, waving. All I want to do is get back to the hotel and go to sleep, but my sense of duty prevents me from ignoring him. Instead, I wait for him to catch me.

'Mr Rourke,' he says, a little out of breath. 'How's things?'

'Okay, I guess. What can I do for you this time, Mr Mayor?'

Saville smoothes his hair back against his scalp. 'I'm just on my way to a meeting – well, an informal get-together – with some of the town's business folk. It'd be good to give them some reassurance about the murder. You know, tell them it'll all be wrapped up and forgotten before long. I wonder if you've got time to meet them?'

I think of my room at the Crowhurst Lodge. I can almost feel the touch of bed linen against my cheek, sense the warm snugness around me. 'I'm kind of tired right now,' I say. 'Maybe tomorrow or some time . . .'

'I'd be really grateful if you could, just to show them everything's going to be okay,' he persists, with just a touch of whining. There's a hint of desperation in his eyes; the once-easy process of re-election suddenly appearing much more of a challenge. Cold-blooded murder in a place as small as Winter's End carries a lot more weight than it does in the city. I think back to what Dale said about Leonard's newspaper articles stirring things up.

'All right. But only for half an hour,' I say.

The Sawmill is quiet, the jukebox turned off. The collection of the town's business leaders amounts to less than a dozen people, all but two of them men, gathered around a couple of tables near the far corner. Otherwise, the place is empty. Saville leads me over and makes the introductions. One seems pretty much interchangeable with another. Someone gets me a beer. Someone else says, 'So, are you guys going to be finished soon so we can all go back to normal?'

I smile, nod, answer, reassure. Yes, we caught the suspect red-handed. Yes, he's going to go to jail for a long time. No, there aren't going to be any more deaths around town. No, I doubt tourist numbers are going to be affected.

The conversation moves on to other matters before long, and I get the impression that these 'meetings' rarely accomplish very much. Just store-owners airing their grievances. The change gives me a chance to blank out the others and retreat into my own thoughts. After a while, I take advantage of a break in the discussions to ask Saville a couple of questions, just on the off-chance he can tell me anything useful.

'What is it, Mr Rourke?' he says, stepping back from the table and lowering his voice so we can talk in relative privacy.

'How long have you been in office?'

'Ten years, just over. Why?'

'You must have known Henry Garner,' I say.

He nods, his face still blank, mind awaiting some clue as to where my questions will lead. 'Yeah, for a few years before the fire; he wasn't a local. I remember when he bought the old Wade House. I was a teenager back then, of course.'

'He must have been pretty young for someone running his own children's home. What kind of person was he?'

'Orderly, I guess you could call it,' he says after a moment's thought. 'He liked everything to be nice and neat, whether it was business dealings or eating lunch. The type that has a proper time and a place for everything.'

'Quite a stern guy, then?'

Saville nods. 'I recall he once nearly went to court after an argument over a maintenance bill for St Valentine's. Wouldn't accept some of the extra charges on it. In the end the company just backed down and he got his way.'

'Was he that strict with the kids?' I ask the question quickly and directly, the verbal equivalent of attacking out of the sun.

'I don't know,' Saville says before he's had a chance to think. He pauses before continuing. 'Some of them used to shift schools now and then, but I guess children in that kind of situation can have problems. Never knew how he ran things at the home, but I doubt he'd stand for trouble. Didn't strike me as the sort.'

'There was never any hint of scandal about St Valentine's, was there?'

'Never. There were a couple of little things that got people chattering about it, but nothing very much. A time when a relative of one of the children tried to abduct her from the home, I think. Got stopped by the cops. Someone from town whose kid ended up there.' He shrugs, then looks back at me. 'Like I said, little things. Sorry I can't be more help. Is this because of what you found up at St Valentine's yesterday?'

'More or less, Mr Mayor,' I say. 'Just some background information, that's all. I appreciate it. Out of interest, I don't suppose you recognize this woman, do you?'

He looks at the locket as I hold it up in front of him. He stares at the picture for a moment, half-frowning and chewing his lip, then eventually shakes his head. 'I don't think so,' he says. 'She maybe reminds me of someone or something, but I've got no idea who. Sorry.'

After another ten minutes or so, I make my excuses and leave. The town's great and good murmur their goodbyes and I trudge back down the road to where my 'Vette is parked.

The Crowhurst Lodge is a dirty white beneath the grey-studded sky. The two faces picked out on the wall seem now to be brooding, pondering on the chances of rain, rather than gazing hungrily at me. The cast-iron door-knocker inside the porch seems to wink at me as I push the door inwards and make my way up through the deserted hotel to my room, which seems more like a sarcophagus than ever. I get undressed and take two of the sedative pills I acquired this morning. Then I lie on the bed, listening to the faint rush of the breeze through the trees bordering the parking lot outside. Fifteen minutes later, I pass out.

# 8

I'm dragged out of blissful sleep by the sound of muffled voices coming from further down the hall. I blink blearily, my eyes feeling as if hot lead weights are glued to their lids, and check the clock to find that it's two in the morning. I've been under for about eight hours, and I don't want to miss out on a single minute of the other five that will pass before the alarm goes off. I lie in bed for a moment, hoping the sounds will die away. Once that hope has been dashed, I struggle out of bed and haul on my shirt, jeans and shoes, then go looking for those responsible.

The stairwell is unlit and I wonder whether there are, in fact, any bulbs there at all. A faint orange glow rises out of the depths from the manager's desk though, and I can see bright light streaking around the edges of a door on the far side of the landing. An engraved wooden sign next to it reads: *The Honeymoon Suite*. It is from here that the noise emanates.

I'm more than a little taken aback when my knock is answered by Rhona Cochrane in a black cocktail dress. In the room behind her I can see Matt, Dale, Laura, Dr Vallence, Jennifer, the pharmacist and others, all holding drinks and dressed for a dinner party. On the wall behind them are portraits of Angela Lamond and the woman in the locket.

'Alex!' Rhona exclaims, ushering me inside. 'We were afraid you weren't going to make it. It's almost time.'

'Time?'

Dr Vallence presses a Martini into my unresisting hand. 'Borrowed time,' he says, looking down his nose at me.

'Borrowed?'

'That's why we're all here.'

The movements of those around me whirl me further inside the room, no matter how hard I try to stop. A blur of faces from around town, almost every one of them recognizable. This vortex of people and voices throws me up against a high school version of Rhona. 'Hey,' she says, 'how are you enjoying the party?'

'I . . . I just got here.' Behind her, the crowd shifts slightly and I can see Sophie Donehan, now wearing a dress of emerald crushed velvet and dark rings of mascara around her eyes. She stares at the two of us, and at me in particular.

'You got a cigarette?' Rhona asks.

I pat my pockets, now thoroughly confused and feeling somewhat underdressed for the occasion. 'No,' I say. 'I must have left mine in my room.'

'Never mind, you can have one of mine.' Beyond Rhona's shoulder, Sophie flashes a look of eager, razor jealousy at me as Rhona hands me the white stick of tobacco. 'If you like, we could go out on the balcony while we're waiting. The others will call us in when it's time.'

'Balcony?'

She's close enough to me for me to feel her body heat. Her bobbed hair hangs back to her ears as she tilts her face up towards mine. When the kiss happens, it does so with surprising force. The tip of her tongue whirls around and against mine like it's dancing the tango.

Then I break it off and pull away. 'This is all nuts,' I say.

I push forward into the throng, roughly in the direction of where Sophie was standing, though I can no longer see her dark, staring eyes. The voices of the crowd are an almost unintelligible babble and I can barely pick out a single recognizable word from the multiple conversations taking place around me. I fight my way past a young couple I don't recognize in outdated clothing, holding hands as they tell Mayor Saville what a wonderful, quiet place this is, through to where the portraits are hanging. Staring at them with the look of an art critic on her face is Gemma Larson. 'What are you doing here?' I say. 'You're not from Winter's End. Why should your time be up?'

'It's not,' she says, giving me her delicate smile. 'I'm here to get everyone's particulars for the morgue.'

I see then that she's not dressed like the others, but is still wearing her lab coat and overalls. 'Oh,' is all I can think of by way of a reply.

'Would you mind if I measured you now? I'd like to make sure you get something that fits.'

I nod dumbly and allow her to run an undertaker's tape measure over me. 'It's a shame,' she says as she finishes. 'I would have liked to have got to know you.'

She squeezes my fingers with one gentle hand, then brushes her lips softly against my cheek before moving away to measure up Dale.

A few moments later, there's a knock at the door. Rhona shushes the crowd, who watch the door with their glasses in hand, then goes to open it. She claps with glee and the other guests cheer when they see Nicholas standing there, naked from the waist up and carrying a pair of knives.

'Hello, everyone,' he says. 'It's time. I'm here to claim my souls.'

As the cheering continues, the killing starts. The twin blades carve through smiling guests, slicing throats and lancing into chests. The young honeymooners are two of the first to drop, then Rhona and the pudgy form of Saville. After that, I can't make out the individual victims; Nicholas is in amongst the crowd and hidden behind a sea of bodies, clapping hands and arterial spray. I turn and run, pushing my way through people still standing as if celebrating New Year. At the back of the room are a set of French windows which open on to a patio at the rear of what has now become St Valentine's Home for Children. Hearing someone behind me, I keep running, across the grass and into the woods. Thorns and twigs whip at me as I plunge on, into the dark maze of under-growth, tree trunks and roots. Footsteps grow closer, gaining on me no matter how hard I try to escape. As they grow louder their pitch changes, becoming higher and higher.

*Beep. Beep. Beep.*

The alarm, hauling me out of the woods and back to the waking world.

# 9

It's just gone eight o'clock as I empty my cup to complete another solitary breakfast in the Crowhurst Lodge's lonely dining room, greatly refreshed after my night's slumber despite the unsettling dreams. My chest feels as if something is burning inside, like bad indigestion, but I ignore it and do my best to bury it in cigarette tar. The day outside is grey and blustery, mirroring my mood. Gusts packed with the scent of rain whip at my clothes as I head for my car.

I stop when I see a folded piece of paper tucked beneath one of the 'Vette's wiper blades. I glance around the deserted parking lot, at the shadows beneath the trees and the light-filled gap that marks the end of the driveway, looking for movement, a shape or silhouette that shouldn't be there. Nothing. I pick up the note.

*Meet me at Martha's at five*, it reads. *I can help you.* My first thought is: help me with what? Then the training kicks in and I look at the note objectively. The paper is cheap plain stuff used by the ream in probably thousands of homes and businesses all over the county. The writing is tight and controlled, but the well-rounded curves of the letters suggest a female hand. The final full stop sits in a noticeable dent in the paper – any harder and it would have punched a hole through it – which suggests that the author has, or believes she has, a serious point to make. The one name that jumps to mind straight away is Sophie Donehan, more because I know she's been watching me than any solid suspicion.

Then my cellphone rings.

'Don't bother heading straight into Houlton,' Dale says at the other end of the line. 'Something's happened here in town.'

'What?'

'A dead body was found at the bottom of Black Ravine in Mason Woods this morning. A guy out walking his dog noticed some bones sticking out of the bottom of one side of the gully.'

'Anything connected to our case?'

'No way to tell, but since Nicholas seems to know the area, there's always a chance. Officially, the remains haven't been identified yet. Unofficially, it looks like this is Henry Garner, the director of St Valentine's at the time of the fire. His wallet was on the corpse. We've got a couple of people out here as well as the CSU and Dr Larson. If you drive down to the old picnic spot I'll have Andy show you where we are.'

From Main Street I hang a left and make for a dirt track that dives into the woods on the eastern periphery of town. The morning's dampness has left the mud beneath my tyres slick and damp. The picnic area is over half a mile through the dank trees, which seem strangely gloomy despite their spring greenery. Shadows cluster around their wet black trunks like young animals suckling at their mother's teat. Eventually the track splits, each arm heading for a different parking spot fifty yards or so along. A deputy is waiting for me at the junction and I follow his outstretched arm to where two Jeeps from the Sheriff's

Department, a State Police crime scene services van and an unmarked station wagon are already waiting.

'Hi,' the deputy says as I lock my door. 'I'm Andy Miller. Sheriff's this way.'

I follow him into the underbrush, feeling droplets of dew splashing against my face and hair with every tree we pass. The damp quickly flecks my jeans dark blue and gives my jacket a waxy sheen. Through a gap in the foliage, I catch sight of one of the other clearings. In it is a red car; I'm not sure of the model but I can just make out the Toyota logo on its radiator. The dog-walker's, I suppose.

Some three hundred yards or so and another cigarette later, the sound of voices reaches me. Gemma, Dale and another guy in deputy's uniform are standing in the leaf litter on the edge of Black Ravine, a twenty-foot deep gash in the forest floor lined with charcoal-coloured stone. The stream responsible for carving it gushes happily away to itself at the bottom. Three forensic technicians are huddled at the base of the cliff opposite, where a jumble of rocks and earth has come away from the worn stone. Tagging and bagging as they go, the trio look to be well into the painstaking process of removing the unfortunate Mr Garner from the rock wall. The Mason Woods spook stories I learned as a boy surface unbidden in my mind, specifically those involving a priest from town who was supposed to have been chased into this very ravine by an angry husband.

'What have they found so far?' are the first words I say to Dale as I step into the small patch of clear ground at the edge of the drop. The watery light leaking through the space above is infinitely preferable to the dim greyness beneath the boughs.

'Morning, Alex,' he says. 'Very little, beyond basic ID. The cliff is undercut at the base and the body was packed in there. Rock and earth; must have been pretty solid to keep out the stream whenever it flooded. You look better this morning.'

'I've got my pills now. Slept since I got in yesterday afternoon.'

Dale grins wryly at me. 'We're not far from Blue Axeman territory here. You don't suppose he might have had something to do with it?'

I smile back. 'I doubt it. Not really his style.' I look back down at the ravine. 'Speaking seriously for a moment, this is definitely homicide?'

Gemma nods and I notice how nice her hair, damp and a little bedraggled, looks in the early morning. 'I'll know more when I've conducted a post-mortem, but there's no way he could have got there by accident. Several of his bones were broken, but I don't know if that happened before or after he died.'

'Anything else? How was the body found?'

'Some of the debris surrounding it seems to have fallen away,' she says. 'It revealed one of the arms.'

'The CSU has come up with a few pieces of evidence which might be usable,' Dale adds. 'Nothing instantly helpful, though. I'll run through it once the scene's been cleared and we know exactly what we've got at hand.'

'Full crime scene procedure? How far have you extended the scene?'

'We're only covering the area immediately around the

body. The site's too old and we don't have enough man-power to try scouring the woods on the off-chance we'll find something else.'

I frown. 'So we're dealing with a death from, what, six years ago, Dale. Why am I here?'

'Everyone thought Garner died in the fire at St Valentine's along with a couple of others. We found some remains, but we couldn't ID everything for sure. We just assumed that was the way it happened. If that's Garner down there' – Dale gestures at the ravine – 'it means it wasn't. Someone took him and killed him, then covered it up with the fire. Angela Lamond worked at the kids' home too, and your guy killed her. What if he'd had practice before?'

'The St Valentine's blaze was arson, wasn't it?'

He nods. 'That's what the investigators from Bangor reckoned. We never nailed anyone for it. Sheriff Kennedy was a friend of Garner's. He had us check anyone with a box of matches who might have been within fifty miles of here at the time. He was pretty worked up about it.' Dale nods to himself, caught up in the memory. 'Half a dozen deputies chasing up and down the county, no leads and no idea where to look.'

'And you reckon Nicholas was behind it?' I don't see a connection. My irritation mounts and the heartburn sensation in my chest grows with it. 'That's a pretty big jump to get to a conclusion.'

'It's a theory, Alex.'

'I don't want you to try and pin this on Nicholas just to save yourself having to face another unsolved murder in your jurisdiction.'

Dale's brows furrow together and his moustache is

pulled away from his nose as he scowls. 'Don't preach at me, Alex. I don't like what you're implying.'

My irritation still won't go away even though I feel like it should. 'I'm not saying you'd do it deliberately. But you know how it goes with cops. You've got two murders. You've got one murderer. If he did one, why not both? It's the outcome that's easiest for everyone.'

'Don't be an asshole, Alex.' He waves a finger at me. 'Don't forget that it was your theory that there might be a connection between Nicholas and St Valentine's. Don't go criticizing me just for believing you.'

I sigh and rub my face with my hands, then spark a cigarette into life and suck deeply on the filter. 'I'm sorry, Dale. It's not your fault; I haven't exactly been on peak form over the past couple of days.'

'Yeah, I know.' He puffs out his cheeks. 'I'm going to check on Andy. I don't want him being overwhelmed by sightseers while we're still working the scene. I'll see you back at the cars.'

I nod and he shoulders his way into the woods. Gemma lifts her gaze from the stream beneath her, at which she had been staring intently and rather awkwardly while Dale and I argued. 'I'll do the post-mortem on the remains when I get back to Houlton. Identification might take a while longer.'

I hold her gaze. 'Any thoughts on what might have happened? I don't know how much of a look you've had at the body.'

'Not enough to suggest anything, I'm afraid. I do know that the techs think someone might have disturbed the burial site. They've got a partial shoe-print for the Sheriff's Department to check. To me, it didn't look like a running shoe, but more like something you'd wear if you were in a suit or dressed smartly.'

I grin at her. 'I didn't realize you were a tracker as well as a pathologist.'

'You say the sweetest things,' she says, laughing softly. This time her quick smile stays.

'Well, I've never been very good with the classic compliments to pay a lady,' I admit. 'The words are there, they all make sense, but when the time comes to say them, they turn to garbage. I try to stick to what I know, and leave the lines of poetry to the experts.'

'You could maybe try them over dinner tonight. If you'd like, that is,' she adds. Her cheeks flush as she says it, pink rising on cheeks left pale by the morning chill.

I smile, but it's just an attempt to mask a sudden attack of nerves. My face feels hot and I can hear blood thumping in my ears. 'Are you asking me out on a date?'

'Um, yes.' Gemma plays with her fingers, keeping her eyes from meeting mine. 'I mean, I don't even know if you're married or something, or whether you'd want to or not, but . . .'

'I'm not married or anything. And yeah, I'd like to have dinner with you.'

'Come by my house at eight? There's a nice little place not far down the road.'

'Okay, yeah, that'd be great. Whereabouts do you live?'

She scribbles her address on a spare piece of notepaper and hands it to me. 'Um, well, I'll see you this evening then.'

'Okay,' I say again. 'Eight. I'll see you later.'

We have one of those awkward goodbyes where neither one of us is quite sure how to end the conversation. Then

I'm trudging back through the trees, still clutching the paper with her address on it. As I tuck it into my pocket, my subconscious reflects that one possible reason I've never managed to keep up a long-term relationship is that my store of witty conversation is, at best, limited.

I push my subconscious back again and tell it to mind its own business.

When I reach the cars, I find Dale and Andy Miller dealing with a couple of interested dog-walkers, a woman of indeterminate age with wide, crazy eyes, and Leonard, the reporter from the *Bangor Daily News*.

'Mr Rourke, Mr Rourke,' he calls out, sidestepping Dale and heading towards me. 'Sorry to bother you, but I was wondering whether there had been any developments in the Lamond case. Is today's incident connected in any way?'

'I'm sorry too, Leonard, but I'm sure you know there's not much I can say about the Lamond case. As to this morning's incident,' I say, glancing at Dale over the guy's shoulder, 'at the moment, we're not treating it as being connected. Obviously that can change, but at present it seems as though this was something completely different.'

The reporter nods. 'Have you spoken with the Lamond suspect? Interrogation used to be one of your specialties at the FBI, right?'

'It did, but again I can't really say anything about the case. I'm sorry, but you know how it is.'

'Sure. Thanks, Mr Rourke,' says Leonard, handing me a card. 'If you do have anything further, would you give me a call? I'm too much of a city boy to be traipsing around in the woods at the crack of dawn.'

'No problem.'

Behind him, Dale is making 'let's go' motions. I step

towards my car. It's then that the woman with the staring eyes screeches, 'It's the curse of the Devil! He's come for you! He's come for us all!'

I stare at her for a moment, taking in the wild locks of dark hair and the hands clenched into fists at her sides. 'It's the Devil!' she wails again, and this time I just shake my head and slide into my car.

The countryside is quiet and disturbingly still as I cruise southward. An atmosphere of brooding seems to have settled on the land around Winter's End as if an unseen presence was released when Garner's grave was found. The sky seems darker, the clouds thicker and more menacing. I don't see any wildlife, bird or otherwise, on the entire trip. Sounds seem distorted, and even the noise of passing traffic is muted into almost nothing. By comparison, the *swish* of the 'Vette's tyres over the blacktop fills the car like heavy breathing, hypnotic in its regularity and strangely biological in its tone.

'How much do you know about the fire?' Dale asks as he puts a steaming cup of coffee in front of me once we're back in his office in Houlton. He settles into his chair and shifts some papers to the side of his desk.

'Just what you've told me and what I saw in the museum.' I sip the hot liquid. 'Arson, three presumed dead, bodies never fully found and identified, no arrests.'

'That's about it. There were a few things that came after, though. At the time, we didn't think much of it. A couple of people in town got crank letters, anonymous threats, nothing much. We figured it was just one of the nuts that always come crawling out of the woodwork after any crime like this. Whoever burnt St Valentine's didn't send any warning.'

'Who received the letters?'

'I remember Sheriff Kennedy got one.' Dale smiles. 'Opened it here in the office, right in front of me. Read it, screwed it up and tossed it in the trash. "Got no time for dumb assholes," he said.' Dale takes a mouthful of coffee. 'If memory serves, the town clerk and Dr Vallence also had letters. I don't think we kept it on record.'

I nod. 'You ever find out who sent them?'

'No, we didn't. There wasn't anything in them that suggested the author knew any more than he could have read in the papers. I never heard of anything more happening to any of the recipients.' Dale looks up as one of his deputies knocks and walks in.

'Initial crime scene report,' he says, placing a file folder on the desk.

'Thanks, Jack. You want a look, Alex?'

I open the file. A batch of photos taken by the CSU this morning are the first things that grab my eye. Glossy shots of the bottom of Black Ravine. The most interesting of these shows the base of the cliff from only a few feet away. A skeletal hand and forearm protrudes from the rock and packed dirt that had hidden the body. A chunk of this mud lies overturned beneath it. I stare at it for a moment, then pass the photo over to Dale.

'Take a look at this,' I say. 'What do you see?'

'Nothing special,' he replies after a moment's thought. 'What is it?'

'Look at the earth that came away to reveal the hand. Look at the cut. It's very clean, aside from a couple of places where individual rocks were. To me, that looks like it was made by a shovel. Someone dug that body up.'

\*

It's half past one in the afternoon when the initial results of Gemma Larson's examination of the remains come through. By this time, I've familiarized myself with the scene at the bottom of Black Ravine and Dale has managed to knock together a short list of Garner's acquaintances, mostly from memory.

'The victim's knees and wrists were both broken,' Gemma's voice floats over the speakerphone. 'There's also a couple of fine cracks around an impact point at the base of his skull. Not enough to kill, but assuming it was made before he died, it would have been enough to knock him out. We've done a preliminary match of Henry Garner's dental records with the teeth of the victim. It looks like they're the same, though we are double-checking just in case.'

'What about cause of death?' Dale says. 'Any sign of what finished him?'

'His hyoid bone is intact, so strangulation is unlikely. There are a pair of scrapes on his ribs just below the solar plexus. I'll be more certain when the remains are examined by the forensic pathologist in Augusta, but I'd say he was most likely stabbed.'

'Any chance that the damage was done during the burial?'

'I doubt it, not from the condition of the ground down there,' she says.

'The arm that was exposed,' I chip in. 'How clean was it? Any moss or other signs that it had been out in the open for some time?'

'The bones were muddy, with no greenery on them.'

I nod. 'Probably fresh out of the ground, then. Thanks.'

'Yeah, thanks, Dr Larson,' says Dale.

'No problem. I'll let you know as and when I've found out more.'

The line goes dead. Dale checks his cup and says, 'I could do with another coffee. You want one while I'm going?'

I nod and he ambles out into the squad room, such as it is. He returns a couple of minutes later with two fresh mugs, which he sets down on the table.

'Thanks,' I say.

He sniffs the aroma rising from his cup and smiles. 'You're lucky it was Corinne's turn to buy a fresh pack during her lunch break. Charlie got the last one, and he buys crap. Not that we have the heart to tell him. At least the guy always pays when it's his turn.'

'Personally, I'll drink anything so long as it's roughly the right colour and isn't decaff,' I observe.

'That stuff's never been much in fashion with the cops up here.' Dale sips his coffee, then returns his gaze to the notes in front of him. 'What are your thoughts on this whole Garner business?'

I pause a while before answering, running scenarios through my mind. 'Why do you break someone's arms and legs?'

'To hurt them. Like kneecapping someone because they owe you money.'

'Or to stop them getting away. It leaves them crippled and powerless, so you can do other shit to them without them being able to stop you, like locking them up or torturing them. If whoever killed Garner just wanted him dead, they'd have cut his throat and left his body to turn to ash in the fire. Instead, they wanted to spend some quality time with him, then stabbed him when they were done.'

'Something personal?'

'Or the killer was a proper nutcase,' I say, shrugging. 'But since the burial site was obviously chosen and the way of concealing the corpse well thought out, I think personal is more likely. The fire, assuming it was connected and wasn't just a freakish coincidence, was simply cover for the abduction.'

Dale interrupts, 'Unless the killer's motives had something to do with the staff at St Valentine's.'

'Sure,' I say, nodding. 'In any case, the guy plans ahead. According to the forensic reports, Garner's wallet was left on him, but his coins, keys and belt were missing. My guess is that it was just in case someone went wandering along the ravine with a metal detector. That would be pretty unlikely, but our killer did it anyway. He didn't want that body found.

'We've got a careful, methodical murderer who's willing to do whatever it takes to get his target. He acts for personal reasons and he's smart enough not to be caught. He's physically tough enough to break someone's limbs and stab them to death.' I swallow a mouthful of coffee; like Dale said, it's good stuff. 'That puts him in the same league as Nicholas. If it wasn't him that killed Garner, I'd say we're looking at someone with a similar mindset.'

Dale smiles faintly. 'I guess I must've won you over to that way of thinking then. So what about whoever dug it up? If they didn't find it by accident, it must've been deliberate. Why would the killer do that?'

'If it was the killer that did it, God knows. If it wasn't, maybe it was an accomplice acting on instructions. I'm pretty good with criminals, Dale, but I've got my limits.' I knock back another slug of coffee. 'Who have you got on the list of Garner's known acquaintances so far?'

Dale slides the piece of paper over to me. The names are few, despite his best efforts and several phone calls to Winter's End. The first note on the list isn't a name at all, just: 'Various staff at the kids' home'. Then, 'Town clerk? Joshua Stern', 'Ian Rourke', 'Dr Vallence', 'Earl Baker' and 'Wife? Not married'.

I look at Dale. 'Ian Rourke? Not much point including my dad here, since he's been dead for just over three years.'

'I was just scribbling down ideas. Stern won't be any help either; he died in a crash four years ago. I checked.'

'What about Baker?'

'He runs a building firm. Done some work around here, maybe on St Valentine's itself. Him and Garner used to go hiking together. No idea where he is now.'

'Garner didn't have any family?'

'Not up here; he wasn't a local and he wasn't married,' Dale says. 'I can't remember if we managed to reach any next of kin at the time of the fire. But if we did back then and we could find them again now, they weren't living locally so they're not likely to know of anyone who might have wanted him dead.'

'What about the rest of the home's management? I saw a photo in the museum of' – I pause for a moment, rifling through my memory – 'Sarah Decker, someone Pierce and Dorian Blythe. Where are they now?'

Dale shrugs. 'No idea. Moved away when St Valentine's shut, I guess. I'll look into it, see if I can turn them up. No guarantees, though.'

I finish my coffee. 'Fair enough. If you see what you can

do to find everyone, I'll go and have a word with Nicholas. Let's see if he knows anything about Garner or the fire.'

The County Jail seems colder than before, its interior seemingly unaware that summer will soon be here. I half expect to see my breath turning to mist as my footsteps echo *click, click* down the bare corridor that leads to the interview room. Two deputies wait outside, hands folded beneath their armpits. I nod at them, then push open the door and walk in.

'Hello, Mr Rourke,' Nicholas says once we've assumed our familiar places. 'You look like you've recovered from whatever was ailing you yesterday. Your eyes still seem a little bloodshot, though.'

'Thanks for the appraisal.' I light a Marlboro out of habit. 'Tell me again about the first St Valentine's, up on Ryland Hill.'

'I didn't think you were interested in ancient history.' No detectable sarcasm in his voice, which is flat and even.

'Maybe it's growing on me.'

'The chapel was struck by lightning during the first sermon there. Twenty people died and the building burned to the ground.'

I lean forward slightly. 'Now tell me about the second St Valentine's.'

'What about it?' Nicholas smiles.

'It also had a fire in which people died.'

'What makes you think I know anything about it?'

I let the cigarette burn itself out in the ashtray and continue to fix him with my eyes. 'You've been there. You left this,' I pull the locket from my jacket and place it on the table, 'in the woods at the back of the building. So tell me about what happened there that was so important that you left a marker for us to find.'

The smile stays, though if anything it becomes a little less friendly and more condescending, like that of a pet owner whose dog has just performed some new trick. 'There was a fire several years ago, like you said. Was your father one of those called out to deal with it, Mr Rourke?'

'Why would it matter if he was?'

'So he was there.' The smile broadens, as if Nicholas is appreciating a joke I haven't noticed. 'I wonder if he ever talked about his work. Did you ever hear stories about the chaos at the building, about the difficulty they had evacuating everyone inside? Perhaps that was why people died.'

I light another cigarette, aware of the irony in sitting here, deliberately inhaling smoke. 'I've never heard of them having that much trouble clearing the building.'

'You haven't listened to the right people.'

'And you have?'

Nicholas leans back slightly as if settling into his seat. 'You've been to St Valentine's, Mr Rourke. What did you see there?'

'A building, corridors, rooms. A lot of mould. A lot of burnt rubble.'

'Did you see the locked doors?' The question is quick and direct, a parry and riposte to my description.

'Yeah.'

'And what did you remind you of?'

'Cells. You're not going to suggest –'

'If there was a fire at a prison, Mr Rourke, do you think the evacuation would be easy? Do you think it would be any easier if only a few people had keys to the cells?'

Nicholas leans forward again. 'When you were young, were you ever caught smoking? You hear stories about fathers locking their kids in the broom closet with a pack of cigarettes and refusing to let them out until they've smoked their way through them all. I doubt it happens for real, not these days.'

'None of the kids at St Valentine's died in the fire, Nick, as you should know. Is there a point to all this?'

'Were you ever caught doing anything bad and told to go to your room without any dinner?'

I sit in silence for some time, watching his face and taking an occasional drag on my cigarette. Once I've finished it, I speak. 'You're suggesting the staff used to lock up children if they were naughty, I guess. I'm willing to entertain the possibility, but how do you know?'

'Plenty of people could know if they did, Mr Rourke. The kids at the home and the staff both would.'

'Do you know any of the staff?'

'Is there anything to suggest that I might?' Like a politician or psychiatrist, answering one question with another.

'You seem to know a lot about the place, and about Winter's End as a whole.' I lean forward, resting my arms on the table as I ask, 'Have you ever met Henry Garner, the director of the home?'

Nicholas raises his eyebrows in surprise, but the look in his eyes tells me he is anything but taken aback by the question. 'According to the stories people tell, he died in the fire, Mr Rourke.'

'His remains were found in Black Ravine this morning, several miles from St Valentine's. He was murdered and his body hidden. He didn't die in any fire, Nicholas. Do you know anything about it?'

The murder suspect's smile returns and a smug look creeps across his features. Not, I get the feeling, connected with the discovery of Garner's body, but rather with something else. 'Death is such a personal subject. Like a piece of music or a movie, our opinions of a particular person's demise vary according to our mood and the nature of their end.'

'And your opinions are?'

'How did you feel when you knew your parents were dead, Mr Rourke?'

Again, I feel the sickening impact of the other car striking my own and anger pumps through me like battery acid. 'That's none of your damn business. Stick to the subject, Nicholas, or this interview and any chance you have of telling your side of the story will be over.'

'Did you know when you lifted your head from the steering wheel that their lives were over, or did you still harbour some hope that they had survived? Did you hate the driver whose car collided with yours, or did you hate yourself?'

The ashtray rebounds from the wall opposite, scattering its contents in a cloud of grey powder. Only my training stops me from vaulting across the table and pounding Nicholas's smiling face against the floor. Instead, I march past him and out of the room, then vent my frustration on the corridor wall. The two deputies watch me, but don't ask questions. Good for them. Punching my suspect could ruin the case against him; punching a deputy wouldn't.

I give myself a couple of minutes to calm down, grabbing a can of Coke from a machine down the hall, which, if anything, seems even colder than before. Then I return to the interview room and Nicholas.

'Let's go back to the subject,' I say as I sit opposite him. 'Did you or didn't you know Garner? Did you or didn't you have anything to do with the fire at St Valentine's? Did you or didn't you have a reason to hate the staff there, people like Garner and Angela Lamond?'

'Those like Garner and the nurse abused their positions, Mr Rourke. Plenty of people had reason to hate them.' He grins, but his eyes are cold and glittering. 'The Devil came to claim them when their time was up, just as he did with others who were equally deserving. You were lucky in your upbringing, Mr Rourke.'

'What's that supposed to mean?'

'You've never been the victim of someone like that.'

'And you were?'

He chuckles. 'Still looking for a motive, Mr Rourke? Casting your bait this way and that, you remind me of the boy struggling to catch fish on Claye Lake under the watchful eye of his beloved father.'

'Just cut the crap and answer the damn questions, Nicholas,' I say through clenched teeth, scowling. 'Tell me about what happened on the fifteenth. The path you took to the murder scene passed through the trees, didn't it?'

'Well, I suppose I had to have got there somehow.'

'But that was hours after Angela disappeared. Where did you take her when you grabbed her off the street? Is there a patch of Mason Woods where we'll find her missing clothes?'

'This is getting tiring, Mr Rourke.'

'Maybe it is, but I'm fed up with fucking around, Nick! If I don't start getting some answers soon, I'm going to give up on this whole case and go back to Boston. You'll go to jail for murder and the rest of our investigation will be forgotten about. You want that?'

Nicholas sighs and shakes his head. 'You can't go back now, Mr Rourke. Sheriff Townsend won't allow it, and you don't want to let go of it yourself. I understand your frustration, but I need you to work this through. *I* won't allow you to go just yet.'

I ask the question even though I've already guessed at the answer. 'What do you mean?'

'Everything that has happened here has done so because I willed it. I am arrested but refuse to talk, forcing the Sheriff's Department to bring in outside help. You used to specialize in interrogating difficult suspects, and you're a friend of Dale Townsend. You've even worked for him in the past. Who better for him to turn to now? You find the children's home, and the tracks and signs I so carefully left. You check out the building, you follow my footsteps, you find the locket *I* left for *you*.' His voice is growing steadily in intensity if not in volume. His eyes harden and their blackness seems to overflow, swallowing the room and leaving me with nowhere to look except his face. 'I told you I was waiting for you, and so I was. Now you're here and you're not going anywhere until I'm through.

'Our lives are so dependent on chance, Mr Rourke. So many little decisions and "what ifs", which added over time completely alter the course of our futures. We are all the products of such a process, but it's rare for a man to make up for the injustices he suffers and punish those who have stolen the life he should have had.'

His eyes burn into mine and I'm almost certain that I'm in the presence of a lunatic. 'Is that what you're here for,

Nicholas,' I ask, 'to punish the people who ruined your life?'

'That's not an issue, Mr Rourke. Remember when I told you that people's actions sometimes put them in the service of the Devil, and that he eventually comes to collect?'

I nod, mouth strangely dry.

'*That's* the issue here. I'd look to yourself, Mr Rourke. It's a rare man indeed who can bargain with the Devil without losing his soul.'

The silence in the room is broken only by the faint hiss of the tape recorder. We sit, staring at each other, as I try to determine what is going on behind the mask Nicholas presents to the world. Did he come to Winter's End for revenge? Does he believe he's the Devil, or just the Devil's agent? Either seems possible, and here, alone with him in the harsh, sterile surroundings of the interview room, I think I could eventually come to believe it too.

Finally, I break the stillness. 'Why should I look to myself? What have I done?'

'If you can't answer that question yourself, I won't do it for you.' Nicholas smirks wolfishly. 'In church, one can't be given absolution unless one first confesses one's sins. Admission is an important step, don't you think?'

'We all commit sins, Nicholas. Mine are probably too numerous to count.' I reach for another Marlboro and return his smile. 'It's interesting to hear you talking about confession, given the sins you've yet to admit yourself.'

'Yes?'

'Thou shalt not kill, Nicholas. But you did just that to Angela Lamond, and perhaps Henry Garner too.'

He gently shakes his head. 'I didn't kill the nurse. She was already dead.'

The look in his eyes tells me that there's an unspoken 'she just didn't know it' at the end of his denial. I try to get him to say it anyway. 'Really?'

'In some ways, it's similar to the fate of the woman in the locket. She wasn't killed either.'

'Who was she, Nicholas? A local? What was her name?'

'I'm sorry, Mr Rourke. If you want to know, you'll have to discover for yourself.' He sighs, and the change in his posture tells me that, as far as he's concerned, the interview is over. I won't be sorry to get out of the room and away from him myself, and so I stop proceedings there and wait for the deputies to take him back to his cell.

# 10

It was a hot day, not quite into the full swing of the Florida summer, but pretty close. The kind of day when the sunlight appears almost white and glare hits you from everywhere you look. A day for air-conditioning and sunglasses, ice-laden drinks and doing nothing but wait for the evening.

I was in Miami to spend a week visiting my parents and relaxing. At least, that's what I told myself. In reality, I had a pile of case folders on my desk, all of them needing my attention, and wanted some support, someone to talk to. So I took a week off and headed for the sun and the only people I thought would understand.

I'd been there three days and was starting to unwind. I still hadn't said anything about work, but I think that both my mom and my dad knew why I was there. There was a lot of non-verbal communication going on at a level deeper than chat about their friends, the city, the weather. Comforting in a way that didn't make me feel like I was running home, looking for a shoulder to cry on.

I was driving them down to a little restaurant by the waterfront they visited every Wednesday, regular enough to know the management. My dad was sitting next to me and the two of us were holding forth on our views on the Red Sox, past and present, with my mom occasionally chipping in with comments from the back.

Traffic was light, but there were quite a few people out

on the streets. Tourists, mostly, to look at them. Everyone was strolling with the same easygoing air, almost sedated by the warmth and the sunlight.

I think that was what told me something was wrong. As I approached one intersection of many on the drive south, the light up ahead green, I could see that most of the pedestrians on the sidewalk to my right were looking away, down the road that was about to meet my own. They seemed frozen, paused in mid-stroll, watching something.

As I passed beneath the traffic lights I heard the roar of an engine running fast and hard, no longer muffled by the buildings that had blocked the noise. I glanced to the right.

Here, the memories get a little confused. I saw a dark car screaming out of the intersection towards me, and I remember slamming my foot on the brakes. I don't know whether it had any time to make any difference. The inside of the other car was in shadow and I could see nothing but dim silhouettes within.

I was thrown about like a matador hit by a charging bull, held only by my seatbelt, and I felt sharp fragments, probably glass, scatter against my flesh. As the car shrieked sideways under the impact and my view began to tilt as its passenger-side wheels left the road, my airbag fired, smothering me briefly in whiteness. I doubt it did anything to protect me. Then I felt the door next to me shudder and buckle as it hit the ground; my car was now on its side. Liquid dripped against my skin. Either I passed out, or I was too dazed to know what happened for a while. Next thing I knew, there were flashing lights outside. I looked across, no, *up*, and saw my father hanging limply in his seat, blood running across his face. The side of the car next to him was shredded and punctured.

The strange thing about my memories of the crash is that I can't remember any sound at all. It's as though one moment my dad was talking about a new pitcher for the Sox, then there was the roar of the other engine, but the next moment everything faded away, leaving nothing but the physical sensations of the impact. The next sounds I heard were the muffled and distorted words of the emergency teams, a couple of paramedics speaking to me, voices coming from the bottom of a deep ocean.

The cops told me later that none of the people they spoke to could remember seeing the driver of the other car. It was a kind of 'situation blindness' I was familiar with. They also said there had been extra padding material in the remains of the stolen sedan, and asked if I had any enemies who might have wanted to kill me. In a daze I rattled off some names – stay with the Bureau for long enough, and anyone makes enemies. I'd never worked a case in Florida, though, so none of them were local. Anyway, most of the ones I could think of were in jail.

The cops eventually decided that the driver might have been planning to ram-raid somewhere nearby and had wanted to make sure he didn't get hurt. Tragic accident, colliding with someone on their way to commit a crime. I didn't really care about their theories, but at the time I accepted them.

From there, I couldn't see any way of avoiding the inevitable. My life as an FBI agent effectively ended on that day, even though the full breakdown took another six months to overcome me completely.

*

'So what do you think?' Dale asks, leaning back in his chair as I spark up a cigarette and settle into the seat opposite in his office, glad to be away from the jail. 'Should we farm out the Garner investigation, or do you want to keep it with Lamond for now?'

I spend a few moments rolling the tobacco smoke around my mouth before answering. 'I think Nicholas has a serious grudge against Garner as well as Lamond. He talked about them "abusing their positions" and about people stealing the life he should have had. Both victims worked at a children's home, and Nick is certainly familiar with the place.'

'Angry ex-inmate?'

'It would fit everything we have,' I say with a shrug.

'And you'd buy him as the guy that torched St Valentine's and killed Garner?'

'Yeah, I would. It happened six years ago, which would make him between twenty and twenty-four at a guess.'

'Young enough to have been in the home during the time Angela worked there,' Dale observes, nodding. 'Which would only leave the question of who dug up Garner's body and why. Forensics report on the partial shoe print we found in the ravine says it was a size ten man's shoe, probably Hush Puppies, not heavily worn. It didn't match those of the guy who found the body, so we're probably looking at the digger.'

'That's good, but we still don't know why he was there.' I pause for long enough to finish my cigarette. 'Has Nicholas sent or received any mail since he's been here?'

'No on both counts. Didn't even take his phone call. You figure he might have someone on the outside?'

'Perhaps.' I lean across and pick up the list of Garner's

associates. The number of names hasn't increased, and I know that two of the people on it have been dead for years. Phone numbers and addresses have been pencilled in for Dr Vallence and Earl Baker, though. 'You keep looking for the digger, Dale,' I say. 'I'll speak to Vallence and this Earl Baker guy and see if they know anything. Have you managed to track down any of the rest of the home's management?'

'Not yet. Every record that was kept in the place seems to have been lost down the years. Charlie's still working on it.'

I pocket the list as well as a copy of Nicholas's photo and stand to leave. 'I'll phone you when I'm done.'

'Do you want me to call you if we get anything back from the pathology lab by this evening?'

'Not unless there's anything spectacular in the results,' I say. 'If they're in, I'll ask Gemma about them.'

Dale chuckles. 'You're a sly one. Still, can't say I blame you. Unless you're in the habit of hitting on the medical examiners in every place you visit.'

'Hardly. Most of them are in their fifties. And male. I'll see you tomorrow.'

'Sure. And, Alex,' Dale calls after me as I reach the doorway, 'don't let Nick get under your skin. He's not worth getting worked up over.'

I nod once, then let the office door swing shut with a click.

The grey and blustery weather turns to rain, a squall charging in from the west, as I head north to Castle Hill, home of Earl Baker. Droplets splash from a heavy sky, keeping my wipers working overtime all the way. Spray kicks up from the asphalt, dancing a grit-laden jig on the road surface. The lush greenery of spring evident in the verges and gardens I pass, as I make my way through the small town, is beaten down under the weight of the downpour, turning it dark and flat.

I run up the driveway of 12 Pulver Street without bothering to stop and check out the house, an indistinct brown shape in the watery murk. By the time Earl, a thickset man in his early fifties, opens the door, I'm busy shaking myself off in the shelter of his porch.

'Can I help you?' he says, raising his voice to be heard over the hammering.

I raise my badge in my left hand. 'Sheriff's Department. I'd like to speak with you a moment.' I glance behind me. 'Inside, if possible.'

'What's up?' Earl asks again once I'm safely ensconced in the relative comfort of his home. The house is a mixture of the bland stylings of an owner who can't be bothered to change what just about works – a look I'm familiar with from my own apartment back in Boston – and the remnants of stray attempts to brighten up the place. A couple of ornaments on top of the TV. A wall hanging printed with an old map of the county.

'It's about Henry Garner,' I say, running a hand through my hair to sweep away a few tousled tendrils that have plastered themselves to my forehead. 'I don't know whether you've heard, but his remains were found this morning, well away from the old St Valentine's building.'

'I heard on the radio that they found a body.'

'Well, I've got a couple of questions to ask, if you don't mind.'

'Sure.'

I'm about to say more when a woman steps in through the doorway in the far right-hand corner of the room and asks from over his shoulder, 'Earl, who was it?'

'Deputy Alex Rourke, ma'am,' I say.

Earl turns to look at the newcomer, who appears to be about the same age and is of a lighter build, with short hair dyed coppery-ginger and casual clothes. 'He's here about Henry's death,' Earl says, turning back towards me as the woman joins him.

'Deborah Pierce,' she says, extending a cold, clammy hand. I recognize the name – she was the nurse at St Valentine's when it opened. 'That was a long time ago. What's happened?'

'They found his body, Deb. It sounds like he didn't die in the fire after all.'

'You both knew Garner well?' I already know the answer to the question, and my guess is that they're more than casual acquaintances themselves.

Earl nods. 'For years.'

'He was such a nice man,' Deborah coos. 'I couldn't believe it when they said he'd died in the fire.'

'You worked at the home. Were you there on the night of the fire?'

She shakes her head. 'No, I'd been gone for a good ten, twelve years by then.'

I turn to Earl. 'How about you, Mr Baker. Were you there?'

'No, I never worked with Henry. I'd been to St Valentine's a few times, sometimes just to visit him, sometimes for work. I was in construction and maintenance.'

'Did either of you know anyone who might have had any kind of grudge against him?'

They both shake their heads, so I take the locket and

the photo of Nicholas from my jacket pocket. 'How about these two people?' I say. 'Do you recognize either of them?'

They look at the jewellery nestling in the plastic bag in my hand. My eyes follow theirs, gauging reactions, judging responses. I'm disappointed. 'I'm sorry, Deputy Rourke,' Earl says.

'I don't know,' Deborah adds. Then she takes a further look at the locket. 'She seems a bit familiar, maybe. Like someone I might have seen around town a few times or something.'

I jump on this. 'Around Winter's End? While you were working at the home?'

'Maybe. I might be wrong, though. It was a long time ago.'

'What about the guy?'

She purses her lips. 'I don't know. There's maybe . . .'

'Yes?'

'No,' she says at last, shaking her head. 'No. I don't recognize him. For a moment I thought his eyes looked familiar, but I can't place him.'

It's something, but not much. I pocket both photos again. 'There's one more thing. St Valentine's had a reputation for strictness. To your knowledge, were kids who misbehaved ever locked up or anything? We've heard a couple of stories that it used to happen, and I noticed some rooms that looked like they could have been used that way while I was there.'

Earl and Deborah look at one another and *there*, there it is. That meeting of stares, the way their eyes twitch as if unspoken thoughts are being exchanged. I see it, and I know without needing them to tell me that Nicholas spoke the truth. The staff used to lock away children who were bad in cells that were probably put together by Earl during his construction days.

Deborah breaks eye contact with me before she answers. 'No, not that I know of.'

'Well, they were just stories I heard. Thank you both for your help, you've been real useful.'

'What's your theory on Henry's death? Do the police have any leads?' asks Earl as he shows me to the door.

'It's a little early to say,' I reply. 'But at the moment, we're treating it as suspicious.' I don't know what prompts me to add what I do next, giving Earl a steady, almost knowing glance as I say it. I guess I just don't like people mistreating children. I had a good time growing up, with decent parents. That other kids aren't so fortunate because adults can be assholes grates with my sense of justice. 'We're treating a lot of things as suspicious right at the moment.'

I return my eyes to the driveway in front of me. 'What do you know,' I say, more friendly. 'The rain's moved on. Must've hung around just to soak me. I'll be seeing you.'

I leave the beefy form of Earl standing statue-like in the doorway, Deborah dangling at his shoulder, a guilty conscience with weak, watery eyes. When I'm back in the privacy of my car, I fumble for and light a cigarette, mostly to give my free hand something to do while my brain ticks over. If the woman in the locket lived in Winter's End, even if it was the best part of twenty years ago, someone must remember her. I make a note to ask Vallence about her again when I see him, as well as trying the older folk in town.

It's getting late by the time I reach Winter's End and

I've more or less made up my mind to leave the rest of my enquiries until tomorrow when, on impulse, I pull up at the Church of St Francis. My eyes take in the whitewashed stone building, a simple construction in the style of the nineteenth century. A quartet of stunted and twisted maple trees are tucked just inside the low wall that lines the base of the gentle grassy slope leading to its doors. In the wall is an equally low wooden gate. The breeze is full of after-rain scent, both fresh and at the same time chill and rusty, decaying. I stuff my hands in my pockets and walk up to the gate. Beneath my touch, the wood feels softened by its recent drenching, and the small metal catch squeals as I open it. As I noticed yesterday, the graveyard of the church is small and simple, and the grounds consist mostly of bare turf with a couple of lonely looking trees and a gravel path cutting through it. The doors are open a crack, just enough to let prospective visitors know that the building is available to them without letting out the warmth within.

The locket, which shares a pocket with my left hand, seems to grow hotter as I trudge along the gravel. I'm about to put it down to no more than body heat when my vision blurs and I again see a woman in the church grounds. Black hair, pale face, and now with no darkness to conceal her, I can see that she *is* the one from the photograph, still clad in her rotting shroud. This time, she doesn't try to lead me further away, but instead points away to the south, eyes imploring. I turn and look, but see nothing except houses and there, in the distance, the tops of the trees bordering town.

When I look back, she's gone. My nerves crackle, a quivering that has nothing to do with the damp. I suck a lungful of cold air and quicken my pace up the path, more worried by the fact that I'm seeing things than the fact that I seem to have been visited by a ghost. I've had hallucinations before, during my breakdown. Departures from reality that generally lasted no more than an hour, when the fear and paranoia that gnawed at the root of my mind suddenly exploded to the surface. There's nothing worse than feeling your hold on the world ebbing away.

Once I'm at the doors I pause, some inner force suddenly very reluctant to step over the threshold. You're not a believer, I tell myself. What are you doing here? I don't have a good answer, but I turn the handle and walk in anyway.

Inside, the church is typical of small town chapels built many years ago and, though well maintained, not wholly renovated since. Faded carpet the colour of red wine, sturdy wooden pews, a simple pulpit and altar beneath a cross and a pair of stained-glass windows. Aside from me, there seems to be only one other person here, kneeling in one of the rows near the front. I walk softly down the aisle, unconsciously adopting the habit of trying to make as little noise as possible when in a place of worship, as if God is sleeping next door and would be extremely annoyed to be awoken.

Getting closer, I recognize the tangled hair and the faded clothing the kneeling woman wears. I saw her in the woods this morning. Hearing my approach, she turns to face me and without unclasping her hands says, 'You've come then. I warn them all, but they pay no heed.'

'What do you mean?'

'You've come to pray for forgiveness for your soul.'

I let it pass; I have a feeling she'd react badly if I argue with her. 'What did you mean this morning, about what happened to Garner being the work of the Devil?'

The woman's eyes don't seem to be focused on me, as if she's looking at something else that I'm unable to see. She says in a calm voice, 'The Devil has come for us, just as I always knew he would. This town is drenched in spilt blood, but the only reward he gives for our sins is everlasting damnation.'

Her words are striking in their similarity to those of Nicholas. 'What exactly has gone on here?'

'They built this place on the bodies of the slain. They murdered one another for greed. They schemed and they worked their evil.'

She seems to be referring to the town's early years, the legends of Mason Woods and the mass pyre on Ryland Hill, so I ask, 'Isn't that all ancient history?'

'Not all of it,' the mad woman says. 'He's cursed this place. He took the woman who died on the highway. Like he took those others. Like he's always taken people here. You don't ask for God's forgiveness and he'll take you too.'

I take out the locket, which still feels strangely warm, and show it to the woman. 'Do you know who this is in the picture?'

The woman brushes the plastic covering the photo with a single fingertip. 'Poor thing,' is all she says.

'What do you mean?'

'You should know, or else you shouldn't be asking me. Now you must pray.'

'I'm not a believer.'

'God doesn't care.'

'Neither do I.' I turn to walk away. Behind me, I hear the woman stand, although she doesn't come after me.

'Throw yourself on the Lord's mercy,' she calls out, voice echoing in the empty confines of the church. 'If you don't, the Devil will take you!'

I look down at the locket. 'No he won't,' I reply. 'He needs me here.'

I make it to Martha's Garden and my meeting with the mystery note-writer with a quarter of an hour to spare. I take a stool and order a coffee, thankful for the reassuringly ordinary human bustle after my experience in the church-yard and the chapel. I sit quietly, smoke, act polite with the diner's staff and let myself relax. The place isn't empty but there are no more than half a dozen people here. None of them look like they've been waiting for me. I knock back black caffeine-enriched restorative and wait. At five, the bell above the door tinkles and I turn to see Sophie Donehan walking a little hesitantly towards me. She's wearing a dark green shirt unbuttoned at the top and bottom and a pair of tight trousers a little lighter in hue than her bobbed black hair. Like many teenagers, she's wearing slightly too much make-up. The dark lines of mascara around her eyes make her look like I feel. She orders a coffee, then moves to a table near the window, watching me as she does so. I pick up my own cup and follow.

'You wrote the note?' I ask, sitting opposite.

She nods, then fixes me with eyes the colour of dark chocolate. 'They say you're investigating the murder.'

'Yeah. Your note said you could help.'

'Did you know that she, y'know, the dead one, used to work at the kids' home in the woods?' Sophie blows on her coffee to cool it, but her eyes never leave mine. It's the kind of gaze an interrogator likes to give their suspect.

'Yeah, I knew that. What about it?'

'Do you know what they were like there?' Sophie asks the question with some force; 'they' is practically spat out in the same kind of tone a priest might use when talking about practitioners of black magic.

'I'm sorry, but I don't have much more than a vague idea. The place shut six years ago. No one's said much about it.'

'They *all* know,' she hisses. 'They pretend like they don't, but they do.'

'Know what?'

The teenage emotional thermostat moves down a couple of notches and Sophie's face settles again. Her eyes continue to burn into mine, hard and piercing. 'If I tell you, will you help me?'

I take a mouthful of coffee by way of slowing the pace. 'Help you how?' I ask once the cup is back on the table.

'Get me out of here. Take me down to Boston with you. I've got money. I can get a place there and find a job.'

'And your parents would probably try to charge me with kidnapping if I did. Why can't you talk it over with them?'

'My mom's dead, so there's just my dad. But they weren't my parents,' she says, hatred running through every word. 'Not my real ones, anyway.'

'How about trying to find your real parents, then? If you still can't get away after that, why not get your friends to help?'

'I don't want to find my real parents. I hope they're rotting in hell!' The hiss is back and, as far as I can tell, her anger at both sets of people is genuine and intense. Her pale skin is flushed beneath the make-up. 'I don't have any friends, either. I hate this place and everyone in it.'

I keep my voice soft and steady, hoping to calm Sophie down. 'Why?' I ask.

'My foster-father doesn't care about me, and I don't care about him. He spends most nights drinking in front of the TV, while I spend most of mine up in my room. When he says anything to me it's usually to yell at me to fix him dinner or something. I've had enough.'

'All right, I'll think about it,' I say with a sigh. As I do so, I have no idea whether I'm being truthful with her or not. 'But only if you're honest with what you know.'

She hesitates, as if making up her mind whether to trust me or not. Eventually, her eyes break away from mine and she reaches for her cup. Once the coffee has gone, she says, 'Do you have kids?'

'No,' I tell her. 'Never got round to it.'

'Uh-huh. But you know that parents are supposed to love their children, right? I guess my real ones must've died or something, 'cos if they loved me they wouldn't have left me in *that* place.' She shows little emotion as she speaks, although she seems relieved to have found someone willing to listen to her. I get the feeling that most people just ignore her. After putting up with the lies from Baker and Pierce and the implied suggestions of Nick, I hope she can give me something more concrete.

'You were at St Valentine's? What was so bad about it?'

'I got out when I was five or six, I guess. Something like that.' She makes it sound like she'd been given parole from jail. 'But it took me ages to get used to living someplace else. It was like the routine they had there. We weren't ever allowed outside the grounds except when the older kids went to school, and they only ever let us out of the *building* in the middle of summer. You imagine that? I never went to kindergarten or anything, never had any friends. They kept us in that place all the time. I guess it would have been harder if I'd been older. The older kids got it worse.'

'What do you mean?'

'You been there?'

I nod. 'I had a look around. There's not much of the home left.'

'If anyone misbehaved, sometimes they'd get a beating, or sometimes they'd be locked in the basement. I never went down there, but we all knew that they could keep you shut up for hours, or days even.' I think back to the cells I'd found in the cellar. 'Even if we hadn't done anything,' Sophie continues, 'the older kids still had to do work around the place. Cooking or cleaning, sometimes laundry. I remember one boy, I dunno how old he was, getting a beating with a ladle from one of the cooks, just for spilling some gravy he was supposed to be serving.'

'Do you remember any of the names of the kids there? Especially the older ones,' I say. It's a long shot, but I'm hoping she'll tell me about a boy called Nicholas. In the end, I'm disappointed.

'No, not really. I remember a few that were my age, but that's all.'

'How about the staff? Anything they were known to have done in particular? Like that kitchen beating you talked about.'

She cocks her head and gives me a calculating smile. 'You want to know about the dead woman, right? I'm sorry, I don't remember much about her, except for the fact she worked there. I think most of the kids only ever went to see her when they'd been hurt.'

'And she never reported what went on at St Valentine's? They could have closed it down.'

'No, she didn't. I guess all the staff were happy with it. If the place was still open today, I'd have told someone and the story would probably have got out. But it's not. Whoever burnt it down saved everyone the trouble. They should be given a medal.'

I know the question I'm about to ask is on a sensitive subject, but curiosity forces me to try anyway. 'Sophie, Sheriff Townsend told me your foster-mom died six years ago, about the same time that St Valentine's shut. What happened? I'll understand if you don't want to talk about it.'

'That's okay,' she says, shrugging. 'I don't care about her, and I don't know why she did it, not really. They didn't get on much, I guess. She was pretty uptight most of the time, and her husband's always been an asshole. One day I came back from school and found her dead on the couch, an empty bottle of sleeping pills on the table.' She smiles faintly. 'Funny, really. I thought she was just asleep at first. Only figured it out when I couldn't wake her up. My foster-father's been on the bottle ever since.'

I motion for another refill for our cups and light a cigarette, offering her one. She accepts.

'I'll tell you what,' I say once the fresh batch of coffee has arrived, 'if you still want to get away from Winter's End when I'm finished and everything's settled, you can come with me. But,' I add, 'you think carefully about this. Leaving home's no small decision, and a fresh start might sound nice but it won't necessarily be all sunshine and roses. Okay?'

'Okay.'

'Here's my card. If you want to get in touch with me, my number's on there.'

She glances at the dark blue print. 'Thanks. Alex,' she adds, a little hesitant in using my first name. 'You think what went on had anything to do with that woman's death?'

'Maybe, yeah. I might find out more tomorrow. Right now I've got too much else on my mind to think about it.'

Sophie nods and seems to be about to say something else. Then she stops herself and walks out with just a plain 'goodbye'. She keeps her head down as she leaves, as if she's worried that anyone saw her talking to me. The scent of drugstore perfume trails in her wake.

I grind out what's left of my cigarette and get some more coffee. I've been sitting there for a good ten minutes, just gearing up to head for home, when my phone rings. The number is that of the office back in Boston.

I press the 'call' button. 'Rob?'

'Alex! How's the Great White North?' my partner bellows through the receiver. 'Getting fed up with moose jerky and whale blubber already?'

'You're thinking of a little way further north than where I am, Rob.'

'Well, you know how I get confused whenever I can see more greenery on the horizon than I can concrete. How's the case coming along?'

'It's going okay,' I say. 'A little more complicated than it was to begin with, but give me a couple more days and I think I'll have everything wrapped up. Has anything urgent cropped up at your end?'

'No, no. I just thought I'd check in with my pioneer

friend. You haven't managed to wrangle a confession out of your suspect yet, I take it.'

'Not yet. We've had a second body turn up, and a few extra connections to take into account. It's no problem.'

A slight pause at the other end of the line. 'Are you all right, Alex? You sound kind of defensive. You are telling me everything, aren't you?'

'Not exactly, but I want to wait for everything to pan out before I start spilling the beans. And you've caught me at the end of a busy day. My brain's still catching up on events.'

'If you say so,' he replies. 'I'll see you in a couple of days. Bring me back a carved walrus tusk souvenir or something.'

I check my watch once the rumble of the 'Vette's engine has faded into nothing. Five to eight. Hell. Early. The worst possible time to arrive. It makes you look desperate and forces your date to rush. Under other circumstances, I'd correct this by sitting in the car for five minutes. Unfortunately, this is a quiet residential street and the 'Vette isn't exactly stealth on wheels. Several seconds are eaten up, however, by the tricky decision of whether or not I should give her the flowers I bought on the way here after all. I don't want to look too eager. Sudden panic, trying to figure out what would be best on a first date. Then I grab them anyway and climb out of the car, making a lot of effort to breathe slow and easy. It's like prom night all over again. I'm just glad she doesn't live with her parents. At least, I *hope* she doesn't live with her parents. I also hope that the restaurant she has in mind isn't going to require me to wear a tie, since I didn't bring one up from Boston.

Gemma answers my ring on the bell within a few seconds. She's wearing a loose red top, a tight knee-length black skirt, and she looks absolutely gorgeous. Her blonde hair is loose, draped around her shoulders like golden cotton candy. Her smile is bright and pretty, but betrays a nervousness that perfectly mirrors my own. This feeling is so obviously shared in both our initial words and body language that we each relax somewhat; we've found our first piece of common ground.

'They're lovely,' she says when I rather awkwardly present her with the flowers, whose exact species escapes me. She places them in a vase on her hallway table, then grabs a slim jacket of brown suede and her handbag.

'I hope they'll let me into the restaurant,' I say, gesturing at my smart-as-possible, but still underdressed, self. 'My nearest tie is a few hundred miles away.'

I grin and she laughs, a genuine sound, soft and tinkling. I know the evening is going to be fine.

We stroll into the town centre, hands knotted together, talking about nothing in particular. The starter before the main course of the conversation, which will have to last over the full stretch of the evening. The restaurant Gemma has chosen is a small place of dark wood, frosted glass and soft lighting. A quiet but friendly atmosphere, and food that's good rather than overpriced culinary art. Not yet into the full swing of the tourist season, it's not packed and we have a corner all to ourselves.

I learn about Gemma's childhood in Bangor, the largest town in northern Maine. Her elder sister, Alice, who moved away to Baltimore while Gemma was finishing medical school, and her younger brother, Ryan, who works at a bank in Augusta. Her student days, her first job as an intern at a pathology lab, the path leading her to the post of part-time medical examiner. I learn that she has friends in town but spends most of her evenings in. I learn that she likes reading so long as it doesn't relate too closely to work, that she watches horror films but likes to have something to cover her eyes at the scary bits, that she listens to music but doesn't have favourites, just whatever comes on the radio.

In return, I try not to bore her with the details of my own sorry life. I cover pretty much everything, good and bad, but don't dwell on anything for long. I wheel out anecdotes from my own student days, then more from my time with the Bureau and after. I tell her about staying at the world's weirdest hotel. I tell her that my choice of car is less about keeping up a macho image and more about demonstrating my taste for the ridiculous. I show her my self-effacing, warts-and-all side. She laughs at the jokes; she gets caught up in the serious stuff. I think she likes me, which is good because I certainly like her.

Hours tick past without us noticing and it's soon time to pay the bill and leave before the restaurant's staff start stacking the chairs on the tables and mopping the floor. We walk home arm in arm, still talking, smiling and happy. Then she asks if I'd like to come inside.

'I would,' I say, 'but I never do on first dates. Not if I'm serious about someone. Maybe it's old-fashioned, but I like to give the girl some time and a second chance for her to decide if I'm really a jerk or not.'

I smile, but I'm aware that this is the final test. If she doesn't like it, then I know that this isn't going to work.

Gemma just smiles back and moves closer to me. 'In that case, are you doing anything tomorrow night?' she says, voice bright and green eyes shining.

I move my hands to her hips, a motion she mirrors, and we kiss, long but softly. Lips like cool satin, breath as sweet as cinnamon. I can feel her hair against my cheek, gossamer-thin gold carrying the scent of vanilla. Her body is warm against mine, gently moving with her breathing.

When we break off, she whispers goodnight and trails her hand through mine as she steps through the door. I stand on the doorstep for a moment like a love-struck adolescent, then amble down the driveway to my car, which is tucked against the kerb. Once I'm inside, I break into a big watermelon grin and let out a long, long breath, happy as I've been in ages. I'd punch the air but it's a low roof, and it's too late to make a whooping noise in such a quiet neighbourhood. Instead, I turn the ignition and pull slowly, reluctantly, away from the side of the road.

On the long, dark journey home, I hum all the way, genuinely buzzing. The grey day has turned into a starless night, and the sole illumination for most of my journey are the twin beams of light spraying from the front of the 'Vette. The damp blacktop has an almost hypnotic TV-static look to it as the tiny cracks and imperfections between every lump of grit in the asphalt flash by, each scattering the yellow-white light in a slightly different direction. The tall grass and foliage to either side appear almost monochrome, such is the difference between the sudden glare of the headlights and the blackness beyond. A feeling of light-headedness steals over me, a sensation akin to having my skull filled with helium and loosely tethered to my shoulders. Elation, doziness, or something altogether different.

I burst out into the empty fields that lie between St Valentine's and Winter's End doing just over sixty, looking forward to getting home. Even the thought of the Crowhurst Lodge and its pale malevolence is a welcome one. Then I catch sight of something reflecting the glow of the headlights up ahead and slam on the brakes.

When the tyres have finished squealing and I've lifted my head from where it rests against the wheel, I'm free to take in the scene in front of me. A man, bare from the waist up and carrying a knife in each fist. Nicholas. In front of him stands a naked woman, Angela Lamond, sobbing, with one hand pressed to her mouth. Phantom rain, translucent in the glow, dances from their skin.

The apparitions stand in front of the 'Vette, oblivious to my presence, after-images of events already passed into history. I can feel the sharp point of light behind my eyes that signals an oncoming migraine even as I stare at this tableau. Despite this, I step from the car to get a closer look. Neither of the apparitions reacts in any way as I creep as far as the front tyres. I can hear, over the ghostly drumming of a downpour that is long since over, Nicholas speaking softly and calmly.

'You understand why this has to be,' he says. 'I wouldn't normally do this sort of thing myself, but I need you to act as a messenger.'

'Please,' Angela whispers. 'Please.'

'I'd tell you that your torment will be less because of the purpose you shall serve,' Nicholas continues. Lightning that exists only for the two actors in the spectral play in front of me flashes from their skin and dances in Angela's eyes. 'But that would be a lie. You must've known how your actions would be rewarded.'

'Please,' she repeats.

'Your fate is set,' Nicholas says, remorseless. He gently turns her around so her back is to him. 'You're no different to the others. Don't think of this as being truly personal.'

He wraps his arms around her like a lover's embrace. Lightning flashes again as the knives in his hands whip out, then back into her ribcage, and blood mixes with the ghostly rain. He lowers her to the floor, waiting until her heart has stopped and the bleeding has slowed, then proceeds to cut and slash with abandon at her chest.

Nicholas stands, lowering his hands to his sides. 'Now, to wait,' he says.

It's quite enough for me. I break out of my stupor and turn and run back to the comforting normality of my car. My fingers twitch and shake as I fire up the engine. I hit the gas, swerving around the phantom vignette in front of me, and don't ease off on the throttle until I reach town.

All I can think about is that I'm seeing things. Again. I desperately want it to be fatigue, or sleeping at the wheel, or some kind of reaction to something I ate, or even the waiter at the restaurant spiking my wine with LSD. My legs feel like they're full of water and every movement of my head produces a tingle at the back of my neck that adds to my fear that I'm falling apart.

The parking lot of the Crowhurst Lodge is darkened and empty. My jumpy eyes, squeezed from behind by the pressure of a mounting headache, fill the shadows beneath the swaying trees with half-hidden figures and shapes dancing jerkily to a tune I can't hear. I stand for a moment on the gravel, reassuring myself that everything is fine and that there is nothing sinister in the swishing foliage. Repeat it often enough and maybe I'll believe it's true. The twisted visages above the hotel door seem to be laughing at me, shaking and shuddering with every guffaw until I blink and look away. I lurch for the front entrance, fumbling my key from my pocket. The ancient iron door knocker at the far end of the porch now wears a mocking grin. I run through, past the reception desk with the single candle-bulb glowing dim and red. Take the steps two at a time, coming perilously close to falling. Into my room, slam the door, turn on every light I can find, and then the TV to drown out the endless noise of the leaves outside.

I pop one of my migraine pills before splashing some water on my face and neck. My head is throbbing and jittering whorls of distortion dance in front of my vision. Take a second capsule. Sit, watch TV, and try to relax again. Take a third. Then a fourth. Knock back my two sedatives for this evening, then follow them up with a fifth treatment for my headache. Shrug out of my jacket and clothes, but make sure my Colt is within reach of the bed.

I pass out to the uncertain noise of the television.


A dreamless sleep is brought to an end by the repetitive tone of the alarm clock. I'm cold, lying on top of the covers. I have a headache, but it feels like a hangover rather than anything more serious. I rub my eyes and pop another tablet anyway. Then I edge rather cautiously over to the window and peep out through the gap in the curtains. What world is waiting for me out there? Awakened or sleeping, dreamscape or nightmare? Has anything changed?

No. It's an ordinary day outside. The clouds are back,

sluggishly blanketing the entire sky like mouldy cotton wool. I still can't see any birds or other animal life, but at least there are no phantoms or strange visitations to plague me. The same world as it was yesterday, as it will be tomorrow.

I shower and dress, lighting my first cigarette as I throw on a shirt. I check myself in the mirror before I leave the room. I don't look well. Skin too pale, eyes bloodshot and red-rimmed, stubble sprouting from a grey chin. I decide not to bother with breakfast today. I can't face another morning in that lonely dining room, feeling like an exiled monarch under house arrest in a foreign land. I wonder how long it will take the mysterious managers of the hotel to notice that none of the food they prepared has been eaten, and whether they will then bother to put out any more tomorrow morning.

It doesn't matter. I trot down the stairs and out to my car, thankful that the emptiness of the Crowhurst Lodge will have prevented anyone from noticing how badly parked the 'Vette is, left skewed across the gravel in the haste of my return last night. The trees bordering the lot are still, silent in the flat air. I glare at them for a moment, daring them to show some sign of the movement that fills the nights, drowning out all else. Then I'm in the car and away, stones skittering behind me.

At 8.15, six miles south of town, my cellphone rings.

'Alex, it's Dale. I've been trying to get hold of you for ages.'

'Sorry,' I say, voice dry and rasping, 'I had my phone turned off. What's up?'

'Nicholas has escaped.'

# 11

I pass through two roadblocks on my way into Houlton. The first is on I-95, a cordon of State Police blue-and-whites and businesslike cops packing shotguns. Traffic is being stopped in both directions, but it's plain that they're concentrating on cars heading west, away from Houlton. The second block is on the town limits, not far from the interstate off-ramp. I'm waved through as soon as the officer who taps on my window sees my badge. I'm glad; if they got a close enough look to see the state I'm in they'd probably pull me over just to see if I'd been drinking or on some kind of drug. I watch two members of the Houlton PD carefully checking the back of an eighteen-wheeler on its way out of town as I pull away.

The Superior Court parking lot is crowded with police cruisers, badly parked cars and reporters. I find a space a little way away from the media circus, then take a deep breath, wishing I was in better shape this morning, and brave the journey to the doors. I'm in luck, and none of the TV, radio and newspaper staff gathered outside seem to know who I am. Until Leonard from the *Bangor Daily News* spots me from where he leans against the wall.

'Mr Rourke,' he calls out, 'over here.'

I don't like the idea of facing a lot of questions, but I'm also polite enough not to ignore him outright. 'Yeah?'

'Any word on the escape?'

'I only found out about it a short while ago, so I guess not.'

He nods. 'But it is the man charged with the Lamond murder who's broken out, right?'

'As far as I know.'

By this point, I can see some of the other journalists on duty looking at us, realizing I'm with the Sheriff's Department and therefore maybe worth speaking to. I start to glance repeatedly towards the doors, hoping Leonard will get the hint and let me go.

The reporter doesn't seem to have noticed. 'Do you know how he escaped?' he asks.

'No, but if you'd stop asking me dumb questions I don't know the answers to, maybe I'd have the chance to find out,' I snap. 'Look, it's going to be a busy morning and I've got to get to work. If I get anything for you later, I'll give you a ring.'

With that, I push past him and into the courthouse as he calls after me, 'You don't look so good, Mr Rourke. You sure you should be hunting people in your condition?'

Up the stairs, legs already tired by the time I reach the top of the first flight, and into the Sheriff's Department offices. In addition to two regular dispatchers, a pair of the department's part-time staff have been drafted in to help deal with the manhunt effort. Dale, Chief Deputy Owen Marsh, a man in a lieutenant's jacket and two guys in State Police uniforms are in discussion around a desk in the centre of the room covered by a large map of Maine.

'Alex,' Dale calls over to me as I help myself to a coffee before heading to the table. 'Come here and I'll fill you in.' He points at the lieutenant. 'Bruce Watts,' he says. 'He handled the first couple of interviews with Nick before I called you in. The other two are Lieutenant Matheson and Sergeant Austin, both from State.' Dale looks at me while the three men nod in my direction. 'Jesus, Alex, you look rough. Pills not working?'

I shake my head. Privately, I think he doesn't look so good either, dog-tired and raw-eyed. 'They're fine. I just had a strange night, that's all.' Dale looks as though he'd like to hear more, but I shrug it off and wash my coffee down with cigarette smoke. 'What've you got so far?'

Matheson gestures at the map. 'We've had roadblocks on I-95 and the other roads out of town at a six-mile radius since within an hour or so of the alarm being raised. We've alerted the Border Patrol and security at Houlton Airport and posted the suspect's details to every police department in the state. Houlton PD are checking in case he's still here. We got a K-9 unit on the scene as fast as we could. The trail was a little confused and we lost it just outside the jail. He may have got into a car or truck. We've got dog teams checking the outskirts of town.'

'That's about all we can do without any kind of lead,' Watts adds. 'There's been no reports of auto theft in town since he escaped, so if he's in a vehicle, he either stole one that no one's missed yet or he had help on the outside; either way we don't know what to look for, if he's in one. Failing that, he might just have been able to cover his scent trail somehow.'

I rub my chin. The pain that's been rebounding around my skull since I awoke is fading now, despite what's happened. 'How did he get out?'

'He jumped one of the deputies at the jail just before lights-out last night and took his uniform,' Dale says.

'Then he triggered the fire alarm and made his way out during the confusion. They realized what had happened when they took a head-count of the inmates and staff. By that point, he was gone. The guard's uniform still hasn't turned up, so he may still be wearing it.'

'And might just as easily be wearing something else. How easy would it be to plan something like that?'

Owen Marsh shrugs. 'The County Jail isn't large and it's not exactly maximum security. We don't take prisoners with sentences over nine months, so it's staffed for that kind of low-risk prison population. If he knew the layout of the building and its fire procedure, it's possible.'

'And he's had a good few days with nothing better to do than get to know the jail,' I observe gruffly, deeply annoyed at the ease of Nick's escape. 'If he hadn't already learned everything he could before he was arrested. It wouldn't surprise me if one of the deputies from Corrections gave him blueprints in trade for a couple of beers.'

'Hey, this wasn't our fault any more than it was everyone else's,' Owen says. He sounds like I've hurt his pride, but I'm in no mood to care.

'Not your fault? It's the department that runs the jail. I don't know who it was that let a prisoner on a murder charge walk out of the front gate during a fire alarm, but if they were any more stupid they'd need to be watered twice a week. Jesus.' I shift my gaze away from Owen, not wanting to get drawn into an argument.

Dale changes the subject while his chief deputy goes to get a refill from the coffee machine. 'You think he's been planning to escape all along?'

'Why not? He's sure as hell planned everything else. He committed a murder, got himself arrested for it, made sure

I'd be brought in – fuck knows why – and arranged someone to dig up Garner's body. Then he broke out.' I gulp back the remainder of my coffee and glare at the map. 'If he was smart enough to put everything else together, my guess is that he was smart enough to have a car waiting by the jail. Maybe his, maybe someone else's. We think he maybe knows someone on the outside; they could have picked him up or left their car in place.

'I'm sorry, Lieutenant Matheson, but your roadblocks and the Houlton PD aren't going to catch him. He's already gone.'

The State Police man frowns and his lips pinch together as he regards me. 'We'll see,' he says after a moment's silence. Then he looks back at the map. 'We've got a helicopter sweep of the countryside around town due to start in a short while. I think we'll head back to headquarters and see if it turns anything up. Sheriff.' He nods at Dale, then leaves, followed by Sergeant Austin.

'Are you feeling all right?' Dale asks. 'You were pretty blunt with Owen and the lieutenant.'

'I'm fine. Just tense.'

'You think Nick's vanished for good?'

My mind's eye flits over the half-burnt ruins of St Valentine's, the dark and tangled forest of Mason Woods, the bare chapel of St Francis. The rattling of the grass bordering Route 11 fills my ears, and with it come the faint echoes of thunder and the barely discernible face of the woman in the locket. For some reason, I hear my father's voice; I can't make out what he's saying, but his calm and measured tones are unmistakable. Then I think of Nicholas, speaking in the same measured tones, dark eyes latched on to mine. I think of his words.

'No,' I tell Dale, 'I don't believe he's run for good, though I think he's well clear of town. He's still in the county, somewhere near Winter's End.'

'Yeah?'

'He came here to punish people for their "sins", and from what he told me, he didn't sound like he'd finished yet. We haven't seen the last of him.' I think of the vast tracts of forest, and all the empty hunting lodges and fishing cabins scattered within. Nicholas would be the proverbial needle in the haystack.

'Any idea who else he might want to "punish" before he's done?'

'Not really. Not that I can think of right now. It doesn't help that we know so little about him.'

'Bruce,' Dale says, 'try and arrange things so that there's always one of our cars within shouting distance of Winter's End. If he's there and he tries anything, I'd like to be sure we can respond quickly.'

The lieutenant nods and goes to speak with one of the dispatchers. 'We're not taking part in the manhunt,' Dale explains to me. 'We don't have the resources, so it's pretty much a State show. Speaking of shows, Owen, could you handle the press outside when Houlton PD check in with the results of their search?'

The chief deputy looks round from the far side of the room. 'No problem. When are they due to tell us how they got on?'

Dale shrugs. 'Give them an hour or so.' He turns back towards me. 'Nick seemed mightily interested in you. If he's here to punish people, you think you might be one of his targets?'

Again, I hear Nicholas's quiet, even tones in my mind.

'No,' I say, 'at least not to begin with. He doesn't like me, I don't think, but it's as if I'm his confessor. If he does anything to finish his business here, it wouldn't surprise me if he wanted to talk to me about it. He doesn't know my phone number, so he might have trouble getting in touch.'

'He knows you're staying in Winter's End, though,' Dale says.

'He doesn't know where.'

'There's only one hotel in town, Alex.'

I shrug. 'No sense getting worried about that now. If I'm going to be spending every minute checking over my shoulder, I might as well go home. I'm not a kid, Dale. I can take care of myself.'

'Sure.' Dale puffs out his cheeks and leads me over to the coffee machine. 'How did everything go with Dr Larson last night?'

'It went fine. Better than fine. Really good evening.'

'Just an evening?'

'I won't grace that with an answer.' I pause for a moment. 'You don't think she might be in danger, do you?'

He shakes his head, looking a little concerned at my edginess. 'You haven't mentioned her to him, have you? Houlton'll be locked down tighter than a bank after the breakout, so she'll be well guarded. We couldn't have more cops on the streets if there was a twenty-four-hour doughnut van making its way around town.'

'Right. Good.'

He turns back to the map. 'You want to focus on the hunt for Nick?'

'He'll either be picked up at the blocks, or it'll be six months before some Tennessee traffic cop pulls him over for a busted tail light,' I say, shaking my head. 'If I can work out why he came here, I might have some inkling of who he is and where he's hiding. I want to keep working on Garner, the kids' home and the woman in the locket. I haven't spoken to Dr Vallence again yet; I'll do that this afternoon. Any luck finding the other management from St Valentine's? I spoke to Pierce yesterday.'

'Not yet, Alex. Decker took a post at a nursing home in New York State a couple of months after the fire, quit four years ago but we haven't been able to find out where she went. Blythe went to help run a clinic in California. His trail goes cold about six months after Decker's. We're trying to track them, but with everything else we can't throw too much effort at it right now.'

'That's okay, Dale. I should have enough to go on with what we've already got.'

'If you need to look at any of our records, they're all upstairs,' he says. 'Check in with me before you decide to head back to Winter's End, and I'll keep in touch with you every so often, just in case. Once the hunt gets scaled down, I'll be able to help you out.'

'Thanks, Dale.' I turn to leave, intending to spend a while going through the records on Garner and St Valentine's.

'Sure. And Alex,' he calls after me, 'take it easy on the pills, huh? It's not a good idea to go overboard on that kind of thing.'

I spend a couple of hours trawling the files, looking for anything the department has that might be relevant to Nicholas's case. It's hard going, navigating by guesswork and instinct more than clear and logical deduction. Every so often I find something on computer or in the collection of file folders and print it out or copy it. Dale sticks his head round the door once, just to let me know that the Houlton PD search has found pretty much nothing, as expected, but apart from that, I'm left alone. It's gone one o'clock by the time I leave the meticulously well-ordered offices with an armload of papers and photocopied reports; some light reading for my spare time. My eyes hurt from the strain of poring over swathes of typescript and I need a cigarette. I head for the doors.

Back outside in the cool but windless air, I light a Marlboro and think about phoning Gemma. Nicholas's escape has left me with nothing to do save skimming my newly acquired material and waiting for the State Police to come up with a lead in their hunt. Since I therefore don't have anything urgent to do, I decide instead to pop up to the hospital and speak to her directly.

Lunchtime is nearly over and the streets are full of people hurrying back to work after whatever fodder the length of their break and the capacity of their wallet have allowed. Pete's Diner is still busy as I pass by, patrons cramming great mounds of food into their mouths as if the world's about to end and they want to go out as full as possible. A growling noise from my stomach reminds me that I've not had anything to eat since yesterday evening, a gnawing sensation made worse by nervous tension. In the end, I have no choice but to satisfy my hunger with something from a sandwich bar in the market square. I munch my selection on the bridge, looking down at the swirling water below.

I reflect that perhaps I would be better off walking away right now, before this case takes any further toll on my system. I could say that with Nick gone, my job is done. Back to Boston and the quiet, harmless day-to-day business I've come to enjoy over the past couple of years. Even as the thought occurs to me though, I know that I won't. My instinct, the primeval desire of the hunter to be there at the kill, probably contributed to my breakdown, but it's a part of my nature and I could no more change it than I could fly. And I have a second reason not to leave, which should even now be coming off her lunch break and going back to work.

I finish my snack and walk to the hospital. I pass straight through Admissions, which holds only a handful of waiting patients with minor ailments and injuries, and head for the elevators at the far side of the room. The basement is church-quiet, the only noise the faint hum of electrics and distant machinery. I see no one else on my walk down to the aluminium doors that lead into the mortuary office. Once there, I knock and poke my head through. Gemma is sitting at her desk with a cup of coffee and a computer printout in front of her. She looks up and smiles when she sees it's me.

'Hi,' I say, stepping fully into the room, 'I hope I'm not interrupting.'

'We don't often have anything urgent down here,' she says.

'You hear about the escape?'

'On the radio.' Gemma shrugs as she says it, I guess unconcerned about Nicholas being on the loose. She changes the subject. 'I've just been on the phone to the pathology lab in Augusta.'

'Anything interesting?'

She shakes her head, setting her ponytail swaying like a

honey-coloured pendulum behind her. 'Nothing beyond what I'd already found. The remains were those of Garner, and he was probably stabbed to death. It wasn't just this you came down here for, was it?'

'Just the opposite. I thought I'd make sure we were still on for this evening.' I grin. 'I also wanted to see you at work; those doctor's greens are a big turn-on.'

Gemma laughs, high and clear. 'I'll have to remember that. Meet me at my place at the same time as last night?'

'Sure. Are we going anywhere nice?'

Her hand slips into mine. 'I thought I might try cooking something at home. You know, just the two of us.'

'Sounds lovely,' I tell her. 'I'll be there at eight.' I lean down and we kiss once, twice. 'I'll have to do the same for you some day. Of course, that will mean learning to cook first.'

She laughs again and gives me a little wave goodbye as I vanish through the doors.

I drive back to Winter's End, Son Seals on the stereo and murders on my mind. The State Police are still out in force on the interstate, and I pass another couple of cruisers on my way up Route 11. I pay them and the rest of the road's other users scant attention, more interested in identifying possible accomplices for Nick, assuming it was an associate of his who dug up Garner's body. And why did they only dig up an arm?

Light bursts through the windows, snapping me out of my thoughts. My hands tighten on the wheel and I'm about to jab the brakes on reflex when I realize that I've just left the forest behind and I'm now in the empty fields between St Valentine's and the town. System jarred, I ease my foot off the gas a little.

*Whoever disturbed Garner's grave only dug up an arm because they didn't know they were unearthing a corpse.*

The image is clear in my mind, newly emptied as it is by the shock of discovering my attention had completely drifted from the road. The scenario is the only one I've been able to come up with that fits. If I'm right, Nick's accomplice isn't another killer, but someone far more ordinary. I press on to Winter's End feeling sharper than I have all day.

Once parked, I climb out of the car and cross Main Street towards the doctor's office. The town centre is almost deserted, an empty shell shrouded in silence and roofed by low, thick clouds. The sound of my shoes crunching on the grit that dusts the road's surface seems almost loud enough to echo from the walls. I come close to checking my watch to make sure I didn't fall asleep at the wheel and it's now dawn and not the Wednesday afternoon it should be. I find it hard to believe that even a prisoner escape could have made everyone want to stay indoors as much as they plainly are, even if the town was already on edge. I guess it's been a while since I worked on a case like this outside the cities. On reaching the doctor's, I find a printed note stuck to the inside of its door.

*Office closed today due to illness. Patients needing to see a doctor urgently should contact Ashland Ambulance Service on 435–6323*

I peer through the glass, but the room beyond is dark and unoccupied. Back at the 'Vette, I check my notes for Dr Vallence's home address.

His residence turns out to be a small house with scarlet-painted wood siding on the east side of town, a couple of streets away from where I used to live. The driveway is empty, but the faint, smudged residue of motor oil on its concrete surface indicates that he owns a vehicle. The front yard is neatly trimmed but little more; the doctor doesn't seem to be much of a gardener. I ring the bell once, twice, a third time, but get no answer. No lights seem to be on and there's no noise coming from inside. I give up on the doctor and stroll back to my car.

Then my phone rings. I don't recognize the number, but push 'call' just the same. 'Hello?'

'Mr Rourke, how are you?'

Nicholas's voice, slightly muffled by the connection, but unmistakable. I rest my free hand on the roof of the 'Vette and look about me, heart thudding, half expecting to see him standing at the corner of the street.

'I'm fine, Nicholas,' I say. 'How did you get my number?'

'It's on your business cards. Very thoughtful of you.'

A dark blue pick-up cruises across the intersection at the far end of the road. It doesn't make the turn towards me. I fight to remain calm and to keep a lid on my paranoia. Act rationally, check your surroundings, keep him talking. Hope to God he's not behind a parked car with a hunting rifle at the other end of the street.

'Thanks,' I say. 'Pleasure to be of service. I guess you have something you want to say.'

'Maybe I just wanted to see how you were doing. Still

chasing old cases? I don't imagine you'd be manning the barricades on the highway.'

The windows along the opposite side of the road are either empty or wreathed in net curtains. I tell myself that any scattered movement at the periphery of my vision is just the twitchiness of my eyes. Even so, I get the same feeling I did as when I walked Angela Lamond's route home. The feeling of being watched. This time, it's not dozens of eyes peeking through the curtains that I'm worried about. It's just a single pair. Part of me, the part that wants to catch Nick, hopes he's here. The rest of me, feeling isolated and vulnerable, thinks the exact opposite.

'Why don't we get together for a drink? We could talk all you want.' It's an old and obvious ploy, but I try it anyway.

'Still fishing for an opening, Mr Rourke? You can do better than that, surely.'

'What's to say I'm not keeping you talking so the cops can trace your call?'

The houses along my side of the road seem just as still as the others, empty mausoleums with bleakly staring eyes for windows. The tops of the trees are just visible at the western end of the street, peeping over the distant rooftops like a bank of thick green-black fog.

Nicholas chuckles. The sound is dry and cold, turned almost metallic by the phone. 'There's no cops trying to trace this. Until you heard my voice, you didn't have any reason to think I knew your number.'

The street seems empty, but I don't relax, can't relax. I feel too exposed. On Main, or in a bar, I'd be able to handle this much more coolly. Hell, I used to talk to killers all the time. Now, it's as much as I can do to keep things under control. Despite that, though, I don't give in to the instinctive urge to get into my car. Outside, my sight lines are uninterrupted and I've got a clear 360-degree view. Inside, it's hard to see anything low down and to the back, leaving me open.

I stay on the line and try not to sound flustered. 'Well, now you've got my number, you want to do something useful with it before I get bored and hang up.'

'Have they told you how Garner died yet?'

'Stabbed.'

With every heartbeat and breath, I expect to hear someone move behind me, a footfall, the crack of a gunshot, the swish of a knife. It's like being a kid playing hide-and-seek, hearing your friend count to twenty out in the darkness before falling completely silent once they've finished. You crouch in the shadows, waiting to feel a hand upon your shoulder.

'Stabbed? True enough, and I suppose the other marks would have gone by now,' Nicholas continues.

'You're saying you killed him?'

'Eventually, yes.' He pauses, probably enjoying himself, knowing that our conversation isn't being taped. 'I found it quite ironic that the path I took with the Lamond woman passed only a short way from his grave.'

'How did you keep us from finding leaf litter on her skin when we examined her?'

'She stripped before we stepped out of the car. Then I wrapped her feet, hands and hair in plastic bags and covered the rest of her in plastic sheeting. I did the same with my own shoes as well. I got rid of the coverings when we reached the highway at the bottom of St Valentine's drive. They're probably wrapped around a tree somewhere by now.' He pauses for a moment. 'I'm surprised you didn't find it. Still, no one found Garner, either. Do you remember him? You visited the home as a boy.'

'Vaguely. I only went there a couple of times. Who dug up his body?'

Nicholas ignores the question. 'Do you remember Garner talking with your father?'

'Who dug him up?' I repeat. Before, I could just about stomach him mentioning my dad. I don't want to talk about it here, particularly since he seems to know so much about him.

'We're not in an interrogation room now, Mr Rourke.'

I sigh, deciding to change tack. 'I'm surprised at you, Nicholas. It's usually only the dumb killers who do this: phoning the police to brag. You've never struck me as one of those. Perhaps I was wrong.'

'Is that what I'm doing?' He chuckles. '"Dear Boss", "This is the Zodiac speaking", you mean? Bad spelling and too many postage stamps?'

'Something like that. Did you send a bunch of letters to people after you set fire to St Valentine's?'

'Why would I want to do that?'

'To try and scare them. Make yourself seem more important than you actually are.'

'I'm sorry to hear you have such a low opinion of me, Mr Rourke.' He doesn't sound surprised. 'Still, I can't say it's anything less than I expected.'

'Because I know you're a nut?'

'Because of who you are. Because of your past. Because of what you've done to me. Because of what we have in common.'

'We don't have anything in common, Nicholas.'

'Are you so sure?'

The phone goes dead, leaving me standing on a silent and deserted street, the words of the killer fading in my mind.

For a moment, I don't move, then I check my phone for the number Nick was calling from and ring Dale. 'I've just been speaking with Nicholas,' I tell him as soon as he picks up. 'He was talking on a cellular. Can you get a phone company fix on the place he made that call from?'

'Jesus, Alex. How did he get your number?'

'Said he read it on a business card, but how the fuck should I know. Can you get a fix?'

'It'll take a while,' he says. 'He'll probably be long gone by then.'

'Yeah, but it'll give us an idea of his movements.' I rattle off Nick's number. 'If they find out he made the call from just outside Boston, we can be pretty sure he's running. If he made it from across the street from your office, we know he's not.'

'Sure. I'll let you know as soon we've got an answer.'

'Good. See if you can get any further calls from that number to my phone diverted someplace else. I really don't want him to be able to ring me up whenever the fuck he feels like it.'

'Will do,' Dale says. 'If it was me, I wouldn't want him calling me in the middle of the night. It'd give me the creeps.'

'You have no idea. Thanks, Dale.'

I hang up and reach for a cigarette. After speaking with Nicholas, I'm in no mood to go through my bundle of notes surrounding Garner, his associates, and St Valentine's. He talked about taking Angela Lamond through the woods on the day he snatched her. A walk in the fresh air might be a good idea right now.

Or maybe it's not, if he's hiding out in the forest. That doesn't worry me as much as the phone call did. Nick's voice caught me by surprise. Me turning up in the place he's gone to ground would surprise *him*. It's the difference between hunter and hunted, and I'm much more comfortable being the former. I take a last look at the empty street, then climb into the 'Vette and start the engine.

A couple of minutes later, I turn on to the rough muddy track that plunges into the blackened, twisted boughs of Mason Woods. I pull into the first parking spot I come to, then sit absolutely still as the echoes of the engine fade and die. It's quite possible that Nicholas could be waiting out here, hoping I'd come. I tell myself that it's quite possible for him to be anywhere, near or far. I make sure I have my Colt with me, just in case, and step out of the car.

The woods are utterly quiet, surprisingly so. There's no wind to stir the trees, and the birds, insects and other wildlife seem to have fled or been silenced. The noise my feet make as I trudge through the leaf litter towards Black Ravine is the only sound to disturb the dead air. Despite the season, the ground beneath the green canopy is brown and dreary, broken by straggles of brambles and other weeds that make apparently empty space a nightmare of grasping loops of wiry foliage.

Before long, I start hearing an echo of the *crunch, crunch* my feet make in the leaves coming from behind me. I spin around once or twice, but the woods behind are empty, so each time I resume my journey. Movement in the dim shadows beneath the trees flickers and swirls at the corners of my eyes. Every time I blink, trying to clear them and sharpen my vision, mostly without success. I hope it's nothing more than birds, woodland animals and the other normal comings and goings I'd expect in a forest.

When I hit the ravine itself, the sudden noise of the stream, confined and amplified by the stony walls of the cleft, sounds harsh and loud in the deathly quiet. The grey skies do nothing to alleviate the close atmosphere of the woods. Below, a thin strand of police tape runs forlornly along the base of the rock face at the point where Garner was found.

I clamber down to the bottom of the ravine and spend a few minutes getting a feel for the site, which is overlooked by a giant splay-limbed spruce on the far side. The climb, although fairly straightforward now, would have been much trickier in the dark, when the remains were dug up. It would have been easier to join the stream at a point where the banks weren't so sheer, then follow its course to the burial site.

There's a sudden burst of movement and a crashing in the leaves above me. I whip my Colt from its holster and wheel around, blood singing. A second burst of movement and a screech like a dying animal and a huge crow or raven, coal-black, bursts out of the trees and lurches into the sky with steady beats of its wings.

Everything falls silent again and I wait, breathing shallowly and running my eyes along the top of the ravine. The gun feels slow and awkward in my hand. A minute or two ticks past with no further interruptions and I relax a little.

I turn south, away from the rockface, and follow the water for a while until I reach a point where the rocks disappear to be replaced by boggy earth on its banks. All the while, the sound of the stream is the only thing to break the air. If my reckoning is correct, it shouldn't be long before the ground starts rising again on the long, gentle slope that will eventually become Ryland Hill. The woods around me have fallen silent again. I can't even hear insects moving. Only the stream keeps up its noise in the background, and I wish it wouldn't as it could be masking other movement. I feel like I'm being watched – no, *stared* at. My stomach tightens.

I glance around at the forest and its mottled foliage, feeling uneasy and cut off from civilization. Maybe I've done enough walking for today. I head back towards my car, alone in the space beneath the green-brown canopy.

When I come within sight of the parking spots at the end of the track, I again see, faint through the trees, the red Toyota, sitting as it did yesterday. Instinctively, I check my gun is within easy reach, then I cut through the under-growth towards the car as quietly as I can.

Emerging from the greenery at a point next to its rear wheels, I can see no immediate sign of anyone within. A spider has spun a web between the wing mirror and the bodywork and now sits, poised but unmoving, waiting for a catch. I glance quickly underneath the Toyota, then move up to the windows and check inside, ready to dive back at the first sign of trouble.

Empty.

Through the smudged glass, I can see an old blanket on the back seat with something underneath it. Nowhere near large enough to be a man, with an irregular shape.

The door is unlocked and, after a quick look around me, I open it. Reach inside, take hold of one corner of the blanket, then flip it back to reveal some of what's underneath.

Cloth. White. A heavy cotton uniform-style shirt, rumpled. A name badge of dark blue plastic.

*A. Lamond, Nurse.*

It's over an hour before the State Police CSU arrives, and another half an hour before I can leave them to the task of meticulously going over the Toyota and the ground around it. According to the records, the car was stolen in Augusta a few days before Angela Lamond's murder. By the time I call at the convenience store on Main Street for some more cigarettes and a bottle of Coke, the sky is darkening rapidly. I'll have barely enough time to get ready for my date before I have to leave for Houlton. Reading the files will have to wait.

I walk out of the store and straight into a familiar figure. Leonard, the reporter, face earnest beneath his balding pate. I'm in no more of a mood to talk to him now than I was this morning.

'Mr Rourke,' he says, bounding up to me like a terrier to its master. 'Could I have a word with you?'

'Sure, Leonard. Fire away. Just make it quick.'

'The escaped prisoner, this "Nicholas" guy. Do you think there's a chance that he could return to the place where he was arrested?'

'Why would he want to do that?'

Leonard shrugs, though it's plain that he has something in mind. 'If he killed Angela Lamond, and he killed Henry Garner, isn't there a risk that, for whatever reason, he could have other targets lined up around here?'

I unlock the car door. 'You'd have to ask him, or find

yourself a psychic. You're asking questions I can't answer.'

'That's fair enough, Mr Rourke,' he says. 'If this guy was responsible for Garner's death and the fire at the kids' home, is there any chance that the police will reinvestigate other deaths from a few years ago?'

I open the door. 'You'd have to ask Dale Townsend.'

'Just one more thing,' he says. 'We're interested in the human side to this story as well. How's this investigation affecting you and the other cops?'

'What are you talking about?'

Leonard shrugs. There doesn't seem to be any malice in his expression, but I'm certain that there's more than just innocent curiosity in his query. 'I understand you've had problems with work stress before,' he says. 'How does this compare? You know, having someone who committed a murder in your hometown on the loose, having to face him in interrogations, that kind of thing. The prospect of having your man escape justice must be eating at you.'

'Leave it alone, Leonard,' I say to him, sliding into my car. My fists are itching, but I tell myself that he hasn't said anything to make it worth punching him. I almost convince myself. 'That's none of your damn business.'

'Come on, Mr Rourke. This is the kind of dimension to a story that the public love.'

'Yeah, maybe. But I don't give a rat's ass about that. It's the kind of dimension that you can keep your nose out of. Now fuck off and leave me alone.'

'What can I infer from your reply?'

'You can infer anything you want, just do it somewhere else where I don't have to see you. Get out of my face.'

He doesn't seem put off by what I'm saying. He just asks, 'Are you threatening me, Deputy Rourke?'

I ignore him and close the door, inwardly kicking myself for getting fired up. More hassle than it's worth, I tell myself as I turn the ignition. He calls through the glass once or twice, then gives up when the engine snarls into life. Half a mile up the road, then on to the gravel driveway and back to the smothering miasma of silence that surrounds the Crowhurst Lodge, which only the neighbouring trees seem able to break.

Eight o'clock comes round and I'm even more on edge than earlier. There doesn't seem to be any sensible reason for it, but the feeling is there nonetheless; a slight tension in every muscle, a taut sensation along every nerve fibre in my body. It feels almost as if I'm trying to quit smoking. I only hope that an evening in Gemma's company, something I look forward to like a drowning man spotting some driftwood nearby, will be enough to banish those feelings.

Now I'm more familiar with the trip to her house, I've been able to time my arrival almost to the minute. With me I have a bottle of what I hope is good wine, plus a couple of things I'll need if I end up staying the night – my razor, which I leave in the car, and sleeping pills, which I keep with me.

I check myself in the rear-view mirror one more time (still scruffier than I'd like), then lock the car and trot up the driveway. As before, Gemma answers the door almost before the chimes of the bell have faded, as if she was waiting there for me. Tonight she's wearing a cotton blouse and tight blue trousers, both emphasizing her willowy figure. She kisses me in greeting, then shows me through to the lounge. Her house is neat and in some ways mirrors my own apartment, insomuch as there is a definite sense of solitary occupation. The film collection next to the TV, for instance, is the obvious result of a single set of tastes. Likewise, there are none of the little oddments couples pick up down the years – photos, souvenirs and presents from friends.

I don't stop in the lounge, however, but follow Gemma through to the kitchen and place the wine on the worktop, next to a big bowl of salad.

'How did you know to get red?' she asks as she checks something steaming in the oven. The smell of rosemary and garlic wafts past her.

'Well, I nearly brought white as well but I figured it might look kind of excessive. One bottle's good for drinking with dinner. Two's good for getting wasted. What's in the oven?'

'Italian roast lamb. You do like lamb, don't you?'

'Love it,' I say. 'And it smells great.'

I go back to the hall to hang my jacket up, then return to the kitchen. We have a glass of wine each and chat about nothing much, continuing where we left off yesterday. I notice that she has a Patriots coffee mug on the draining board. 'I didn't realize you were a football fan,' I say.

'Oh, that. No, I'm not. It was a present from a friend when I was at medical school. How about you?'

'I had a case a couple of years ago involving one of the team's staff, got a couple of free tickets out of it. Can't stand the game, though.'

Gemma looks at me as she hands me a couple of plates, perhaps picking up on the vehemence of my tone; I must sound as if I've been grievously offended by the world of professional sport.

'Still,' she says, 'it must have been a nice job to have on your books. High profile, especially in Boston.'

'High profile isn't all it's cracked up to be. Damn reporters.' I describe my afternoon encounter with Leonard, and what I think he was insinuating in his final questions. The thought alone is enough to make me feel hot and prickly as the pressure builds up inside. 'He practically came out and said I was cracking under the strain. As if the son of a bitch doesn't have enough to write about without trying to poke around in my head.'

'It's just what he does. It didn't sound like he said very much.'

'Well, maybe not now but it did at the time. Asshole!'

Gemma shrugs, looking a little confused at my sudden change in mood. 'He was only asking. He probably didn't mean anything by it.'

I remember a lot of other people, my fellow FBI agents, who also didn't mean anything by what they said. I remember their looks of concern, not for me, but for the quality of my work, as my mind began to crack. I also remember the way they looked at me after I left the hospital. To them, I was a basket case. Someone to be pitied, not out of genuine charity, but because pity is so often our way of hiding disgust.

The memory turns the pressure inside to sheer rage. As before, I can't seem to control it. 'I don't think they understand what it's like,' I snap at Gemma. 'I spend hours at a stretch talking with a psycho. I haven't done anything in my spare time since I got here except read police reports. Then my goddam suspect escapes from under everyone's nose and people look at me like it's my fault and I should be doing something about it. That's when they're not trying to say I'm cracking up. If they'd get off my back and leave me the hell alone I'd be fine!'

'They're just concerned. And you do look a bit . . .'

'A bit what? Are you starting as well? I've had Dale hassling me, saying I should lay off the medication, as if he knows what he's talking about.'

Uncertainty creeps into her eyes. 'Alex, what's wrong? I just said I was worried about you. I'm sorry if that bothers you.'

'Worried about me? Why? Do you think there's something wrong with me? Is that it, are you siding with them?'

'Well, yes,' Gemma says. 'Listen to yourself!'

'You don't like what I'm saying?'

'Not the way you're saying it!' she says, eyes blinking rapidly. If I notice how baffled and upset she is becoming, I don't care.

'So how would you like me to say it, eh? Come on, let's hear it,' I snarl, arms folded in front of me like a schoolteacher talking to a particularly stupid pupil.

'Alex, stop.'

'Stop? Yeah, why don't I?' I snap. 'I'll stop bothering you, so you can stop pestering me. I've had enough of your bleeding-heart sympathy, you and everyone else! Thanks for a wonderful fucking evening. I hope you have a nice life!'

With those words I storm out of the house, leaving behind a confused and tearful woman who I know, deep in my gut, I have badly hurt. By the time I've reached the bottom of the driveway the fit of madness has passed and I realize what an asshole I've been. I've screwed up badly, hurting someone that I care about over nothing, ruining something truly good. I lean against the car and let my head slump on to the roof, trying to figure out what the hell came over me. Something's not right, not this evening, not the whole day.

I should go back and apologize. Would she believe me? Would she even want to speak to me? Would it make things better if I did?

I climb into the car, realizing as I do so that I've forgotten my jacket, still hanging in Gemma's hallway. Some time spent cold, in nothing but shirtsleeves, is probably no more than I deserve. I take a last look at the house, where I should even now be having a great evening, then turn the ignition and drive away.

By eleven, not only am I back in Winter's End, but I've ditched the car at the hotel and I'm in Larry's, the bar at the north end of town, frequented by truckers and other passing workers for the logging companies. I've been here for two hours, getting steadily drunker at a rate which surprises me. Larry's doesn't have the relative respectability of the Sawmill; in fact, it's a dive. Smoke-stained ceiling, beer-soaked floorboards, country music. But I'm in no mood for a quiet night's drinking. I want to get hammered; to wash away whatever it was inside that made me flare up at Gemma's house. I want to shoot pool and work out a little aggression. I want to get in a fight with a couple of truckers and have the shit beaten out of me.

Steps one and two are complete. Three gets going when I return from taking a leak to find my bar stool occupied by a big sweaty guy in a check shirt and jeans that could easily fit a couple of trees. In retrospect, I could have chosen something more tactful than my opening line of, 'Get your goddam ass out of my seat, you fat fuck.'

I could also have chosen a fat fuck who *didn't* have two friends with him.

Could have, but didn't.

The guy slowly turns to look at me. Dark hair thinning from the temples back. His jowls hang down over the line of his chin, unevenly covered with stubble and sweat. His gut mirrors this, drooping down over his belt.

'What?' he says, more a grunt than a word. Over his shoulder, I can see two guys by the pool table taking an interest. One is about the same build as Fatty and the two could almost be brothers. The other is a little younger and a little leaner; years of truck stop dinners and beer have yet to take the same toll on his figure.

I lean, somewhat unsteadily, towards Fatty's ear and say, louder, 'Get your ass out of my seat, you fat fuck!'

The guy stands up. He's a couple of inches shorter than me but carries a distinct weight advantage; plenty of natural padding to soak up punches. 'You got a big mouth, pal,' he says, regarding me with puffy eyes narrowed in righteous anger.

'Not half as big as your butt. What do you do for a living, taste tester at a doughnut factory?'

Fatty's two friends join him to stand at his shoulder. The thinner, younger one is in the middle and he looks as if he's being squeezed into shape. 'I think you've had enough,' he ventures, still holding his pool cue.

'Yeah, why don't you leave and find yourself some fresh air,' number three says.

The anger that overcame me earlier in the evening, now dulled a little by the alcohol, starts building again. I want a fight, whether I triumph or get hammered into sense-lessness. I want ribs to crack; it doesn't matter if they're mine or theirs. I want to hear the sickening hollow thud of someone's skull rebounding off the wooden floor. A penance of blood for what I've done.

I smile or, at the very least, bare my teeth. 'What are you guys, a family or something?' I slur loudly – not shouting, but not far off. 'I guess', and here I point to the thin one, 'that would make you the bitch, right?'

I'm aware through the haze that our little quartet is now the centre of attention. The bar's other patrons are watching with expressions that suggest they're trying to make up their minds whether to run, stay out of it, break it up, or pitch in.

Off to my right, the barman leans across the counter and says, 'That's enough, pal. Get out of here and go sleep it off.'

When I don't budge, he starts making his way around to kick me out by force. I just keep on looking at the Three Stooges. I've noticed, though, that the beer bottle in my hand would make a handy weapon.

'Well, c'mon, assholes! What are you waiting for?' I snarl.

Luckily for me, they never get a chance to reply. Just as the trio look like they've collectively decided my apparent bravado isn't anything they need worry about, a voice yells from the back of the bar, 'Sheriff's Department! Leave it alone, guys, or I'll have every damn one of you off to the cells!'

No one moves as Dale shoulders his way through the throng. He looks like he hauled on his uniform in something of a hurry. 'Take it easy, Alex,' he says to me. Then he turns back to the rest and yells, 'Go on, it's over! Haven't you got drinks to go back to?'

I sigh and place my empty bottle on a nearby table. 'Hey, Dale. What're you doing here?'

Following my lead, we move further down the bar and order another couple of beers. The barman hesitates to serve me but Dale gives him a nod and, aside from a couple of dark glances, I'm left alone.

Dale swigs a mouthful of Bud. 'Gemma Larson called me. I checked the hotel and the Sawmill before I came here.'

'Gemma,' I repeat, rubbing my face with both hands. 'What did she say?'

'That you were acting kind of strange. She asked me to look out for you.'

He's obviously holding back on most of the details of their conversation, but I don't blame him. I knock back a quarter of the bottle, then watch the light playing off it as I turn it in my hands. Around and around and around. Self-pity has won out over anger.

'I screwed it up, Dale. Just like I screw up everything.'

'No you don't.'

I down another long gulp of beer, and wave at the barman for a fresh one.

'Yep,' I say, sighing and finishing off the rest of the bottle's contents. 'The FBI – fucked that up. You bring me up here to speak to some guy and all I could get out of him before he ran off was riddles and bullshit, so I guess I fucked that up too. Now Gemma.'

Dale considers this for a moment, then has another mouthful. 'You want my advice?'

I shrug. 'Sure.'

'You're not a screw-up any more than the rest of us. And you're also not at high school any more, so just deal with it. Go home, sleep this off, and think again in the morning.'

'Ain't going to be able to sleep,' I say unsteadily. 'Left my pills in my jacket.'

Dale drags me to my feet. 'Believe it or not, a gallon or two of beer works just as good as any sedative. Let's go.'

'You haven't finished your drink.'

'I'm driving – first you home, then me to bed.'

Dale helps me unlock the door to the Crowhurst Lodge, but I'm left to navigate the darkened stairs on my own. Despite the state I'm in, I have little difficulty climbing from one step to the next, as if the building is welcoming back an old friend by shifting its own structure to help my unsteady feet. My key slides into the lock on the first attempt and then I'm in my room. Although I don't drink regularly, I remember enough from my college days to knock back as much water as I'm able before I finally collapse on the bed, bloated and dizzy.

# PART THREE
# All Things Left Undone

'The hour of departure has arrived and we go our ways –
I to die, and you to live. Which is better God only knows.'
                                                    – Socrates

Sleep comes quickly, but it's an uneven and increasingly fragmented visitor. As the night goes on and the effects of the alcohol wear off, the periods of waking become increasingly pronounced and uncomfortable. The trees have resumed their chattering outside; the bedclothes are too hot, the room too cold. I need to take a leak, I need to drink more water.

During one of my too-brief bouts of unconsciousness, I find myself standing in a corridor in St Valentine's. I blink once or twice, for the mildewed run-down present I'm familiar with seems semi-transparent, overlaying the bright paintwork and clean linoleum of the past like a ghostly second skin.

Children's voices echo faintly from the walls, giggling and laughing, the sound high and piping. I move down the corridor to an open doorway. Beyond, in the dusty remains of the playroom, two young boys are kneeling on the floor, their attention caught up in some sort of game. Despite my proximity, I still can't hear what they're saying as their voices echo just as badly as before, turning words into unintelligible babble.

Stepping closer, to where I can see over their heads to the ground in front of them, I see that one boy has twin miniature knives in his hands. The other is holding a toy pistol. They are turning over, one at a time, a stack of photographs that sits between them, and are trying to be the first to stab or shoot the person or place depicted. The images on the photos are in black and white, and hard to make out, so I bend down and pick one up.

It's me. The two boys look up and their eyes, eyes I recognize, meet mine. One has the same deep blue irises as Nicholas. The other has the same as my own.

'Bang,' says the boy with the gun, pointing it at me.

The blue-eyed boy smiles as he thrusts his knives at my gut.

Opening my eyes, I find that the night has finally dragged on long enough to reach half past five in the morning. The sky outside is starting to lighten. I feel tired, but not in the remotest bit sleepy. My mouth is dry and sticky, a leftover of yesterday's drinking binge, but I'm glad to find that I don't have much of a hangover. My emotions seem to be more in check today, too, as if I've been under the influence of something that has now worn off. I take a piss, shower and brush my teeth, then sit in front of the TV for an hour or two with a glass of water.

I eat another breakfast alone in the Crowhurst Lodge's archaic dining room, feeling now more than ever like the guy at the end of the film *2001: A Space Odyssey*, trapped on my own in some alternate dimension where time and ordinary reality hold little meaning. At least the food is good.

I step out of the still-unoccupied hotel, rubbing in turns at my weary eyes and my stiff neck. I try stretching, but all that does is make my shoulders hurt. For a minute or two I sit in my car, gathering my thoughts for the day ahead. I think about phoning Dale to find out if there have been any developments in the hunt for Nicholas, but I figure if there was anything important, he'd have called me.

I fire up the 'Vette and hit the road on the short jaunt into town.

On Main Street, I find the doctor's office closed with the same note on the door as yesterday. Mail is starting to build on the mat inside. I try Vallence's home phone, but all I get is his voicemail, leaving me with no choice but to head round to his house again.

The building is the same as when I left it yesterday and the street feels less deserted, even though I still seem to be the only person out of doors. I ring the bell twice before I move to the living-room window and cup my hands against the glass, trying to see inside. Aside from the rhythmic movement of a carriage clock on the mantel, everything is still. There's a coffee mug on the table as well as a half-eaten sandwich.

I walk round the side of the house, through an iron gate with hinges that squeal as it swings open, to the door at the rear. The tiny back yard is a mirror of the front, neat but plain. I knock a couple of times on the door and kitchen window, which also shows nothing much inside, but neither that nor calling Vallence's name earns a response. I return to the front and try again. When I still haven't had an answer, I try the front door. Unlocked.

'Dr Vallence,' I yell through the opening. 'Sheriff's Department. Anyone home?'

Silence. My fingers instinctively reach out and touch my pistol, seeking reassurance. They find it, but I leave the gun holstered. No sense scaring the wits out of him if he's home, but bed-ridden with flu.

I step into the cream-carpeted hallway. At the far end of the corridor I can see the kitchen. The door to the living room is open at the foot of the stairs and it's here that I head first. The room is devoid of life, but I check the coffee mug on the table to see if it still retains any warmth. It doesn't, and the bread of the half-eaten sandwich next to it is dry and stale. I move through to the kitchen, which is as tidy as I would expect from someone like Dr Vallence, then return to the stairs, walking on the balls of my feet like a burglar.

At the top is a short landing. Ahead, an open door into the bathroom. To the left, two others, both ajar. The first leads into an unoccupied bedroom. The second opens on to what seems to be Vallence's den. There are a pair of black steel and wood bookcases holding a mixed collection of hard- and soft-backs, a set of shelves holding mostly personal crap – photos, souvenirs, old keys – and a desk covered in papers, computer equipment, and the remains of the late Dr Vallence, face down in the dried remnants of a fantail spray of blood. I don't need to check for a pulse to know that he's dead, and it doesn't look like it happened just a moment ago.

Training and experience might keep me calm, but my fingers still instinctively brush the grips of my Colt again before I call Dale.

'Alex, I was just about to ring you,' he says. 'We've heard back from the phone company with a fix on Nick's position when he called you.'

'That's great, Dale. I've got a dead body in front of me.'

I hear the hiss of an in-drawn breath. I flash a glance over my shoulder in case it didn't come from the phone. I'm alone.

'Who is it?' Dale asks.

'Dr Vallence. I'm at his house right now. It's hard to say from where I am, but it looks like whatever killed him did so somewhere around his neck. There's no sign of an exit wound, so I'd be willing to go out on a limb and say he was stabbed.'

'You might be right. The phone company fix had Nicholas calling from inside, or very near to, Vallence's address. Is there any sign of him at the house?'

'Aside from the corpse, you mean?' I think back to my conversation with Nick, looking up and down the street in a haze of subconscious paranoia. All the while he was probably watching from Vallence's window not ten yards behind me while the doctor's body slowly cooled upstairs. The thought makes my muscles tense and my nerves fizz in a mixture of apprehension and anger. I should have noticed something wrong. If I had, Nicholas might be back in custody. Vallence might even be alive.

'The house seems empty,' I tell Dale. Deep down, I wonder whether I really believe that. 'I've only given it a quick sweep, not a proper search, but I've not found anything to suggest Nick's been back since the phone call.'

'Okay, stay there and I'll have a unit join you at the house. The CSU should be with you in an hour or so.'

As I hang up, my eye is drawn by the papers on the desk. Although they seem at first glance to have been what Vallence was last reading or working on, I notice that the text faces my side, not his. I don't want to contaminate a crime scene, but I want to know why this little vignette was arranged, presumably by Nicholas. I move closer, but touch nothing.

Accidental injury logs marked with the St Valentine's emblem. Type and cause of injury suffered, countersigned by Vallence. They look old, and there aren't many of them. Personal records, maybe, or maybe something stolen by

Nick when he torched the kids' home, now put on public display.

Printouts of what look like prescriptions issued by the doctor, his copies of the documents given to the pharmacist. I recognize some of the drug names – morphine and diazepam being two of these – but not all.

Some extra sheets of paper clipped to the back of these lists, unreadable without moving them.

Bank statements for at least two accounts in Vallence's name.

A voice calls up from the front door, 'Deputy Rourke? It's Sergeant Elliott.'

'I'll be right with you. Check the rear of the building's secure,' I reply.

As I back away from the desk, a photo on the shelf behind it catches my eye. It shows Dr Vallence standing somewhere in the woods alongside a short man with thinning hair and Henry Garner. All three are dressed for the outdoors, in sweaters and jackets that were last in fashion a good thirty years ago, and are grinning broadly at the camera. Garner and the short man are proudly holding some sort of fish, pretty heavy to judge by looking at it. A label stuck to the frame reads: 'The gang at Claye Lake – Josh's beauty'.

The short man is familiar from somewhere, and even the photo itself sparks something in my mind. I'm almost certain I've seen his face, but I can't place it for the moment. I make a mental note to take a copy of the photo when the CSU has finished with the scene.

Downstairs, a Sheriff's Department Jeep is waiting outside with a beefy guy in sergeant's stripes leaning against it.

'What's the picture?' he says as I walk over to him.

'Victim's in his den upstairs. Looks like a cut throat. You check the back of the building?'

'Jack's keeping an eye on it right now.'

I make my way to the 'Vette and leaf through the police files on Garner I copied yesterday, looking for the short man's face. It takes a couple of minutes of flicking, but I eventually catch sight of someone similar, but older, in a single, blurry photo taken from a ten-year-old newspaper. The caption underneath names him as Joshua Stern, town clerk for Winter's End.

I take the page back into the house to compare it with the picture in Vallence's den. It takes a little imagination to unravel the changes wrought by the twenty-odd years between the taking of the two photos, but I'm pretty sure I've found a match.

'I'm going to head back to the department's offices in Houlton,' I tell Sergeant Elliott once I'm outside. 'There's something I've got to check. Dale's got my number if I'm needed for anything.'

I drive as quickly as I reasonably can on the return journey, over the limit but no one pulls me over; I guess the cops know the car. For the entire trip, I think about the photo in Vallence's den. Everyone in it is now dead, two of them murdered and Stern killed in a car crash. If it really was an accident. To be sure, I need to know about Stern. Back in the archived police reports, I find the four-year-old file on the crash that killed him. In it is a much clearer photograph, more recognizable as the same man in Vallence's picture.

Stern was driving home from a get-together with some old friends in Presque Isle when his car skidded off the snow-covered road and went over an embankment. Twenty feet down, it hit a tree.

The photos taken at the scene show the twisted and battered remains of Stern's vehicle with the town clerk's body still wedged behind the wheel.

Massive cranial damage was the official cause of death. There was no sign of mechanical failure on the car, so investigators concluded that Stern probably fell asleep at the wheel. He had a clean driving licence and not so much as a parking ticket to his name.

This would have seemed an open-and-shut death on the roads, perfectly common during the winter months. But I can think of another scenario.

In my mind's eye, I see Stern driving home in the ice-hard darkness. His headlights pick out a car apparently stranded by the side of the road, its driver flagging him down. He stops, and the driver staves his skull in. Then he wedges Stern's foot on the gas and runs the car into the trees at speed.

When I replay the images in my head, over and over again, the driver who stops Stern is Nicholas.


'Dale, it's Alex. What's the situation with Vallence?'

'Forensics are still going over the house, although the ME's left. It looks like he died from a single cut to the neck, though there were a couple of bruises here and there. We've got some clear latents from around the house, at least two sets, and some other stuff that might be of use. Including his shoes.'

'What about them?'

'The sole of Vallence's right shoe matches the print we found at the place where Garner's body was dug up.

There's a spade in the garage, still with mud on it. We're going to have it analysed, just to check it matches.'

'So Vallence was Nicholas's accomplice?' I say, cradling the phone with my shoulder so I can gather my cup of coffee from across the desk I'm sitting at. 'I guess that's why his car wasn't at his house.'

'Reckon so. No keys, either. I've put out an APB on the car. It might help the State boys in finding him.'

'Still no luck then?'

'Not yet. There's more, too. Vallence had a couple of pictures of Angela Lamond in his bedroom, along with some other things. It looks like they were seeing each other on the quiet.'

'Angela's rose buyer, huh? Why the big secret?'

'I dunno. Maybe Vallence didn't want to upset the town's great and good by letting everyone know that he was sleeping with one of his nurses. Maybe they just liked it that way. It might be that Nick killed her as a way of threatening the doctor.' I hear the sound of the breeze across the connection as Dale moves outside. 'While you were at Vallence's house, did you see the papers on his desk?' he asks.

'I had a quick skim. They looked like we were meant to find them, the way they were arranged.'

'Yeah, I thought the same. Interesting stuff, some of it. One of our people's going through his computer now to see if there's anything more.'

'What did you find?'

'It looks like the doctor was arranging for people to get hold of drugs on prescription, for a price. Had a few steady customers — not enough to arouse suspicion, but enough to give him a healthy bonus on top of his salary. We're trying to find Arthur Tilley, the pharmacist here in town, right now. Seems he may have left in a hurry.'

'Makes sense, if he was in on it. I guess word about cops being at the doctor's house wouldn't take long to get round.'

'He was also one of Vallence's regulars. Morphine, according to the lists. The doctor also received money from St Valentine's, possibly for overlooking the way some of their kids were treated, but we've got no way of knowing for sure.'

'If Nick knew that, he might have been blackmailing Vallence into helping him. Anything else?'

Dale pauses, and I hear him hold his breath for a moment. 'There is,' he says eventually, 'but you'd be better off hearing it from someone else. Have you spoken with Dr Larson at all today? I mean, did you try and patch things up at all?'

'Not yet. I've been busy and I thought she'd still be at the scene.' I'm also afraid of having the door kicked in my thoroughly deserving face, but I don't want to admit it.

'Go talk to her at the hospital. She'll explain.'

I puff out my cheeks. 'If you say so. Oh, and thanks for sorting me out last night,' I add. 'I don't know what came over me. And I can usually drink more than that without falling over.'

'Don't worry about it. Everyone has that kind of trouble now and again, even me and Laura,' he says. 'Actually, that's not true. We've had hardly any tough patches since we've been together. Lucky, I guess.'

I chuckle. 'Thanks for the understanding, Dale.'

'If you want understanding, don't act like such a jackass,' he says, but with a wry tone to his voice. 'I'll see you later.'

He hangs up, so I pluck up my courage and drive down to the hospital. Houlton seems relatively unaffected by the jailbreak, with no sign of the nerves affecting Winter's End. The town's police are out and about, but there's no sense of fear here. The hospital itself is reasonably busy, in a relaxed, late-in-the-week kind of way. To my relief, Gemma is alone in her office downstairs; her assistants must be elsewhere. I knock and walk in. She looks up at me without smiling, green eyes unreadable.

'Hi,' I say, like a kid about to admit to their dad that they broke the kitchen window. 'Can we talk?'

'I was worried you wouldn't want to,' she says. I can't detect any hint of blame in her tone; a good sign, or so I hope.

'Oh, I do.' Nerves lend my voice speed, even if the flow of words is a little uncontrollable. 'I'm really sorry for what I did and the things I said last night. I acted like a total asshole over nothing. It's been burning me since it happened that I hurt you and screwed up what was going to be a really great evening with someone I care about.'

I run my fingers through my hair. 'I know you might think I'm a jerk,' I tell her, 'but I want to say how bad I feel, and to ask whether you'd give me another chance. Could we have a second shot at this?'

For what seems like an hour, Gemma sits in silence, eyes locked on mine. Then she looks away and her face relaxes.

'I don't think you're a jerk, Alex,' she says. 'Not yet, anyway.' Relief floods through me like cold water. 'And I think maybe I know what came over you last night. You've taken drugs for insomnia for ages, right?'

'Years, yeah. On and off.'

'Have you ever taken any of the quick-acting ones, or just those for long-term use?'

I shrug. 'I don't know; I don't pay much attention to their names or what the difference is between one and another. Some work, some don't. Why?'

She holds up the bottle of pills I left in my jacket pocket. The jacket itself is on a worktop in the corner. 'And you've been taking these according to the instructions?'

'Two a night, just like it says.' Suspicion of what's been happening begins to creep over me. 'Dr Vallence gave me the prescription after he spoke to my doctor back in Boston.'

Gemma steps around her desk to stand next to me. She looks at my eyes, checking them as if she's examining something inside. 'How do you feel right now?'

'Okay, I guess. A bit tired, and getting kind of worried by all these questions. What's wrong with the pills? I mean, they get me to sleep and everything like they're supposed to.'

'When the Sheriff's Department read through Dr Vallence's notes this morning they found your name in the copied prescription records on his desk,' she says, breaking eye contact and toying with my fingers. 'On the back he'd scribbled a note which suggested he told the pharmacist to give you a different type of drug than what was on your prescription, in secret. I said I had your jacket, with the pills in, so Sheriff Townsend asked the hospital lab to check them.'

She looks back up at me. 'What you've been given is

called triazolam. It is used for treating insomnia, but it can have side-effects, particularly if you take twice the normal dose.'

'Twice? What side-effects?'

'Psychotic behaviour, increased irritability,' she says. 'The label on the bottle says that it contains fairly weak lorazepam tablets, a completely different drug, two pills to be taken at night. But that's not what they are, so you've been taking double the limit of something much stronger.'

'That sounds bad,' I say, a deliberate understatement.

Gemma nods. 'It is. Someone was trying to make you overdose, either to kill you or to make you useless as a cop. You're lucky it didn't have any worse effects on you than what I saw last night.'

'Well, I have had some pretty strange dreams.'

'Dreams?'

'And one or two hallucinations. I thought I might be on the way to another breakdown,' I add with an embarrassed smile. Gemma's eyes widen slightly.

'Hallucinations?'

'Nothing bad, I promise. Look, I am going to be okay, right? I mean, this stuff doesn't fry your brain or kill your liver or anything?'

She smiles, showing the dimples in her cheeks. 'You'll live,' she says.

'Good. And you don't think I'm an asshole?' As I say it, instinct telling me that things aren't over between the two of us, uncertainty blows across the surface of my memory. Did the drugs trigger my episodes, or was I already having them? Did I have the dreams and suffer the visions before I'd seen Vallence? Have I been seeing ghosts, or am I heading for another breakdown?

Questions I can't face right now. Maybe ones I don't *want* to face right now. In any case, I've got other things on my plate. Plenty to deal with aside from my mental condition.

*Exactly what I thought before I had my breakdown: too much work to get done to worry about what was happening to me.*

'No,' says Gemma. 'I don't think you're an asshole.'

I smile too, and put an end to the internal debate. 'It's a real relief to hear you say that,' I tell her. 'Things have been complicated enough without ruining the one really good thing that's come out of being here. I don't, well . . .'

'Yes?'

Feeling a little bashful, I continue, 'I don't suppose you're free tonight, are you? We could maybe have another go at a second date.'

Gemma answers with a kiss, a lingering touch with little force and a sense of distant sweetness, cotton candy against my lips. When we finally break away she says, 'Eight o'clock again?'

'I wouldn't ask you to cook for us two nights in a row.'

'We'll send out for pizza.'


I head back to Winter's End with the intention of grabbing a couple of hours' sleep before getting ready for seeing Gemma. When I pull up outside the silent, dead-looking form of the Crowhurst Lodge I rest my hands on the wheel for a moment, tired mind still ticking over what I've learned. The outer glass door of the hotel is ajar, which I optimistically take as a sign that the management is, at the very least, still in the land of the living. Not that this has encouraged anyone to man the front desk; the foyer is as empty as ever when I walk through the inner door. I am surprised, though, when I discover that the door to my room is unlocked. Perhaps I've caught whoever passes for cleaning staff here at work. I turn the handle and step inside.

The TV is on, playing MTV or one of the other music channels, and the air carries the scent of a drugstore perfume I recognize from a couple of days ago. Sophie Donehan is on the bed, lying against the headboard with her knees hitched up in front of her, TV remote by one hand and an open bag of jelly beans by the other.

'Hi,' she says without looking round, as if I should be expecting her. 'I told the guy at the desk that I was a friend of yours and he let me in.'

'I haven't seen anyone at that desk since I got here. You must have struck lucky.' I don't mean to sound suspicious, but I do. Sophie just shrugs.

'Okay. I had a look at the guestbook and took a spare key from behind the desk,' she says in a flat, uninterested voice. 'It doesn't matter. I'll drop the key off on my way out.'

'Which only leaves the question of why you're here.'

'I heard about the doctor and that guy they found out in Mason Woods.'

I nod slowly, not yet able to see the relevance to her visit. 'And?'

'And you've been asking questions around town about them and everything else.' She says all this far more calmly than I've heard her speak before, as if I'm now a trusted confidant that she's happy to share her secrets with.

'Right again.' Another thought strikes me. 'Shouldn't you be at school?'

'I *hate* that place. Besides, I'm almost finished there. I'll be graduating in a couple of weeks. And don't talk to me like I'm stupid, Alex,' she says, a young woman still getting used to talking to her elders on a first name, equal, basis. 'I think maybe what I know might help you. Otherwise I wouldn't be here.'

'Okay, I'm sorry.' I perch on the end of the bed. Sophie straightens her legs so I'm no longer hidden by her knees. I'm now sharing my end of the covers with her sock feet; I notice that she's had the decency not to trail her shoes all over my bedclothes but has instead left them on the floor at the side. 'What've you got?'

'There's something else I remembered about that place. Something specific, y'know? It was just before I left. I was in one of the dormitories not far from some of the offices – you've been there, right?' Her eyes are no longer fixed on the TV screen or me, but have the unfocused glaze of reminiscence. 'It was night but I couldn't sleep because I had a cold and my throat hurt. We'd all been shut up in bed early because someone had stolen something – I don't remember what. Anyway, I was lying there when I heard a man yelling, but it was muffled, like there was a thick door or something in the way. Then there was another voice, not so loud, talking back.

'I crept out of bed and opened the door a little, so I could peep out into the corridor. I remember there was a light coming from one of the rooms further down, and I could hear the voices more clearly. The man was shouting, I guess to one of the older kids; I couldn't hear what he was saying back. The man got louder, then the kid said something else, real low, and everything went quiet. Then the crying started. It went on and on, sobbing and stuff, until I finally went to sleep. You don't forget a noise like that, especially in a big old house.'

It's interesting enough, but doesn't seem to be especially relevant. 'What does this have to do with the case?' I ask. 'Aside from adding to what you already told me about St Valentine's.'

'You asked me if I remembered anything about the older kids,' Sophie says, shrugging. 'Anyway, all next day the nurse's office was shut because she was treating someone. I couldn't get any medicine for my throat because she was too busy. The doctor came out in the end. I know because he dropped off some cough syrup when he came.'

That seems to be about it. 'Thanks for telling me what you have, Sophie,' I tell her. 'If you think of anything else, give me a ring.'

'Sure.' Sophie slides her legs off the bed and slips her feet back into her shoes. I stand to show her to the door. 'Thanks for listening to me, Alex,' she says as she passes me on her way out. 'Most people round here think I'm crazy.'

'I know that feeling.'

She glances up at me, scanning my face with her dark eyes. 'You look kinda tired.'

'The job's just been catching up on me, that's all.'

'Okay.' Sophie shrugs, then reaches up towards me as if to give me a goodbye peck on the cheek. Instead, she plants a kiss firmly on my lips before leaving with a wave and a sly smile.

I close the door behind her, shaking my head. Then I go and wash my face under the shower for a minute or so to kick my brain into gear again. I spend half an hour scribbling down what Sophie told me, then, before dropping thankfully back on to the bed for some well-deserved rest, I reach for the boxes of stuff my dad left with Ben

Anderson, now sitting by the wall next to the bed. The photo from Vallence's den reminded me of something, and the only place I can think of is the bundle of pictures in my dad's things.

I untie the yellowed string binding them together and spread the photos out around me, running my fingers over each, looking for anything that stands out. After a minute or so, I pull two prints out of the mess and stare at them.

The first interests me because I don't recognize the person in the photo. A young boy, probably no more than five or six years old, looking uncertainly at the camera with wide, staring eyes. He doesn't feature in any of the other shots, even those that depict distant relatives and scattered branches of the Rourke family.

The second grabs me because it shows my father. More specifically, it shows him in outdoor gear, with a belt of trees and a sliver of lake behind him, exactly the same as the picture in Vallence's den. Standing with him are Henry Garner and the doctor himself. A note in pencil on the back says: 'Claye Lake. Josh's big catch (his turn with the camera)'.

My skin pricks and tingles as I look at the faces of the men, all of whom are now dead, two almost certainly killed by Nick. And what about the third – my dad? Is that why Nick seemed to know so much about him and the way he died?

Before I pack everything away, I lift up the last couple of items in the box and find, at the bottom, a single sheet of paper gone brittle and yellow with age. It seems to be some kind of memo or report, headed with the St Valentine's name and emblem.

*Some of Matthew's schoolteachers have complained about his behaviour. While he is not openly disruptive, they report that he has refused to do his homework on several occasions and pays little or no attention in class. There have been other incidents as well, and while they haven't openly blamed Matthew for them, they do suspect his involvement.*

*We may have to transfer him to another school. Our staff are doing their best to instil a sense of discipline in him as well as keeping an eye on him in case his behaviour is a symptom of anything more serious.*

The note is signed: 'Henry'. I have no idea what it's doing in my father's things. Maybe he did some legal work for St Valentine's, or maybe one of the kids there had an inheritance coming to them that his firm was looking after. I don't know, but the possibilities frighten me. The skin of my hands feels taut and prickly and my eyes blink in unison with each fresh thought that sleets across my brain.

The image of Vallence's fishing photo dances before my weary eyes. Garner, dead at the bottom of Black Ravine. Stern, in the wreckage of his car. Vallence, pitched forward in his office. My father, in the passenger seat next to me, blood running from his forehead. And the woman in the locket . . .

*The woman in the locket was a victim of a crime which went unpunished for a long time . . .*

A doctor. A town clerk. The director of a kids' home. A small-time lawyer. All dead.

An anonymous woman. What did they do, kill her?

I abandon that suggestion as soon as the thought strikes me. My dad was about as far from being the murdering sort as it's possible to get. He had his failings, like anyone, but he wasn't a criminal.

That doesn't leave me with much. I need to know who the woman in the locket is, and for that, I need Nicholas. I try phoning the cellular number he called me from, but the automatic message tells me that the phone I'm trying to call is turned off.

Did he really kill my parents? Was he the driver of the car that wrecked mine? Once more I fight to recall what I saw of the man behind the wheel of the sedan. In the split second before the impact, I caught the briefest of glimpses of the other car. But with the reflection from the windshield, and the indistinct view through my passenger-side window, everything inside was dark and blurred. Was my foot jammed on the brakes for long enough to really affect my speed? Would the sedan have had to turn to make sure it smashed cleanly into the side of my own like it did?

Why? And what does it have to do with the photo in my father's things, and the memo from St Valentine's?

I lie on the bed, the photo of the three men overlaid by that of the nameless woman. She hovers, just out of reach, eyes wide and trusting, smile strong but somehow uncertain. A face now with a touch of familiarity about it. The cheekbones, maybe, or the nose. The shape of the eyes.

Similar, so much so that I can almost believe there's a family resemblance, to the boy whose picture my father left in Ben's attic.

Another evening, another check on the time to see whether I'm late, early, or spot on. Another ring on the doorbell.

My hands, damp with nerves, clasp a bunch of flowers and another bottle of wine.

Gemma makes me wait a little longer on the doorstep before answering this time. She's wearing a tight black top, in deep contrast to her blonde hair, and a matching skirt. She smiles to see me and shows me in.

As promised, we send out for pizza. We lie back on the sofa, Gemma nestling in my arms, and watch *Hannibal*, eating take-out and drinking wine. About halfway through, we lose interest in the film, our attention occupied solely by each other. We make love slowly and gently, a tender but passionate entwining of bodies. Then again later, this time beneath her cool-smelling sheets. Gemma dozes off first and for a while I watch her as she lies still against me, feeling my heart beating in time with hers through the warmth of her chest.

I've always thought that it's when we sleep that humanity's true face is revealed. Our daily cares and worries disappear, the lines around the eyes fade and our features soften as we find the kind of peace that's a rarity during daylight hours. No matter whether the effect is good or bad, there's no longer any duplicity in our appearance; nothing hidden or buried. I've never really taken time to appreciate it though, at least until now. Gemma, with her tousled hair lying on her cheek and a faint smile on her lips, breathing softly against my skin, is perhaps the most beautiful sight I've ever seen.

Even during the rare, short-term flings I've embarked on in the past, when I was alone in the night all I'd see would be darkness or, at best, images from work. Victims, suspects, clients. Flat and lifeless. Now all I can see is her and the difference is extraordinary. I'd do anything to be able to distil and bottle the way she looks and the way I feel, and carry it with me wherever I go like a St Christopher's medal for my soul.

My sleep that night is natural, blissfully deep and dreamless, something I haven't experienced since returning to Winter's End.

# 13

The dawn arrives and for the first time in what seems like for ever, I don't have to face breakfast alone in the echoing confines of the Crowhurst Lodge. Freed, I feel relaxed and happy, revelling in the rediscovered joy of human company. Gemma and I part on the driveway as we each go our separate ways. The kiss we share is long and deep.

I reach the office to find Dale already there, along with Lieutenant Matheson. Dale gestures at the papers in front of him. 'Here's how things stand,' he says, more for my benefit than Matheson's. 'The prints we found at Vallence's belonged to Nicholas. Time of death for the doctor was some time between two and four in the afternoon two days ago, during which time we know Nick called you from the doctor's house. Vallence was killed by a single cut to the throat with a blade we still haven't found. His car is gone, and, according to his neighbours, it's been missing since the afternoon before the prison break. This fits with what else we found at the doctor's home.

'There were three notes in his desk, all delivered at specified times by courier firms. One warned him that if anyone came asking about St Valentine's or carrying a locket with the photo of a woman in, he was to "take measures" – I figure that's where your fake prescription comes in, Alex. The order was backed up with the threat:

"Look at what I did to your girlfriend if you're not convinced of my sincerity." It looks like Nick used the Lamond murder as a way of adding to the pressure on Vallence. He would already have been under some if Nick was blackmailing him over his drug sales.'

'Maybe he just hates women,' Matheson chips in. 'The extra wounds he inflicted, the fact that he stripped her. It could be that he's pathological and gets off on killing, even though he tried to justify the murder to his accomplice.'

'For now we'll have to hope he isn't,' Dale says. 'We don't want any more murders. He seems to have planned ahead, which might be a good sign on that score. The second note he left for Dr Vallence told him to dig at the site of Garner's grave on the night in question, though it didn't tell him what to expect there. The last told him to leave his car in Houlton, half a block from the prison, and go home without it. We found Nick's prints on each of them.

'According to the phone company, the cellular he called you from hasn't been turned on since, so they can't get its location. No one's reported seeing Vallence's car, a stranger matching Nick's description, or anything we might use to narrow down his location. The State Police are no longer setting up roadblocks, though they're keeping their eyes peeled. Border Patrol haven't seen him and we've had nothing from the local PDs.

'On the bright side, we now have a much better idea of how he abducted Angela Lamond. The stolen car that Alex found in the woods is the same model and colour as that of one of the residents on Carver Street. She wouldn't have known it wasn't one of her neighbours until she was in a position for him to grab her. As far as we know, he took her straight to Mason Woods and from there to St Valentine's.

'While that's good, though, we've still got dick to go on until someone spots him.' Dale drains half a cup of coffee in a single swallow, then scratches his moustache with an air of concentration.

'Who was that nutcase who was out in the woods when we found Garner?'

Dale raises an eyebrow. 'That's just Ellie Naylor. She's harmless. Why? You don't think she's anything to do with what's happened, do you?'

'I don't know,' I say, thinking back to her wide, staring eyes. 'I ran into her again at St Francis. Some of the things she said were similar to what Nick said in our interviews.'

'She knew about the murders?'

'No. At least, I don't think so. But she came out with the same kind of "work of the Devil" shit that he did and she seemed to recognize the woman in the locket.'

Dale shrugs and reaches for his coffee. 'Just crazy talk, most likely. She was probably just pleased to have someone listen to what she was saying for a change.'

'How did she get like that?'

'She's Sophie Donehan's aunt. She lost it after her sister killed herself. Lives with Rose Alford. She pretty much depends on her for everything. Like I said, she's harmless.'

'Could she have any connection to Nick, do you think?'

Dale looks at me pityingly, then shakes his head. 'You must be working too hard on this if you reckon that's a serious possibility.'

'Working too hard, huh?' I say. 'It's not often I get accused of that. She might have met him, though, if he ever came up to town for some reconnaissance before he killed Angela Lamond. It would explain why she sounds like he does.'

'It would, but how would I know?' Dale replies. 'Unless she tells you directly, there's no way to be sure if there even is a reason. We can try asking Rose if she's had any visitors, but I doubt we'll hear anything to back up your theory. All I can tell you is that every time there's a car crash, a bad storm or the town gets snowed in, she's out there saying it's the work of the Devil, or God, or Walmart, or someone else. She's a nut, Alex. Just like every other nut you've ever run into.'

I sigh, unconvinced even though Dale does have a point. 'Yeah, I guess.'

'Any other ideas?'

'How about coming up with a list of possible victims?' I suggest. 'Even if he only killed Vallence to tie up a loose end, there might be more to go before he's finished his business.'

Matheson shrugs. 'Surely he'd only kill to cover his tracks or if someone tried to stop him stealing a car or something. We'd never be able to list individuals.'

Dale looks at me, but I shake my head. 'No, he came here to finish something. I don't know what yet, but he's thought this through. When he killed Garner, he did it cleverly enough that no one even knew it had happened. I think there's a chance he's killed since, as well, but made the deaths look like accidents. This time, he got himself caught. Someone like that doesn't show himself unless it's not going to stop him doing what he's set out to do.'

'Who are you thinking of for these previous victims, Alex?'

'Joshua Stern, the town clerk, and,' I hesitate a second or two, a little unwilling to face the possibility, 'and my father.'

Dale stays silent for a moment and just raises his eyebrows. Eventually, he says, 'You think he killed your parents?'

'My dad was his target. My mom was probably just a bonus.' I realize what I've said. 'Jesus, I feel bad for making it sound like that.'

I now understand why cops aren't supposed to get involved in personal cases if they can avoid it. Not because the thirst for revenge is too strong – though if Nick did kill my folks, I aim to see him go down for it – but because it becomes harder to think like a cop. Unpleasant as it may be, victims tend to be no more than a collection of vital statistics and a photograph or two when they reach your desk. Caucasian male, age sixty, white hair, and so forth. Start getting caught up in who they were and some of the things you have to think, talk about or go through become even more unpleasant than they already are. And you feel guilty every time you act like you would in any other case. It's a hell of a position to be in.

Dale seems to understand, and continues as if nothing's changed. 'Stern died in a car crash,' he says.

'And my dad was killed in a hit-and-run collision. Both of them were friends of Vallence and Garner. The four of them used to go fishing together.'

'Were there any other deaths around that time that might have been connected?' Matheson asks.

'I'd have to check the records,' Dale says. 'If I remember rightly, Stern died in the same year that Bob Kennedy, the Sheriff before me, had his heart attack. He used to know

Winter's End pretty well. Had a cabin by the Aroostook River. I don't remember any others.'

'Sheriff Kennedy, huh?'

'No sign of foul play. Guy just had a weak heart.'

'Didn't he get one of those notes after the fire at St Valentine's though?' I say.

Dale shrugs. 'Yeah, but that was a couple of years before he died.'

'Even so, you don't think it might have been connected in some way?'

I don't get an answer. At the back of the squad room, I hear the phone ring and the dispatcher answer. Then he calls Dale's name out loud. I turn to see him standing with his hand cupped over the receiver and an excited look on his face.

'I've got a forest warden on the line, Chief,' he yells. 'He says he saw a car matching the one you're looking for up at the McWirren hunting lodge near Purser Lake.'

Half an hour later, rain is beginning to fall as I step out of my car and on to a dirt road hemmed in by rank upon rank of trees heavy with spring foliage. The ground between their thick dark trunks is dim and indistinct, shadows made worse by the gloom of the day. Not countryside that makes you feel welcome, far from it; it reminds you how little you belong out here. The track follows the shoulder of the ridge we're on for another couple of hundred yards before diving off to the west, downhill towards the lakeside and the McWirren cabin.

Today may have begun on something of a high for me, but the sight of the empty forest drags at my spirits again, like a soldier seeing the first machine-gun nest on his way back to the front lines after a week's leave. A sight that tells you you're back on the job, an assignment that never seems to have an end.

I pull my collar up against the cold water falling with increasing force and join Dale, two of his deputies and four state troopers next to one of their cruisers, skewed to block the road. I find him talking, water running in a steady trickle from the brim of his hat, with one of the troopers, apparently the first to arrive.

'Where the hell is the forest warden?' he asks. 'Didn't he say he'd meet us here?'

The younger man shrugs. 'He did, but he's not here now. You don't think he might be closer to the cabin?'

'Maybe, but I don't see his truck anywhere, either.'

'What's going on?' I ask Dale.

'The warden – something or other Hudson I think his name was – is missing. He did say he was going to sit tight and let us know if anyone came or went this way. I guess we'll have to go down to the cabin without his input.' Dale raises his voice a little to be heard by everyone. 'There's a chance that if our man is down there, he could have a hostage. Don't go shooting unless you're absolutely sure of who you're shooting at. Let's go.'

'We're leaving the cars here?' I say as we march briskly, but as quietly as possible, along the road.

'Best not to alert him if he's there. Half a dozen vehicles will be easy to spot somewhere as quiet as this. A couple of blue-and-whites are going to follow us in a few minutes, which should give us time to get to the cabin before they're heard.'

I nod and draw my pistol from my jacket. The Colt, old but well cared-for, is cold to the touch but comforting in its weight and solidity. I take the safety off and rack a round into the chamber. 'I don't like the sound of the warden being missing,' I say, quietly enough that only Dale will hear me.

'Neither do I. He might just have gotten nervous and bugged out.'

'I hope so.'

We fall silent again. The TV static noise of the rain hitting the leaves is the only sound to accompany us as we walk through the growing mire to the point where the track bends to the left. No one speaks any more, even when the foot of one of the state troopers plunges into a shin-deep mud hole covered in water.

The McWirren hunting lodge, a large log cabin of the sort rented out to vacationing families, squats darkly at the bottom of the hill within spitting distance of the grey waters of Purser Lake. On the far side, a mile or two away, the black, forested mass of Doubleback Ridge rises like a wall, as if it's trying to encircle the cabin and hold its occupants in place until we can reach it.

'No car outside,' Dale mutters. 'Could be round the back.'

'Still no sign of the warden, either.'

We fan out into the trees, three of us on either side of the road. The air beneath the leaves is damp and earthy, and the inch-thick carpet of pine needles that covers the ground deadens our footsteps as we sidle towards the building. The ground is clear, free of the kind of under-growth that entwines Mason Woods, strangling it and tying it in knots. The mostly evergreen woodland around the lake has no such entanglements, and only the occasional exposed root gives me any problems.

The low drone of the twin police cruisers' engines sounds behind me as I reach the last line of trees before the cabin. Beyond, the lake is a ruffled grey sheet masked by a curtain of rain. The lodge itself still seems to be asleep after the winter lull, with heavy shutters over its windows and a thin carpet of twigs and old leaves covering the ground outside. If there have been any motor vehicles down here recently, someone must have expertly covered their tracks. Everything about the cabin seems to be shut tight, waiting for the owners to reopen it as summer draws on.

I glance across at Dale and shake my head as the cruisers reach the bottom of the hill and come to a stop. Our half-dozen-strong force emerges from the greenery and advances cautiously towards the building, guns out.

'He's not here, Dale,' I say, holstering my gun.

'What makes you so sure?'

'Look at this place.' Two state troopers move slowly up to the front door, which turns out to be locked. 'No one's been here in ages. Search all you want, but if he was ever here, which I doubt, he's gone. This has been a damn wild goose chase.' I turn and start trudging back towards the slope alone.

'What about the warden?' he says after me. 'What happened to him?'

I stop and look over my shoulder. 'How the hell should I know? There probably never was a warden. It's a hoax, maybe, or Nicholas giving us the runaround. I'm going back to the cars. If I'm wrong and there's something here, give me a shout.'

I slog grimly uphill through the mud to where my 'Vette sits wholly out of place amongst the police vehicles and the forest. A pair of deputies whose names I forget are perched in their four-by-four, enjoying a cigarette while they wait.

'Any news?' one of them asks as I pass.

'Not yet. Place looks deserted.'

I slump into the 'Vette, sitting sideways with the door open and my mud-covered shoes outside while I have a smoke, glaring at the massed battalions of trees in front of me. This might have been a waste of time, but I feel a little guilty about giving Dale a hard time for it. I should probably apologize, and probably will once my mood improves.

Then the radio in the deputies' Jeep crackles into life, audible despite the patter of the rain. I can't make out every word from where I sit, but this ceases to be a problem when one of the deputies calls me over. 'You'd better hear this,' he says.

'What is it?'

'This is Deputy Traynor over in Winter's End,' the voice on the other end of the connection says. 'I got called out to a report that someone was vandalizing the graves at St Francis's church.'

'Uh-huh.'

'Turned out it was just one tombstone pushed over, but it had a note addressed to "Deputy Alex Rourke, Sheriff's Department" laying on it.'

My fingertips begin to tingle. 'Which would be me. Who phoned up with the report? Did you get a description of the vandal?'

'A woman living across the street called it in about half an hour ago. She didn't get a good look, but she said it was a guy with dark hair and casual clothing. He drove off in a red or brown pick-up. You want me to open the note?'

'No, no. There's not much chance, but it could always be a letter-bomb or something. Are you still up at St Francis's?'

'Yeah.'

'I'll be there in half an hour or so.'

I tell the two deputies to let Dale know what's happened before I jump in the 'Vette and spin it around, back up the trail. I keep my foot down almost all the way to Winter's End, eager for a fresh scent of my quarry.

*So sorry to have missed you, Mr Rourke. It must feel strange to have your life suddenly ruled by the actions of someone else. Are you enjoying the hunt, or is the pressure starting to get to you? I take it you know about the doctor and how he had your pills switched. I wasn't sure what he'd come up with, but I have to say I admire his efforts.*

*Don't feel sorry for him, though. The man was scum, a criminal, though his worst offence wasn't in the records I left for you.*

*Do you know what it's like to have a loved one taken from you? I'm not talking about your parents here; even if the impact of that sedan hadn't finished them, old age would have had them soon. No, I'm talking about someone truly close to you, that you spend hours with every day, that'd you do anything to protect. Do you know how it feels when they die?*

*Do you know how it feels when they're killed by your own blood?*

Reading the words brings back the same sense of isolation and vulnerability I felt when Nicholas and I spoke on the phone outside Vallence's house. I run each sentence through my mind, looking for meanings, suggestions, conclusions. Then I look up from the note, which lies open on the front seat of Deputy Traynor's Jeep. Traynor himself is hovering next to me by the open door, as if the presence of the vehicle will shield him from the damp.

'Bag the note and the envelope,' I tell him, still running its words through my head as the rain drips from my hair and trickles down the back of my jacket. 'Where did you find it?'

'There's a turned over gravestone near the right-hand edge of the churchyard,' he says. 'You can't miss it.'

'Any other witnesses who might have seen him plant this?'

'Not that I could find. Ellie Naylor's in the church, but I don't think she saw or heard anything. Hard to tell with the way she rambles.'

Through the gate, past the straggly maple trees now bowed and dulled by the drizzle, on to the sodden grass of the graveyard. The dreary space feels lonely and cold, like a big, damp room in an abandoned house. The Church of St Francis huddles like a pale old man off to my left, its windows his sunken eyes, lined with dark slate. The whole place is depressing, less a house of worship than a stark reminder of a time when the town tried to reach beyond itself with the building of St Valentine's Chapel. The church is a living monument to the deaths that occurred when Ryland's dream burned to a cinder, a smug edifice that says, *look what happened when you tried to replace me. See what your folly cost you.*

I return my gaze to the dark, flat grass of the graveyard.

Near the wall that borders the eastern side of the grounds, amongst a small collection of plots laid out like a grid, I find the vandalized tombstone.

As I reach it, the wind suddenly gusts around me, driving ice-hard specks of rainwater against my skin and tearing at my clothes. It whips around as if I'm standing at the heart of an invisible tornado, carrying with it a sound like distant screaming. I shift my weight to help my balance and duck down to get a closer look at the marker. I have to keep blinking away as tiny shards of water slap into my eyes, giving everything a strobelight feel to it. I sway and for the briefest moment dizziness floods through me.

Then the wind drops just as suddenly as it came and I'm free to get back to the job at hand. From the straight-edged gouges in the earth, it looks as if Nicholas used a spade to help him topple the stone, which is plain and unadorned, like the grass-covered grave itself.

*Joanna Thorne*
*Be at peace, free at last of life's trials*

The pale grey stone is spattered with moss and lichen; from that and the lack of fresh flowers or other personal offerings, I guess that Joanna hasn't had any visitors in a while. In which case, what made Nick choose her grave? There are others that would be easier for him to topple without being spotted, and others more easily seen, which would have made sure his note was found.

The part of my mind still turning over Nick's words settles on the last section of the note. I turn and jog back to the Jeep, then pick up the sheet of paper, now safely sealed in an evidence bag, and run through it again.

Heart jumping, I reach for my cellphone. 'Dale, it's Alex.'

'We didn't find anything at the cabin, and we haven't been able to trace the warden –'

'Yeah, well it was probably Nick trying to get us haring all over the countryside while he was up here in town. He left a message for me on a tombstone at St Francis's church. I need you to do two things for me, Dale.'

'Sure, Alex. Sounds urgent.'

'It is. I want you to get a unit – I don't care if it's your guys, Houlton PD or a State Police blue-and-white – but I want you to get a couple of people down to the hospital and keep an eye on Gemma for me. We'll have to figure out somewhere safe where she can stay, but that can wait.'

'Nick threatened her?'

'Yeah, maybe.' I read the note out loud for his benefit. 'All that stuff about your loved ones dying sounds pretty threatening to me.'

'How did he find out about you and her?'

'Fuck knows. Maybe he's been following me around, or bugging my car, or maybe I'm getting worried over nothing and he doesn't know at all. But I'm not willing to take that chance.'

'Okay, we're getting hold of Houlton PD right now. There'll be a couple of uniforms with her in a few minutes.'

I allow myself to breathe out and do my best to relax. 'Thanks, Dale.'

'That's all right. What was the second thing you wanted?'

'Joanna Thorne. Died twenty-one years ago, buried here in Winter's End. Can you get hold of some information for me – who she was, how she died, that kind of thing?

I'll come down to Houlton and do some checking of my own, but it'd help if the ground's been prepared.'

'No problem.'

I'm about to hang up when I think of something else. 'Oh, Dale,' I say, 'I'm sorry I was a bit grouchy this morning. Guess it's just eating at me that we haven't caught him yet.'

'Forget it, Alex,' he says. 'We all get like that sometimes. If you like, I'll give you some traffic duty while things are quiet. You could take out your frustration on the travelling public.'

'Tempting, but then they might not re-elect you. I'll settle for catching the son of a bitch.'

'You and me both. I'll see you later.'

Deputy Traynor looks at me as I replace the phone in my pocket. 'That everything you need from me?' he asks.

'There's one more thing you can do,' I say after a moment's thought. 'Call in at the Crowhurst Lodge and see if anyone's turned up there or left messages for me. If you can find the manager, that is,' I add.

Before leaving for Houlton, I walk back up to the church itself. The building is as empty as last time. The only occupant is the mad woman, Ellie Naylor, Sophie's aunt, kneeling in the same pew as before. She looks around as I approach, hair snarled and knotted.

'Back?' she says, hands still clasped in front of her. I can see her fingernails pressing and grinding against each other. 'For God's forgiveness, or your own satisfaction?'

'I told you before, I don't believe in God.'

'A poor deity he would be if that bothered him.'

I shrug. 'Actually, I came to see you. You remember when I showed you the photograph of a woman and you

261

said that she was what started all this? How did you know?'

'I know her face. I saw when they found her, cold and asleep and dead.'

'So you remember her?' I say, more urgently than before. 'What was her name?'

'It doesn't seem important any more. I don't remember.' Ellie turns away from me and lifts her eyes towards the stained glass ahead of her. I don't know whether she's praying or not. I'm not even sure who she's praying for. Or to.

'Do you remember where she was buried?'

She shakes her head and in a firm, dismissive voice says, 'The dead have no more cares in this world.'

'That's a nice saying,' I tell her, trying my best smile and kindly voice. 'Where did you hear it?'

'I don't remember,' she says, and sounds like she means it. Bang go my hopes of finding out whether or not she's spoken with Nick.

'And you think God is punishing those who killed the woman in the locket? Was her name Joanna, do you think?'

'God does not punish such things, and in the same way Satan does not forgive. God would not wash the sin from their souls, and so they are his.'

Joanna Thorne. Born in Bangor fifty-three years ago. Became a secretary at a law firm in Houlton after leaving college. At first, I think this might prove to be the link between her and my father along with the rest of his circle of deceased friends, but it turns out that she worked for a rival group of lawyers. Left her job and moved to a small apartment above a clothing store in Winter's End four years before she died at the age of thirty-two. Held a handful of low-pay jobs around town – store clerk, cleaner, kitchen assistant – but ended up spending most of the last couple of years of her life on welfare. She apparently became an alcoholic and eventually passed out drunk in the street one January night and froze to death. Never married but had one child, a son called Matthew, to an unknown father nine months or so before moving to Winter's End. He became a ward of the state after his mother's death. The last scrap of information on Joanna and her offspring says he was sent to St Valentine's Home for Children. Any record of him leaving the home must have vanished in the fire.

Or did it? I think back to the note I found amongst my dad's things which mentioned a child called Matthew. Could they be the same, and if so, how was my dad involved in his stay at St Valentine's? It could be that his law firm dealt with Matthew when he was placed into care, or it could be that he took a liking to the boy during his visits to the home. And there are other possibilities, far darker, that I'm unwilling to consider. Nevertheless, they prowl like sharks in the gloom beneath the surface of my thoughts, threatening to surge upward and drag me down with them whenever I think about Matthew and his mother Joanna.

From what little information exists about her, I can't work out why her life changed so dramatically after the birth of her son. I guess it's possible she couldn't handle being a working mother, but the slide seems pretty extreme. Unfortunately, there's no way of telling what else was going on in her life at the time.

Matthew would now be about the same age as our estimate for Nicholas. His familiarity with the area, the burning of St Valentine's and his choice of gravestone to leave his note on would all make sense if Nick and Matthew Thorne were the same. But then why desecrate his mother's grave?

*The dead have no more cares in this world.*

'Not interrupting, am I?'

The voice startles me out of my thoughts and whisks my attention back to the Sheriff's Department records office. Gemma, stepping quietly through the door, a half-smile, half-frown on her face.

I put down the notes I've been reading, or pretending to read, and stand to meet her. I give her the best smile I can manage. 'No, I was just thinking, that's all.'

She moves as if to kiss me, but instead fixes me with her eyes and says, 'Alex, why am I being escorted every-where by a pair of cops?'

I can't think of an easier way to put it. 'Because there's a chance that Nicholas knows about you and might try to, well, get at me by doing something to you.'

'Oh,' she says, blinking a couple of times and lowering her eyes.

'He hasn't threatened you outright,' I tell her, trying to cushion things a little. 'But he talked about how it feels to lose a loved one, and I didn't want to leave you in danger. Hence the cops.'

I tell her what the note said.

'What about going home?' she asks. 'Or going to work? Am I supposed to take a break somewhere away from here?'

'At work, you should be okay. There are all sorts of people surrounding you – while that would make it easier for him to get at you, it will make it harder for him to do anything without being seen. Staying at home is dangerous. Without round-the-clock protection on the building as well as on you, he could break in and hide himself inside while you were out.'

I realize I'm lecturing her without meaning to and apologize. 'Sorry,' I say, 'force of habit. It's my "lay it on the line" voice. Won't happen again.'

'That's all right,' Gemma says.

'I'm sorry for getting you into this, too.'

'It doesn't matter.' She loops her arms around my chest and kisses me softly. 'But since you've got everything worked out, where am I meant to stay?'

'Dale's made up one of the spare rooms here in the courthouse. You should be comfortable enough for a couple of days. He says the department will even cover the expense of getting breakfast from one of the places down the road.'

'You think it'll be over in a couple of days, by the end of the weekend?'

The image of Nick sending us out on a bogus tip, just so he could tear up a grave in broad daylight and leave me a message, hangs in my mind. 'Yeah, maybe. There's a couple of things I have to find out first, though.'

That night I sit in the darkened chamber in the Superior Court building, Gemma breathing softly on the couch opposite, and repeatedly run through everything I've heard. The quiet, controlled tones of Nicholas blend and spill over into the older voice of Dr Vallence, Dale's gruffness, Earl Baker's lies, the woman at the museum.

If Nick was Matthew Thorne, an embittered former inmate of St Valentine's, I could understand why he'd kill

Garner on the night of the fire. If Vallence helped the home's management cover up the abuse it inflicted, I'd also understand why he killed the doctor after blackmailing Vallence into helping him. But what about the other two people in the Claye Lake photos: Joshua Stern and my father? Did Nick murder Stern and make his death look like an accident? Was he really the driver of the car that killed my parents in Miami? I wish I knew why anyone would want revenge on my dad. I don't remember him doing anything that would make anyone want to kill him.

Anger dies over time, and I've had my therapy and I think I've more or less come to terms with their deaths. I just wish I could somehow make up for all the times I didn't go and see them, or didn't feel like talking to them. I wish I could have patched things up with my dad quickly, before I'd even joined the FBI. I'm not the vengeful sort but if Nick killed them, I'd at least want to know why. And I'd want to see him stand trial for it. And I'd want him to lose.

Most of all, I want this whole affair to be over so I can go back to my normal life and forget about killings and faces in the dark.

But to do that, I need to understand him better, and what happened to make him the way he is. What ties Stern and my father to Matthew Thorne and St Valentine's? For that, I'd have to ask someone who knew my dad, and knew him well.

The sun may be up, but I can't see it through the thick bank of dark grey cloud that hangs low over the woods near the McLean River. My watch tells me that it's just past nine o'clock on a cheerless Saturday morning as I push through the thick, leafy foliage with Gemma in tow. A stiff breeze sends ripples through the treetops, showering us both with fine specks of water shaken from the leaves above and bringing with it the promise of another sustained soaking before long.

Twenty minutes' hike from where we left the 'Vette next to Ben Anderson's battered RV, we start to hear the sound of water pouring over the flat black rocks of the riverbed. A hundred yards or so further and we're standing on a low bank of stone and heavy earth at the outside of one of the wide, dark river's sweeping curves. I can make out Ben a good distance downstream and some way out from the water's edge, casting his line expertly into the water.

'Hey, son,' he calls out as soon as we're close enough. 'See you've brought a friend, too.'

'Ben Anderson, Gemma Larson,' I say, making the introductions.

'Pleased to meet you. You two feel like joining me?'

'Afraid not. I haven't been fishing since I was a kid. Are you having any luck?'

He shakes his head. 'Not today. Haven't had time to get a feel for the water, know where the fish are. What's on your mind? You anything to do with that shit I heard on the news?'

'I am, but it's not that I'm here for. You and my dad were pretty close, weren't you?'

There's a *swish* as the line arcs back across the water, the fly on the end dancing just above the surface. 'Yeah, we were,' Ben says, keeping his eyes on what he's doing as he speaks.

'Do you remember him ever mentioning a woman called

Joanna Thorne? It might have been something to do with the guys he used to go up to Claye Lake with.'

The line swoops to the old man's hand and he turns to regard me, eyes dark beneath his bushy brows. 'What do you want to go asking after her for? No need to go digging up the past now, son.'

'I think the guy I'm looking for might be her son,' I say. 'I've got a suspicion he was involved in my father's death as well as that of Joshua Stern, and we already know he killed Henry Garner and Dr Vallence. Somehow, Joanna Thorne is linked to them, but it's only someone like you who can fill in the blanks for me.'

Ben stays still for a moment, just another rock in the river, before his eyes drop and he wades towards the bank. 'Let's head back to the van,' he says. 'This kind of talk's better in more homely surroundings.'

The interior of the RV is in better shape than the outside, with the kind of personal touches that only come with years of steady ownership. Take off the wheels, hide the bodywork behind brick walls, and you wouldn't be able to tell it was anything other than a small house. Gemma and I sit at a table spread with a cream cloth decorated with tiny embroidered geese in flight, while Ben potters around in the tiny kitchen, making coffee. Eventually he emerges with three steaming mugs and sits opposite.

'What do you want to know about Joanna?' he asks, blowing gently on his drink to cool it down.

'How she knew the four men. Anything that could lead her son to murder. I know he grew up in St Valentine's after she died, but that wouldn't explain why he killed Stern or my father. If he killed them,' I add.

Ben nods. 'First, you have to understand something: your dad loved your mom. He really did. But he had his weaknesses, too.'

'And Joanna was one of them?'

'He had an affair with her what, twenty-five, thirty years ago now. Didn't last long, you understand. Figure he realized what an ass he was being and ended things. A few of us knew – Josh, Nathan, Henry, me, a couple of others. I didn't have much to do with it, but I know some of them used to cover for him, saying they were all going up to the cabin they used to rent for a weekend's fishing. Then they'd head somewhere else – usually for two days in a bar out of the way – while he and Joanna had the cabin to themselves. Lasted a couple of months, I think, then he broke it off.'

The thought of my father cheating on my mom all those years ago leaves me feeling strange, a little unnerved. 'And that was it?'

'Not exactly,' Ben says, almost apologetically, and drains his mug. 'A little while after it was over, she got in touch, said she was pregnant and that he was the father. Guess that'd make her son your half-brother.'

# 14

A hole opens in my chest and my senses begin to drain away through it. This must be how it feels to be told you're adopted and that your biological parents aren't the ones you've grown up with. Everything you thought you knew about your upbringing, childhood – hell, your whole life – falls down and there's nothing there ready to take its place. You think you know your parents, but you don't. You think you're comfortable with being Alex Rourke, only child, no living relatives. But you're not any more because it's not true any more. Ben has no reason to lie to me, and I have no reason not to believe his words, spoken in that slow, steady drawl of his.

I have a brother.

Not only that, but I have a brother who's a killer. A brother who might well have murdered my mom and my – his – *our* dad. I've always liked to think of myself as a nice enough guy, and now I have to come to terms with the fact that almost the same genetic path has created a monster, and that this was hidden from me for nearly thirty years.

'What did he do?' I ask, gulping down a couple of swigs of coffee to ease the dryness of my throat.

'We all had our opinions about whether he should come clean or just cut her off completely. I don't know whose advice he followed in the end, but he wouldn't have anything to do with her again. Didn't want to break up his family, I guess, not with a kid of his own already.'

'Which is why she moved from Houlton to Winter's End,' I say quietly. 'She was trying to stay close to him.'

'Used to see her around town sometimes. We never spoke – I don't think she even recognized me – but I knew who she was. Used to try and help her out in little ways if I could – generous tips when she was waitressing, that kind of thing. Sweep the path outside her place in winter. Work dried up, I guess, and I stopped seeing her so often.'

'And she hit the bottle.'

'If you say so,' Ben says, shrugging. 'Like I said, I stopped seeing her around after a while. But I heard what happened when she died. Not from your dad, but from Josh. Your dad told him she'd come to see him, called at his house, desperate for money. He reckoned she was trying to blackmail him or something, and I guess he didn't want a long conversation on the doorstep with his family inside and all. Anyway, he told her to leave him alone, shut the door on her. A couple of days later, she was dead.

'She didn't have no family, so the boy was headed for the children's home. I guess he would've been about five or six by then. Your dad wanted to be certain there was never any record of the father's identity, so he asked Josh, being town clerk, to make sure his name was never mentioned. Nathan and Henry kept quiet about what they knew, and I think one of them might have said something to old Bob Kennedy 'cos he didn't look too hard at what she was doing with her evenings before she died.'

I turn the mug in my hands, running my fingers over the warm china clay. 'My dad used to visit St Valentine's every so often when I was a kid,' I say softly, looking back with new light on old memories. 'He used to take toys and stuff for the children. I thought he was just being kind to less fortunate kids. But he did it because he had a son there?'

'I guess. Your dad was a good man,' Ben says, equally softly. 'He wanted to make sure the boy was all right, but he didn't want to lose your mom and you because of the mistake he'd made.'

'I went with him a couple of times,' I continue. 'I played with some of the kids. That could have been my brother I was with, but he never told me.'

'He was trying to work things out as best he could.'

I think of what Nick – Matthew – has become. His words: *Do you know what it's like to have a loved one taken from you? Do you know how it feels when they're killed by your own blood?* He blamed my father for the death of his mother. He hated the others for helping brush the past under the rug and for his treatment at St Valentine's.

He said he came back to bring me here. Why? Because I'm the last member of the family he felt himself outcast from as a child? For having the life he didn't?

I sit in silence for an age, staring blankly through the mug, into the distant past. Gemma lays her hand on my arm and, after a while, says, 'Are you all right, Alex?'

'Hard news to hear now,' Ben adds from the opposite side of the table. 'Some things are best left forgotten. Wish they could have stayed that way.'

It's nearing the end of a warm day. The sky is clear blue flecked orange by the thick rays of the early evening sun. An indistinct murmur of conversation and occasional words of support are coming from the makeshift stand by the side of the grass, where some forty or fifty people are sitting, waiting for the game to begin. Most of them are parents here to watch their kids, and quite a few have younger or older siblings with them, eating ice cream and talking with the high-pitched enthusiasm of their years.

I'm eight years old, playing at second base in my first appearance for the team. Like every boy in his first ballgame, I'm scanning the faces of the crowd as I go to take up position by the plate, looking for my parents, hoping to catch their smiles and hear them shouting for me. I see my mom, who waves and blows me a kiss, but she's alone and there's no space next to her for my dad.

I know then that he's not coming, and the knowledge fills my eight-year-old heart with disappointment. We win the game, I play okay, but none of that matters to me. What matters is that my dad missed my first ballgame.

Later, Mom told me he had called to say he had to work a couple of hours late, and that he was really, really sorry to miss the game. I told her I didn't mind, lying and brushing it off as easily as I could, and that was that. Dad took us all out for dinner when he got home an hour or two later, let me order whatever I wanted, and I forgave him; kids aren't good at holding grudges. I never forgot, but it wasn't a big thing, there were plenty more games and it became just one of childhood's little ups and downs.

Now I no longer know for certain that my dad really did miss the game because he was working late. Was he with Joanna Thorne for that extra couple of hours? Was he lying naked with her by the time I pulled on my team strip?

I don't know what prompted Dad to be unfaithful, just as I don't know what made him break off the affair. Did he leave Joanna because he loved my mom, or because of me? I think maybe Ben was right, and that he'd tried to work things out as best he could. He didn't want to risk losing his family by acknowledging Joanna and her son, but he couldn't turn his back entirely on his offspring, illegitimate or not, after she died. That's certainly what I'd like to think.

Years after my first ballgame, I'd sit with him on our occasional fishing trips and I'd believe we were close, that I knew him better than almost anyone. But only now do I realize how much he hid inside, and how little I understood what was going on as I grew up.

'Dale, it's Alex. Any developments?' My voice sounds hollow in the quiet left by my now stilled engine. The 'Vette is parked at a gas station not far from Smyrna Mills. I've been driving without urgency, though not entirely aimlessly, since returning to Houlton. Thinking, mostly. About a brother I've never spoken to outside jail. About a life I never knew existed. About the people who hid it from me.

I need to go somewhere quiet and clear my head, and there's only one place I've got in mind to do it. Where it all started, and where my dad tried to end it. First, though, I guess I should check in.

'Hi, Alex.' Dale pauses. 'Everything okay?'

I stare through the windshield, eyes focused on nothing much. 'Yeah. It's fine. Have you got anything new on Nick?'

'You mean our boy Matthew? Nothing current, but we're building up quite a life history on him; assuming we're tracking the same Matthew Thorne.'

'Social security number?'

'And money too. The banks have been quite cooperative.' I hear paper being turned over at the other end of the line. 'Matthew Thorne, twenty-six. We're still tracing his early educational history, but he doesn't seem to have gone to college. First employment records start at the age of sixteen. Mostly low-key stuff and he didn't spend too long in one place. Some nothing jobs: store clerk, delivery driver – driver's licence issued in Colorado – but then things get more interesting.'

'Yeah?'

'Worked at a locksmith's in Milwaukee for four months, then a stint with a demolitions firm in Detroit. After that he skipped to Atlanta and worked at an auto-wrecking yard, then a library in New Jersey. That takes him almost up to the time of the fire at St Valentine's, and he can already pick locks and knock down buildings. Some unsavoury types in some of the businesses he was working, too,' Dale observes. 'God knows what else he learnt.'

'Then what?'

'There's a blank around the fire itself. He pops up about six months later at a mail order company based in Pennsylvania selling military surplus to wannabe soldiers. A stint as a mountain guide in Nevada then, ah, let's see' – I hear more paper turning – 'he became a librarian at a college in New York State. Then there's another break, but credit cards seem to have him staying at a couple of motels further north for a few weeks.'

'At the time Joshua Stern died, right?'

'Right,' Dale says. Then he pauses and the line goes silent, so I ask the inevitable question.

'Where was he when my folks were killed?'

'Miami. Working as an auto mechanic.'

'Jesus fucking Christ.'

Dale doesn't comment, just continues with his list. 'After that he goes back to wandering again. Store clerk in Virginia, bartender in Kansas City for a while. Small-time stuff.'

I blink once, twice. 'Kansas City? When?'

'About six months after your parents died. Stayed for a few weeks.'

'Jesus *fucking* Christ. I was in hospital in Kansas City then.' My mind is doing cartwheels, trying to work out how long Nick – Matthew – has been stalking me, working on his revenge. 'Son of a bitch.'

'Anything you want us to do?'

'Not right now,' I say, shaking my head. 'I just need some time.'

'Sure, Alex.' Another pause. 'The guys said you and Dr Larson took off somewhere this morning. Anything new crop up in your investigations?'

'I'll tell you later,' I say. Then I hang up. 'Maybe.'

The stony track that winds up to Claye Lake. I bring the 'Vette to a halt beneath a slate-grey sky and spend a moment looking through the trees, mostly birch and fir, to where a stream tumbles down the hill in flashes of white foam and silvery water. The cabin is somewhere out of sight beyond the crest of the slope, not far from where the stream begins its journey.

I'm not sure why I'm here, what I hope to achieve. Some kind of half-assed idea of revisiting the ghost of my childhood at one of its symbolic anchors, maybe. The lake is perched on the rugged shoulders of Brightwell Mountain at the eastern end of the Appalachians, a deep pool of cold snowmelt and run-off from the slopes, drained by a dozen small streams which eventually join the main rivers to the north. The view from the track leading up the slope is one I've carried with me since the first time I saw it, filled with excitement at the thought of spending a weekend up here with my dad, just like his friends did.

The first drops of rain, fat and heavy, hammer against the windshield as I debate whether to drive all the way up to the cabin or leave the car here and walk. Somehow, like a pilgrim in ancient times, completing the journey on foot seems like the right thing to do, as if the sight of the 'Vette outside the cabin would forever dilute the strength of my childhood memories. Without it, maybe I'll still be able to picture my dad's car standing by the door, its ordinarily dull brown suddenly seeming perfectly in tune with its surroundings. Maybe I'll be able to stand on the jetty at the back of the building and hear him recounting stories from his own childhood, trading them for my jokes that I'd normally be afraid of telling in front of my folks.

All private feelings, and I'm both glad and a little unhappy that Gemma isn't here to share them. She couldn't understand why I wanted to come here, though she tried.

'Are you sure you need to do it?' she asked when I dropped her back at the Superior Court in Houlton. Then she rested her hand against the side of my face and added, 'If Nick's on the loose out there, you shouldn't be wandering around the woods on your own.'

'I'm not worried about him,' I replied after a moment's silence. 'But I need to do some thinking, get my head straight. Maybe it'll help me figure out where he is.'

'At least tell Dale where you're going.'

'He's got my number if he wants to check on me.' I

leaned across and kissed her as she reached for the door. 'I won't be long,' I told her, trying a smile. I lost sight of her as I pulled out of the parking lot.

I sigh as the rain beats down harder on the 'Vette, drumming a tattoo on the pale blue bodywork. I expect Gemma will tell Dale what we learned from Ben Anderson, and that I've gone haring off into the middle of nowhere so I can contemplate my navel. I half expect him to call before long, asking what the hell I think I'm doing.

Maybe not. Maybe he'd understand that our childhood is important, that it's the beginning of everything we later become.

*Childhood events shape the rest of our lives, Mr Rourke.*

Nicholas's words, back in the interrogation room. A shudder runs through my body as other things he said come back to me, called into being by a chain of thought that had nothing to do with the crimes he committed.

*Claye Lake. A small cabin thirty yards or so from the lake.*
   *Trees running all the way down to the water's edge.*
*You remind me of the boy struggling to catch fish on Claye*
   *Lake under the watchful eye of his beloved father.*
*Have you ever been fishing, Mr Rourke?*

Claye Lake, where my father used to take Joanna Thorne for their secret trysts. Where he and his friends would spend the occasional weekend. Where the others would claim to be if he needed a cover story. Where the lies began. Where Matthew, now Nicholas, was probably conceived.

*She was a victim, Mr Rourke. A victim. 'One of yours?'*
*Laughter.*
*How did you feel when you knew your parents were dead, Mr*
*Rourke?*
*It's rare for a man to make up for the injustices he suffers and*
*punish those who have stolen the life he should have had.*

Is this the hiding place he prepared before killing Angela
Lamond? For a moment, I think about calling Dale and
letting him know my suspicions. But I don't know if he'd
be willing to send back-up out all this way on no more
than a hunch, particularly after yesterday's wild goose
chase.

And there's a part of me that doesn't want him here, if
Nick is at the cabin. This is my place, and if anything is to
happen here, I don't want to share it, as if I owe it to the
memory of my father. I take my cellphone out of my
pocket and turn it off.

I check my Colt and make sure I'm carrying a spare clip
before opening the door and stepping out into the rain,
feeling the same anticipation I did the very first time I was
here. Then, gun in hand, I jog in a hunter's half-crouch
into the trees, up the hill towards the lake and the cabin
from my childhood.

Still hidden in the sodden, moss-lined woods, I crest the
top of the slope not far from where the stream begins its
downward journey. In front, Brightwell Mountain vanishes
into the clouds at the far end of the granite-coloured
waters of Claye Lake. The cabin, tough and seasoned
wooden boards over stone, stands thirty yards or so from
the water's edge at the end of the track. Next to it, what
looks like Vallence's ageing Honda and a dark red pick-up.

Light spills dimly through the front window of the building and the frosted glass set in the solid wood of the door.

I tighten my grip on the gun and break across the short stretch of clear ground between me and the truck, careful to keep low and make as little noise as possible. A quick check on the bed and cab of the pick-up – empty – and I'm past and tucked next to the Honda, which also seems unoccupied. Rain rattles from its hood as I risk a quick look at the cabin before scuttling forward to the shelter of the wall by one of the smaller windows.

Keep low, to the rear of the cabin. The straggle of trees leading down to the water looks empty, and the wooden jetty that runs ten yards or so out on to the lake seems to be deserted.

Back to the front. I lift my eyes cautiously over the edge of the window. No sign of Nicholas, so I try the door.

Unlocked. I cautiously push it open and step inside.

The living room runs all the way to the western wall of the building on my right. Someone has tacked papers up above the mantelpiece, some kind of plans or notes, perhaps. A TV is on, but silent, at the far end of the room. On my left is the door that I remember leads to the kitchen, ahead is another, standing slightly ajar, that will take me into a short corridor which runs to the bathroom and bedrooms at the back of the cabin. The building is quiet save for the sound of the rain thudding against the roof.

First I check the kitchen, pushing the door and swinging through the opening just as I was taught so long ago, gun ready but not held too far from the body, careful to check the corner behind me. The door at the other end of the long kitchen, which leads into the dining room and pantry, is open. The kitchen itself shows signs of occupation for some time: clean washing up on the draining board, plenty of food, coffee and the like on the worktop.

I move through and into the dining room. Like the small pantry off to one side, it is empty, but again shows signs of habitation. A pair of muddy boots sits on the mat by the back door.

I return to the living room, intending to head next for the bedrooms, when a voice says, 'It's amazing what you can catch in these waters, if you're patient enough.'

Nicholas. The sound has a slightly scratchy, metallic edge and seems to be coming from the far end of the living room, next to the unlit hearth. A speaker, I guess. Gun raised, senses tingling, I move closer. 'Hello, Nicholas,' I call out. 'Or should I call you Matthew?'

'At last you've managed to work out the truth, brother. I was wondering how long it would take.'

A chill that has nothing to do with my rain-soaked clothes or the voice steals over me as I get my first good look at the papers on the walls. While some are newer – notes on the layout of the county jail, handwritten scrawl about the shift times the Sheriff's Department works – many are older and have obviously travelled with him, folded and unfolded time and again. Photographs, newspaper clippings, records both typed and written. The black-and-white mugshot from my high school yearbook sits next to an article from my college newspaper about baseball. My graduation photograph sits below it, along with a list of everyone in my year. Further along are a string of clippings from local newspapers, all of them about cases I worked on at the Bureau. A couple of blurry pictures of me in my FBI days are interspersed between them. At the top of the display is one of my business cards and a set of printouts from the material on the Robin Garrett Associates website. Almost my entire life is plastered on the walls, the object of an obsessive's focus. I swallow, trying to get some moisture back in my throat. I can't believe how much digging Matthew has done, how much he's shadowed my life. I feel like my past has been pinned inside a display case like a museum exhibit.

'How do you like my current home, Alex? Appropriate, don't you think?'

'How did you know I was coming?'

There's a dry laugh. 'Smile, brother. You've been on candid camera.'

I look at what I had taken for a TV, in reality a closed-circuit camera monitor, and next to it, the cabin's phone. The light next to the 'speaker' button glows red. It is from here that Nicholas's voice emanates. The glowing screen shows a colour view of the track leading to the cabin. A couple of hundred yards from wherever the camera is hidden – up a tree in all likelihood – I can see my 'Vette sitting in the rain. He must have called the cabin's number from his cellphone when he saw me coming, and he's just been waiting for me to find his nest, with my life history on display like a hunting trophy.

As I look up from the screen I notice the two colour pictures that lie at the heart of Nick's montage. They're not framed, but they've been hung with pride all the same. The first shows my parents' headstones up close, their names nice and clear above their freshly filled grave. The second is a more distant shot, but clear nonetheless. An orderly little crowd wearing black, most of them facing away from the camera. A priest in white and black robes, reading a passage from the leatherbound book in his hand. And me, standing next to him, looking down past knotted hands to a pair of identical coffins, each of which bears a single wreath.

'You might be my father's son, Matthew,' I say, staring at the photos until they fill my vision, 'but you're a long way from being my brother.'

Perhaps it's a whisper of air as the door leading towards the bedrooms opens, perhaps the faint sound of a foot landing on the carpet, but I hear something move behind me.

I turn quickly, but only quickly enough for Nick's fist to hammer into my jaw. I feel a couple of teeth wobbling as my mouth fills with blood and I stagger backwards into the wall. Before I can regain my wits and fight back, Nick follows up with a punch to my gut that knocks all the wind out of me and leaves me slumped on the floor, fighting for breath.

'I could have killed you before, Alex,' he says, slamming his foot into my ribs. Pain lances through my chest as at least one of them cracks. 'I thought about finishing you off in Miami while you were still passed out in the wreckage of your car. I knew our father was dead, so why not you as well?'

'Why didn't you?' I rasp, blood rattling in my breath and dribbling down my chin. Hearing Nick admit that he killed my parents, coupled with the images on the wall from their funeral, threatens to bring back the pain and anger I felt over three years ago. Somehow, I've managed to keep hold of my gun, but I don't have the strength to lift it.

'I decided to learn more about you, the brother I never

knew, who had the life I should have had. I thought I should learn more about what I'd missed.'

'I didn't kill your mom, Matthew,' I say. 'And I never knew you existed.'

'Sins of the father, Alex.' Nick takes another kick at my ribs, but on reflex I bring my knees up and the blow catches me on the shin.

'You didn't have to kill him, you son of a bitch!'

'No, but I hadn't thought of a suitable alternative back then. Besides, I'd already dealt with the others. I figured Vallence might still be useful, particularly once I'd decided what to do with you.'

He turns away from me and walks across to his wall display. I can see the butt of a pistol wedged behind a clock on the mantel, within easy reach of where he stands. I cough once, twice, as life begins to return to my battered muscles. The pain in my face and chest rises and falls like a heartbeat.

'This is your life up here on this wall, Alex. High school, the FBI, therapy, going private. Your parents.'

I manage to climb to my knees. 'Yeah?'

'Falling apart, wouldn't you say?'

I use the wall at my back to help get to my feet and start to lift the gun.

'Your career tanked after your breakdown, didn't it? You've got no family – except me, of course – and few friends. I couldn't ruin your past, but I could dig up some old secrets that would destroy people's memories of it.' He looks back at me and smiles. 'The image of our beloved hometown will be tarnished for years, and our father's reputation as a pillar of the community will be in tatters once they all know what he did.'

'Bullshit, Matthew. You're under arrest,' I say, cradling the Colt in both hands to keep my aim steady. 'Get your hands —'

'My mother, an innocent woman, died because of your father. I spent years putting up with the abuse of people like Garner because of him, and the people who helped cover his tracks.'

'Put your hands —'

'Do you have any idea how that feels?' he yells, cutting me off again. 'But I'm not done with you, brother. There's one more thing I need you to do for me.'

'Shut up and place your goddam hands on your head before I blow a hole through it!'

He takes a short step forward, smiling. 'That's exactly right. Do it, Alex. You must want to pull that trigger. So do it, kill me. I want you to. There's no one here to see you.'

'What the hell are you talking about?'

'I want you to become a murderer, a failed cop who shot an unarmed suspect for his own satisfaction. It'll destroy everything you've got left, and you'll have to live with it for the rest of your days.' He raises his voice a notch, pride and bitterness in equal measure. 'At last you'll have to face everything I did. No life worth speaking about. Trapped for ever, wondering what might have been. I don't know if I'll be able to watch you from where I'll be, but if not we can always compare notes when you get to Hell.'

'Shut the fuck up and stick your hands on your head.'

'It's not like there's any point to my life, once I'm done with you.' He lifts his gaze from the barrel of my gun to meet my stare. I blink as sweat runs past the corner of my eyes. 'I killed your mom and dad, Alex. You wouldn't believe the amount of planning I had to put in to make sure I smashed into your car at that intersection with enough speed to waste them both. I even had to pay some Puerto Rican kid to phone me when you were a couple of blocks away.'

I blink again, tasting the metal tang of blood in my mouth as I struggle to keep focused on the man in front of me and remember my training and upbringing. My knuckles are numb with the effort of holding the Colt and my hands feel clammy and damp.

'I had a look at your car once I'd picked my way out of the airbag and all the cushioning I'd packed into mine. I leaned in through the hole where your windshield was and checked Dad for a pulse. You know what I'd have done if I'd have found one?' His smile widens and hardens. 'I'd have grabbed the back of his head and slammed his face into the dashboard, over and over again until all you'd have seen when you woke up would have been a mass of pulped flesh where your father's face used to be. And I'd have enjoyed it.'

My pulse sounds loud in my ears, a roar not quite loud enough to drown out his voice. The rest of the cabin fades to nothing, leaving us alone in a bright tunnel surrounded by darkness. The gun feels hot and heavy in my grip. The trigger seems to be drawing itself back beneath my finger.

'Then I would have done the same to your mother,' he says. 'I'd have pounded her shattered skull until it split. Every snap of bone, every hollow ripping sound of the sharp fragments being driven into her head, I'd have savoured and enjoyed.'

I can't seem to breathe or break my gaze away from

Nick's. Killing him seems so easy. Then I start to hear a voice, my father's. I can't make out what he's saying, but the level, calm, soothing tones are unmistakably his. A fragment of memory, perhaps, synapses firing without reason or warning in my battered brain.

'Maybe you'd have heard the noise, wondering what it was.' He smiles. 'It's just a shame you didn't have a wife or some kids I could have dealt with next. It'd be nice to see your face when you found the remains of your loved ones. Of course, I've got the chance to do that now.' He pulls out a blurred Polaroid of Gemma walking into the Superior Court building with her police escort and adds it to the display on the wall. 'I like her, Alex. I think I'll kill her next, leave her somewhere nice and open, if you don't stop me. How'd you like to come home to find her head wedged on the banister rail? Maybe I'll even fuck her first. I guess we'll see.'

I blink and swallow dryly, then adjust and tighten my grip on the gun. Nick's smile broadens. I breathe in. 'Maybe I've got more of my father in me than you have,' I say through a parched and sticky mouth. 'Maybe it's something else. But there are places where we differ. I'm not a murderer. I'm taking you in.'

The room bleeds back into view as I breathe out. Nick's smile fades and twists as he realizes that I'm serious. 'Perhaps you're right,' he says. 'You might not be a killer. But I am.'

With that he whips around, grabbing his pistol from where it sits on the mantel. I can see the darkness down its barrel as it swings towards me. The rage in my half-brother's face is clear to see as I squeeze the trigger once, then again. Blood blossoms from his forehead and chest and for a moment he seems to hang still, frozen in the split second before his muscles fail and gravity takes over. Then his knees fold beneath him and he slides to the floor, gun falling useless at his side.

I let out a long, shuddering breath, wincing with the pain that flares from my broken ribs. Then I take a last look at Matthew Thorne before trudging towards the front door.

Outside, I take out my phone and turn it on again. Then I call Dale.

'Alex!' he says as soon as he picks up. 'Where are you?'

'I'm at the cabin by Claye Lake.'

'Gemma said you'd gone somewhere up there. I tried calling but I couldn't get through.'

'Nick's here.'

'We're on our way.' I can hear his chair scraping back and his footsteps against the floor of his office. 'Does he know you're there?'

'Yeah, no, it doesn't matter.'

I put the phone away and sit on the ground by the front of the cabin, trying to keep my ribs still. I feel empty, drained. It's a hard thing to kill someone, even more so when they're family. Did I do right? Could I have hit him in the shoulder or something and disarmed him instead? I lean my head back against the wall of the cabin and let rain splash against my face. The droplets don't let up, if anything falling harder as if the sky itself is in mourning.

It barely seems a moment later that Dale's Jeep crests the hill, going flat out with its lights blazing. Dale jumps out, followed by one of his deputies, and I can hear more engines coming up the slope towards the cabin. Both men are packing shotguns.

'Alex! Are you all right?' he says as he reaches me. The deputy jogs past, heading for the cabin.

'I'm alive,' is all I can say in reply.

## 15

Dale drives me down to the hospital in Houlton. I entrust Deputy Miller with the keys to my 'Vette and he promises to deliver it to the Superior Court without wrecking it. I spend most of the journey staring out of the window in silence, watching the trees flash past and, later, the miles of lonely green fields through glass streaked by the rain.

As we approach the I-95 interchange, Dale tries to draw me out of myself. 'He was a murderer, Alex,' he says. 'Whether he was really your brother or not doesn't matter. You did right.'

'Yeah, I guess,' I reply, watching oncoming traffic kicking up spray from the road. Having said my piece, I lapse back into silence.

'What made you think he was up by the lake?'

'I didn't think he was until I got there.'

Dale glances across at me and asks a question I'm sure Gemma has already given him the answer to. 'So why did you go up there?'

'I wanted to be close to my dad. I wanted to feel like he was there so I could understand. I wanted to sit with him and talk, like we used to.' I look at Dale. 'Why do you think Nick and I turned out so different? He was so full of anger over things I never even knew about. I don't think I could ever get like that. But we came from the same place and the same source. I don't get it.'

He shrugs. 'You're asking the wrong person. Just be thankful you weren't both the same.'

'I guess.'

'Look, Alex,' he says. 'Nick chose to be the way he was. There were hundreds of kids lived at St Valentine's, and even if it was run badly, there's only one of them that I know of who turned out to be a murderer. He didn't have to be that way. He seemed smart like you, so he could have been anything he wanted. It was nothing to do with you or your dad.'

Gemma comes to see me while my injuries are being treated at the hospital. She doesn't say much – I guess she knows I'll talk if I want to – but clasps my hand and rests her head on my shoulder. I ignore the complaints from my battered ribs, three of which are broken. What few words she does share with me are soft and genuinely warm. They haul me out of my melancholy, even though I can't seem to recall exactly what they are once I'm out of my daze.

Dale drops by again later on, to see if I'll be up to answering the questions and filling in the paperwork for the State Attorney General's Office that follows any police shooting. I tell him I'll do it tomorrow, and he seems happy with that. In fact, he seems pretty happy all round, I suppose because he's managed to wrap up the Lamond case without help from another police department or agency. His stock must have risen quite a bit in the county, and no doubt Mayor Saville is singing his praises to anyone who'll listen. I don't begrudge him his success.

Gemma takes me home and I'm asleep almost from the moment I pull the covers up around me.

I dream that I'm eight years old again, and the last of

the warm afternoon sun once again floods the ballpark. When I walk out to second base, I scan the faces of the small chatting, cheering crowd here to watch the game, and find my parents sitting near the end of one of the rows. My mom waves and blows me a kiss, while my dad just smiles, happy and proud.

I don't remember how the game ends. It doesn't seem important.

The following morning I drive back to Winter's End to collect my things, which gives me the distinct pleasure of checking out of the Crowhurst Lodge. I walk down the silent staircase for the last time, my bag slung over one shoulder. As usual, the front desk is unoccupied. Rather than attempt to summon someone by ringing the bell, I can't help but sneak up to the thick wooden door behind the desk, then turn the handle and push it inwards, unsure of what awaits me.

It opens on to a narrow room, cluttered with papers, mouldering ledgers and handwritten notes. At the far end is a table. On it are an old portable TV, an electric kettle and a huge collection of coffee jars, milk powder and bags of sugar. The whole room smells dark and sour. The old man who manages the hotel is sitting in front of the TV, watching re-runs of M*A*S*H.

'What are you doing back here?' he says, startled by my presence. 'Guests aren't allowed here.'

'Um . . . I'm checking out. Send the bill to the Sheriff's Department; they're paying.' I look at the TV. 'You do this all day, every day?'

'Not always the same programme,' he says, as if that explains everything. Maybe it does. 'Why, what business is it of yours?'

I shake my head. 'It's just . . . nothing. I'll be off now.'

Outside, the clouds have passed and the sun is shining once more. The twin mosaics, which on closer inspection are badly worn by time and the elements, are little more than green and red shapeless forms. The trees around the parking lot are a vibrant, healthy green. I drive down to the blacktop of the highway and turn southwards. Winter's End seems cheerier, and perhaps a little busier than it was. I can't tell whether it's really that way, or if I'm just looking at it differently.

I'm about halfway through town when I see Sophie Donehan walking down Main Street, dark hair glinting in the sunlight. I pull up in front of her and wind down the window.

'Hi,' she says, her smile an upturned curve of dark lipstick.

'Hi. If you're still set on getting out of here, I'll probably be leaving at the weekend.'

'Yeah, I heard everything was finished. They said you shot a guy.'

I nod. 'I did,' I say. 'Though I don't know if I'm happy or not about killing him. So, do you want to go or not?'

'No, I think now I'll stay for graduation and the summer break. I'm starting college in the fall.'

'Yeah? Whereabouts?'

Sophie gives me a sly smile. 'Boston,' she says, 'so I'll probably see you later, Alex.'

She gives me a peck on the cheek, then walks off with a backward glance and a wave over one shoulder. I start up the car again and pull away from the kerb.

The familiarity of Winter's End still stirs up memories, but no longer with the same force as when I first returned here over a week ago. The streets are just rows of houses, the shops nothing but businesses. The people are strangers, for the most part, just ordinary folk from an ordinary town. I no longer find the past intruding on the present.

I spend a week attending to the paperwork from Nicholas's shooting, and watching Dale tie up the remaining details of the case. The department sifts the stuff he left at the cabin, finding more than enough to prove Nick was behind the Lamond and Garner killings. On the Tuesday, the State Police announce that they've found and arrested Arthur Tilley, the pharmacist from town who switched my prescription on Dr Vallence's orders. He breaks down completely during questioning and admits changing the pills, working with Vallence in the prescription drugs trade, his morphine addiction, everything. I suspect he'd have confessed to killing JFK and making off with Jimmy Hoffa if he'd been asked.

The department's efforts to track down the other senior staff from St Valentine's bear a little more fruit. Sarah Decker, under her married name of Sarah Weir, turns up on a missing persons report filed by her husband nearly four years ago. Dorian Blythe's fate remains a mystery. My guess is that the remains of both of them are buried somewhere in New York State and California, or lying at the bottom of a lake or river. Maybe I'm wrong, and Matthew didn't go after them or couldn't find them. People lose track of one another all the time.

A couple of other former inmates of St Valentine's come forward as the story hits the press and give their own versions of what life was like there. Dale manages to keep any mention of Matthew being my half-brother out of the papers, and no one much bothers me with questions.

I stay with Gemma at her house in Houlton for the entire week, an arrangement we both find surprisingly comfortable, and one which allows us to learn ever more about one another. The days are glorious, the evenings beautiful and the nights wonderful, aside for some discomfort from my ribs. Our time together is by far the happiest I can remember in a long while.

At noon on my last day in Houlton, Dale and Laura show up at Gemma's house to see me off. The four of us have coffee, then I reluctantly lug my bag out to the 'Vette. 'I'll let you know how the case goes,' Dale says, shaking me by the hand. 'There shouldn't be any leftovers from the shooting. The guy was armed, and no one's going to miss him. Everything else should take care of itself.'

'Good,' I tell him.

'I guess this is goodbye for now. Try to keep in touch this time.'

'It shouldn't be a problem.' I smile, but it's Gemma I'm looking at. 'I'll be up here as often as I can manage.'

When the time comes, Gemma and I say nothing to one another. We just embrace long and tightly. The colour of her eyes, the brightness of her smile and the warmth of her body are already safely locked in my memory, keeping me going until the next time I see her. Not perfect, but they'll do.

I climb into the car and fire up the engine. Matthew's locket now dangles from my rear-view mirror. As I head west, I find myself staring at it now and then, wondering about Joanna Thorne and the other family, the other past, I so nearly had.

I drive up the stony track to Claye Lake again, this time under the brilliance of the springtime afternoon sun.

There's some police tape on the door to the cabin, but it's not enough to distract me from the beauty of the place. At the far side of the mirror-smooth water, swathes of evergreens blanket the slopes of Brightwell Mountain. The bare patches of rock above and between them look purple in the light and the streams down its slopes resemble flashing rivulets of quicksilver. The forest around the cabin is airier now the rain has gone, and is full of the scent of leaf mould, rising sap and old, healthy wood. Birdsong of a dozen different types chimes from the branches.

The cabin itself is now much more as it was in my childhood, now that all trace of Nick's presence has been taken away. The walls are the same solid, honest boards, and the building itself looks sturdy and compact. I can almost forget everything that happened here.

I walk around to the back and on to the jetty. I sit on the weathered wooden planking with a can of my dad's favourite brand of beer and look out across the lake, silver-blue beneath the sky. Then the two of us talk for an hour or so, just like we used to before we fell out, drinking beer and watching the world grow older. It's what we should have done when I left to go to college, and what I never got the chance to do again after the crash. We don't talk about anything much, just father–son stuff, but I feel better for it.

When I'm ready to leave, I take the locket from my jacket and look at it one last time. I draw back my hand and fling it as far as I can, into the lake. The tiny piece of scratched gold arcs away from me, glinting in the sun until it hits the water. It disappears leaving barely a ripple, taking the past with it.

Then I say goodbye to my dad and walk away.

'It is always better
to avenge dear ones than to indulge in mourning.
For every one of us, living in this world
means waiting for our end.'

– Beowulf

*Read on for a taste of*

# THE TOUCH OF GHOSTS

By John Rickards

Coming in hardback in August 2004

(Michael Joseph, £12.99)

# Prologue

A jewel-clear summer's day. The kind they photograph and sell to tourists on postcards for fifty cents apiece. The late morning sun is a burning ember, a single relentless, blazing diamond pinned against the empty blue. Acetylene-white light washes over weathered mountain crags that pierce a vast rumpled green blanket of forest. It glitters like frost from dozens of lakes and rivers in the folds of a landscape rarely broken by towns and highways.

Closer, the same light flashes from the glistening plumage of a bird diving for fish in one of these lakes and from the struggling rainbow-scaled catch in its beak. It dances from the wings of dozens of insects flitting through the trees surrounding the lake. It sparkles in the hair of a running woman.

She sprints across an open stretch of wild grass, a narrow break in the tangled forest, carving a swathe of darker green bent and broken stalks in her wake. Her heart pounds against her ribcage, threatening to punch through it with every beat. Her breath burns her throat as she gulps for air. She can feel her backpack slamming into her spine with every stride, flattening her shirt against her sweat-soaked skin. She ignores it all, waiting instead for the sound she dreads.

Running footsteps, behind her. Sneakers smashing through the grass. He has followed her downstairs and out through the doors, no shouting, no calls – silent all the way. She knows he's no cop – they shout 'Freeze!' or 'Hold it right there!', don't they? They *pursue*, they don't *chase*.

More than anything, she wishes she'd never taken a look at the old building with the sagging roof, wishes that her will alone would be enough to rewrite the past, to change events. Wishes she could wake up from what *has* to be a dream.

Thin, spidery branches rattle from her jeans and whip against the skin of her face and arms, tracing needle-thin lines of fire. The air changes, becoming cooler and carrying the musty acid scent of leaf mulch. The ground beneath the canopy is rough and uneven. Roots and tough, wiry vines lurk in the plant litter that covers the floor, ready to snag her feet as she pounds through the undergrowth.

She could have run for the dirt track, but the man had a car. She could have made for the lake shore in the hope that someone from town would see her from the opposite bank, but she knows how far away it is. She can feel the distance, the open gulf between her and safety. Her only hope is the highway, north through the woods.

Muscles burning as her legs pump up a gentle incline, eyes concentrating on the ground in front of her. Breath increasingly ragged, hacking and blowing. Trying to maintain her pace, to ignore her tiring body. Can't even hear the man's footsteps over the roaring of blood in her ears.

A flash of blackness explodes from her jaw and suddenly she can taste dirt, feel dry, dead leaves against her cheek, head swimming. Her mouth feels warm and coppery, one of her teeth shakes and pulls sickeningly as she squirms, trying to drag herself to her feet again. Weight, heavy against the small of her back stops her and her limbs feel awkward and rubbery. It's not the man – she can hear his running footsteps coming to a halt a couple of yards behind her – it must have been someone else who landed the punch.

As she opens her mouth and the first notes of her scream erupt from within, a hand snatches at her hair, hauling her head back by a thousand tiny points of white-hot pain. Metal, cold, thin and sharp touches the skin of her neck.

In the microseconds it takes for the knife to draw a line of liquid ice across her throat she thinks about her parents, waving as she pulled away in the taxi bound for the airport. She thinks about her two-year-old cousin Charlie, playing with his birthday presents. She pictures her friends from college and how she won't be able to enjoy graduation with them. she tries to remember them all, one last time.

Her ravaged arteries pump and sputter blood across the forest floor, leaving a clear path for her soul to follow after.

Crying bundle of newborn joy.

Photo in a yearbook.

Face on a milk carton.

Name on a grave.

# I

A lecture theatre much like any other. Rows of padded benches spread up towards the low, wide windows at the back of the room, surrounding the dais at the bottom like the seats of a Roman amphitheatre. Forty, maybe fifty men and women are scattered around the auditorium although, I note with an inward smile, they are concentrated in the first five or six rows. If I'd been holding this presentation at college, I could guarantee that the back couple of rows would be packed and only half the students in attendance would actually be listening. Here I can't see anyone whose eyes aren't on the man speaking next to me or on the notepaper in front of them. Times change.

'Your instructors at the Academy may have told you that there are two broad types of suspect,' Robin Garrett, the man next to me, is saying. He's technically my boss. In reality, he's a friend I just happen to work with. 'There's those who just want to get their guilt off their chest. Even if it takes you a while to get the whole story out of them, you'll get your confession, because they want to confide in someone. And there are those who will clam up and won't give you a damn thing.'

The people who've shown up here on a dreary Thursday evening at the start of November to hear our words of wisdom are mostly trainees from Boston's Police Academy. The rest are newly graduated police officers willing to sacrifice an hour or two of their spare time on the chance it'll boost their conviction rates and help them make detective.

'The ones who eventually break down and give you everything they've got aren't a problem,' Rob continues. 'It's the second kind, whether they're experienced criminals or just plain stubborn, that'll make you work for every ounce of truth you can get.'

If I listen hard every time Rob pauses for breath, I can hear hail smashing, handfuls of pebbles against the windows at the back, even over the electrical hum of the projector illuminating the screen behind us. Every gust of wind outside brings a fresh batch. Rhythmic, like a heartbeat or the sound of a hundred hourglasses being turned over at once.

'Alex will speak in a little while about interrogation techniques and matching your approach to the individual suspect. That's his field. Mine is the proper preparation beforehand to maximize your chances of success, whether you're after a confession or just information.'

Every once in a while we do this. Boston PD pays us a small but reasonable amount to give evening lectures to rookie recruits and patrol division newbies desperate to get their detective's shield. We pass on our experience – Rob as an ex-FBI field agent, myself as a one-time specialist in the Bureau's NCAVC violent crimes division. In return, we maintain our good relationship with Boston PD, and they get cops with a slightly broader degree of training. Everyone's happy.

'If you make sure you have as much relevant evidence and information to hand as possible before you even open your mouth, you'll have more chance of cutting through any bullshit and lies they try to feed you. You may even be able to make them think you know more than you do and trick them into giving themselves up.' He pauses for effect. 'Just make sure you get it right.'

Rob taps a key on the laptop in front of him and the glow from the screen behind me changes colour. I know without turning around that he's showing them a picture of twenty-three-year-old Bernard Leon, charged with murder in Phoenix two years previously. This is Rob's part of the show. Now that the introduction is out of the way, he'll run the audience through two cases where police have had to rely on confession evidence to make their case, one failure and one success. After the story of the botched Leon investigation, he'll tell them about Dan Rothman, a career criminal suspected of holding up a Detroit jewellery store. The detective who eventually wrung a confession out of Rothman, along with the subsequent successful prosecution, was given a promotion as a result.

I glance down at my watch, trying to hide the motion from the people listening to Rob. Like the rest of Boston, it's non-smoking here, so I'll have to wait until the lecture's finished and we've gone through all the usual questions and chat at the end before I can light up again. My girl-friend recently began trying to persuade me to cut my thirty-a-day habit, so far without success. I just don't have the willpower, although the inclination is growing as it becomes harder to smoke anywhere but at home.

Look back up at the windows. Three feet high, six across. Black mail-slot gaps gazing out onto darkness. Tiny silver lights twinkle and flicker across them as though there's a clear starlit night out there, not specks of sleet reflecting the lights of the city as they dribble down the glass. I let my mind wander as I watch countless drops of icy water trickle and die. I think about groceries I've got to buy, laundry I've got to do. I think about the weekend.

'And now Alex Rourke will discuss the different interrogation techniques themselves,' Rob says, bringing me back to the present. 'They're all yours, Alex.'

I stand up and quickly run my part of the lecture over in my head. A hundred-odd eyes blink and glitter at me as I begin.

An hour and a half later, the last of the latest additions to Boston's police force have filtered away, leaving the two of us to pack up and head for home. I've just finished dropping the laptop back in its hold-all when the door at the side of the room opens again to admit Lieutenant Aidan Silva, a man who always reminds me of a bear given human form. A mop of chestnut hair matched by a bristling beard flecked grey by the advancing years, and between them a round, heavy nose and a pair of dark, sunken eyes. How and when he and Rob became friends, I don't know. They shake hands before Silva leans over and offers me a paw.

'I don't know what your people have been putting in their food, Aidan,' Rob says as he stuffs our notes into a bag, 'but we actually had some intelligent questions at the end. Caught me by surprise.'

Silva grins, baring his teeth. 'I hear there's a couple of them can walk and chew gum at the same time, too,' he responds. 'Better hope it's not the start of a trend, otherwise I'll be obsolete in a couple of years.'

'You and me both. We'll end up in a retirement home together. Alex can come look after us and make sure our copies of *Sports Illustrated* are kept up to date. What's on your mind?'

'Jolene's decided to invite some people round for dinner and drinks on Saturday night,' the lieutenant says. 'I figured I'd see if the two of you were free. She doesn't want it to be an all-Department gathering, so I need as many non-cop friends there as I can lay my hands on. Otherwise, I'll have to make small talk with the neighbours.' He shudders.

'Sounds good to me,' Rob says. 'How about you, Alex?'

I shrug. 'I'll have to check. Gemma's coming down tomorrow night so it'll be up to her whether we're there or not.'

'Well if she fancies a drink Saturday, my place at eight,' Silva says. 'I'll see you guys then, or not.'

I give him a wave as he ambles back out through the doors, then go back to making sure we've not forgotten anything. Rob and I head out to the parking lot, instinctively hunching once we've left the shelter of the building and face the full fury of the elements.

'You got anything else planned for this evening?' Rob asks as though we don't both have cold water seeping rapidly past our collars and under our shirts.

'Tidying,' I say, sweeping back my hair where it's become plastered to my forehead. 'I've got to get the apartment neat before Gemma gets here.'

'Don't wear yourself out. You've got to meet a client first thing tomorrow.'

I grimace in mock pain as he drops into his car, then hurry over to mine, trying not to drown. Even in the downpour, my pale blue 1969 Stingray Corvette – a gas-guzzling piece of history that I hardly ever use in Boston – cuts a sleek form, its almost aquatic lines making it seem totally at home in the wet. I dive into its welcoming interior and sit for a moment, wiping water out of my eyes and trying to think warm thoughts. Run-off from the roof sluices down the windshield in front of me, laced with ice crystals that melt and vanish as I watch. Rob's tail-lights blur red as his car pulls out of the lot, then vanish altogether.

Only then do I snap out of my trance and fumble in my well-worn tan leather jacket for a pack of smokes.

At two minutes to nine the following morning I reach the doors to the building that houses our company. A five-storey red brick edifice that, although not hugely inspiring, is at least smart enough to look good on the brochures Rob occasionally throws together for potential clients. There are a couple of copies of that very same promotional literature in the lobby, alongside similar efforts belonging to the other five firms renting space here.

*Robin Garrett Associates*, the copperplate text on the cover reads. *Licensed private investigators, process servers, business security and criminal consultants.* Most of these end up in the hands of nervous small corporate outfits with problem employees, suspected low-level fraudsters or other sources of the white-collar work which is one of our two main money-spinners. The second field we specialize in – again, something the police would in theory handle if they didn't usually have more pressing problems on their hands – is missing persons. Being a college town, Boston has its fair share of students who drop out and, once their parents have made their feelings on the matter clear stop keeping in touch with their families back home. Once things have cooled down, people sometimes need help locating their errant offspring, which is where we come in.

Then there are non-student missing person cases, which

are much more difficult and which have a much smaller clearance rate. I'm pretty sure this morning's is going to be one of those, if the preliminary information our secretary Jean gathered over the phone is correct.

Jean herself has just settled into her seat when I step out of the elevator and head for the office. I doubt that Rob or any of our three junior staff are in yet. She smiles at me and says, 'Morning, Alex.'

'It is, and I'm certainly feeling it,' I reply. 'My body clock keeps telling me I should still be dozing.'

'Rough night? How did the lecture go?'

'Okay, same as usual. But then I had to spend three hours tidying my apartment. It was midnight before I got to sleep.'

She shakes her head. 'Next time a client calls I'll tell them we can't make any early appointments because none of the staff crawls out of bed before noon. I hate depriving you of your beauty sleep.'

'Thanks, Jean. That sounds like a great idea. I'll mention it to Rob.'

She laughs as I walk past her, into our airy squad-room-style office. Relatively uncluttered, but still with all the furnishings any self-respecting small business should have. I'm a little disappointed to see that Kathryn, one of our junior staff – 'the kids' – has beaten me in. The feeling quickly fades when I realize it's given her time to get the coffee machine on and ready, allowing me to help myself to a cup before I've even sat down.

I've barely had time to find a place to put the cup amongst the drifts of paper that cover my desk when the phone rings on its internal circuit. The client is here.

I look as the door at the far end of the room opens and

a woman somewhere in her forties steps a little hesitantly over the threshold. Dark hair now going grey, neatly tied back out of her face. Steel-rimmed glasses sitting on a lined, tired-looking face. Emerald green wool coat, charcoal sweater and matching pants. Sensible shoes. All of it looks fairly new. Over her shoulder is a brown leather bag.

On the desk in front of me is a short list of Jean's handwritten preliminary notes, based on what the client said when she called us.

*Colleen Webb.*
*Son Adam (25) last heard of nearly two months ago – Burlington, VT.*
*Husband dead – car wreck – six months ago.*
*Moving out of old neighbourhood – insurance money.*
*Can't find son to tell him/discuss with him.*
And, in Rob's handwriting: *Don't think she's a time-waster. See what you can do.*

At the bottom is her phone number and address in Roxbury, part of Boston. I slide the note underneath a stack of old paperwork and stand to greet her. When she shakes my hand, her palm feels damp and papery but her grip is a firm one. I give her my best professional smile and offer her a seat.

'Mrs Webb, I'm Alex Rourke. How can we help?'

# WIN A WEEKEND IN WASHINGTON, DC AND VISIT THE INTERNATIONAL SPY MUSEUM!

If you've enjoyed *Winter's End*,
here's your chance to

## WIN A WEEKEND IN WASHINGTON, DC

and revisit the haunts of ex-FBI interrogator,
Alex Rourke.

We've teamed up with leading travel experts **FUNWAY**
The leading US specialist

and Hilton Hotels **Hilton** to bring you this amazing competition.

Just send in your details and you and a friend could be jetting off on a fantastic weekend break to Washington, DC.

*The prize includes:*

- Two return scheduled flights with United Airlines from London (Heathrow) to Washington, DC
- Three nights' accommodation at the Hilton Washington on fashionable Connecticut Avenue
- Two tickets to the International Spy Museum
- Two tickets for an Old Town Trolley Tour of the city
- Airport and hotel taxes
- Macy's discount shopping card, giving 11% off all shopping

TURN THE PAGE FOR MORE DETAILS!

- Washington, DC is a beautiful city of Paris-inspired boulevards and parks, with white marble buildings overlooking the well-planned streets.

- Hop on an Old Town Trolley Tour – a two-hour narrated trolley bus ride – or take a free guided tour of the US Capitol.

- To make your trip to Washington, DC even more authentic, we've included two tickets to the International Spy Museum at historic 800 F Street NW, adjacent to FBI headquarters. This exciting new museum features the largest collection of international espionage artefacts and interactive exhibits ever placed on public display.

- When you've had your fill of history, head for the shops and restaurants at Union Station, beautifully restored to its former glory, the art galleries and sidewalk cafes of stylish Dupont Circle or colonial Georgetown, with its bustling bars and boutiques, for great shopping and nightlife.

---

**TO ENTER THIS EXCITING COMPETITION
SIMPLY FILL IN YOUR DETAILS BELOW AND SEND THIS PAGE
(OR A PHOTOCOPY) TO JOHN RICKARDS COMPETITION,
PENGUIN GENERAL MARKETING, 80 STRAND, LONDON, WC2R ORL.
CLOSING DATE: 31ST NOVEMBER 2004**

**NAME** ...................................................................................

**ADDRESS** ..............................................................................

**EMAIL** ..................................................................................

**For information on Funway Holidays please go to www.funwayholidays.co.uk
or call 0870 22 00 626 and for Washington, DC go to www.washington.org.**

---